Books by Tracie Peterson

*with Kimberley Woodhouse
**with Karen Witemeyer, Regina Jennings, and Jen Turano

For a complete list of Tracie's books, visit TraciePeterson.com.

A CHOICE CONSIDERED

TRACIE PETERSON

BETHANYHOUSE

a division of Baker Publishing Group
Minneapolis, Minnesota

© 2024 by Peterson Ink, Inc.

Published by Bethany House Publishers
Minneapolis, Minnesota
BethanyHouse.com

Bethany House Publishers is a division of
Baker Publishing Group, Grand Rapids, Michigan

Printed in the United States of America

Library of Congress Cataloging-in-Publication Data
Names: Peterson, Tracie, author.
Title: A choice considered / Tracie Peterson.
Description: Minneapolis, Minnesota : Bethany House, a division of Baker
    Publishing Group, 2024. | Series: The heart of Cheyenne ; 2
Identifiers: LCCN 2023056624 | ISBN 9780764241086 (paperback) | ISBN
    9780764243059 (cloth) | ISBN 9780764243066 (large print) | ISBN
    9781493446575 (e-book)
Subjects: LCGFT: Christian fiction. | Romance fiction. | Novels.
Classification: LCC PS3566.E7717 C48 2024 | DDC 813/.54—dc23/eng/20231221
LC record available at https://lccn.loc.gov/2023056624

Scripture quotations are from the King James Version of the Bible.

Cover design by Peter Gloege, LOOK Design Studio
Cover image from Joanna Czogala / Arcangel

Background images: Shutterstock

Baker Publishing Group publications use paper produced from sustainable forestry
practices and postconsumer waste whenever possible.

24 25 26 27 28 29 30   7 6 5 4 3 2 1

1

APRIL 1868
CHEYENNE, WYOMING

What do you mean they stole the fire ladder?" Melody Doyle asked her father over breakfast.

"Well, just what I be sayin'," her father replied. "Judge Kuykendall has run an ad in the paper sayin' somebody stole it, and he wants it back immediately."

"Seems like sneaking off with a large ladder would be difficult—and even harder to hide." She poured hot coffee in her father's cup.

"For sure it would be, now." He downed half the cup in one gulp, then folded the paper. "No doubt someone will be findin' it. Hopefully before the next fire. Oh, I forgot to be tellin' ya, I'm gonna go to the prizefight tonight."

"Are you sure you're feeling up to it, Da?"

Ever since late January when her father fell at work, his back had been giving him nothing but trouble. He couldn't even get clearance from the railroad to return to work because of the problems it was causing him.

"I'm sure to be just fine, daughter. Don't ya be worryin' none."

But Melody did worry. Da wasn't his usual self. All her life, he had been the very image of strength and resilience. These last few weeks, however, he'd seemed so weary, and Melody was certain he was in pain.

She knew her father was frustrated after taking that fall. He'd been quite high on the ladder when he'd lost his balance and hit the ground on his back. The doctor said it was a wonder he hadn't hit his head, but Da had only laughed and said if he had then there wouldn't have been any injury at all. He was a hardheaded Irishman who'd definitely gone through worse, but for some reason, this fall had taken its toll.

"There is something I was hoping we could discuss." Melody pushed back her empty plate. "Do you feel up to it?"

"For sure I do. Don't be worryin' about me. I won't be coddled."

She smiled and reached out to place her hand over his. "You've never allowed anyone to coddle you, and I won't insult you by trying to start now. In fact, what I want to say is about as far from coddling as I can get."

"Then speak. What would be on yar mind?"

For as long as Melody and her father had lived in Cheyenne, they'd called a tent home. It was the way of most section hands and their supervisors since the railroad kept them moving along the line.

Melody hadn't minded in the beginning. It was fairly comfortable—at least as much as they could make it. The entire tent wasn't much bigger than ten by ten, but it was all Melody had known for some time. Now, however, she was more than ready to enjoy the comforts of a real house with windows she could look out of and a nice large fireplace. Da seemed most content when he was living like a nomad, but not Melody.

Melody straightened. "I want to stay in Cheyenne. I know the railroad is moving out and that your job will take you west with it, but I've had my fill of moving from place to place. I like Cheyenne and the people we've come to know. Marybeth and Edward, the Taylors, Dr. Scott. They're all good people, and I want to be a part of their lives. So I'd like to remain here when you go.

"And you won't be that far away. They won't get down the track more than a couple hundred miles, and you can always take the train back here on the weekends. I could find a nice place to stay and have room for you as well. Just think how pleasant it would be for you to leave the chaos of the end-of-the-tracks town and come back here to rest. You wouldn't get to go to church with me since services are still held in the evening, but at least we'd have some time together."

"So ya have yar heart set on staying in Cheyenne? I cannot say that this is surprisin' to me," Da began.

She nodded. "It's been on my mind since Julesburg."

"I cannot be holdin' against ya the desire to settle yarself near friends. The folks ya named are good and godly people." He tossed down the other half of his coffee and held out the cup for more. "But I cannot have ya stayin' here without a man to protect ya. There will still be dangers even after the rowdies pull out."

She refilled his cup. "But our friends will keep an eye on me. Marybeth even said I could come and live with them. I could stay in the house or in the little shed out back where they were living before the Hendersons sold them the house."

Her father shook his head. "No, ya'll be needin' a husband, Melody. I've been feelin' that way for a long time now. Ya need a man of yar own and children. Yar made for love and family—like yar ma."

Melody only had vague memories of her mother. She'd died when Melody was barely ten years old. Now, almost sixteen years later, the memories were cloudy. She could hardly remember what her mother looked like, although Da said she was the spitting image of her mother.

"And while I know yar old enough to decide for yarself, I'm still yar da."

"I respect that, Da. I don't want to do anything against your wishes. I just hadn't thought of marrying anyone. You'll soon be heading west, and finding a husband in that short time is going to be difficult. After all, there's no one special in my life."

"Not that I don't have men askin' me all the time if they can be courtin' ya. Of course, they know there's a risk in approachin' me, but that's the first part of the test. If they're brave enough to come and discuss it, it shows strength of character." Da chuckled. "Yar a beauty like yar mother, and ya could have yar pick of suitors. We've only to put out the word."

"Advertise for a husband? Is that what you're suggesting?" She was surprised not to feel more appalled by the idea.

"And for sure it could work. We could be lettin' folks know that yar of a mind to marry and live here in Cheyenne. I could take this time away from me job to inspect each man and listen to his story. Then I could be pickin' a few suitors for ya to choose from. Ya know for yarself that I have God's gift of discernment. I can be tellin' when a man is truthful or false."

Melody shrugged. "I suppose we could give it a try. It's not like I must marry any of them. I can always head west with you if none of them appeal."

"And for sure ya could, and ya would, for I'll not be leavin' ya here without protection and security. After all, how would ya make yar way and pay for all that life costs ya?"

"Well, I supposed I'd get a job. I can clean house, and I'm a fair cook, as you well know."

"Aye, that ya are, and I know ya enjoy workin'. It's havin' ya alone that torments me."

Melody knew he was just concerned about her well-being. She patted his hand. "If you want to pick out some suitors for me, then I'm not opposed. I love and trust you. I don't want to stay here to be rid of you. I'm hoping, in time, you might even want to come back and settle here as well. My children will need their grandda."

"Could be. But ya know me wanderlust." He beamed her a smile. "Yar a good daughter, Melody, and God has given ya sound judgment. If ya have a young man who has caught yar eye, ya might be lettin' me know. I can talk to him and give ya my opinion. After all, the choice is gonna be yars."

She got up and kissed his cheek. "Thank you, Da. I know that together we should be able to figure it out."

He nodded and picked up his paper. "Now, didn't ya say ya were gonna go visit Marybeth?"

"Aye. After I do up the dishes, I'll be on my way."

"*Is é do mhac do mhac inniú, ach is í d'iníon d'iníon go deo.*" He went back to reading.

Melody smiled at the old Irish saying. *Your son is your son today, but your daughter is your daughter forever.*

"Aye, Da. I'm yours forever."

"And so Da said he'll put out the word that I'm looking for a husband. I figure we have about forty-five days to find one because the doctor said Da can rejoin the workforce in June." Melody glanced from Marybeth Vogel to Granny Taylor. These two women were her dearest friends in the world.

"That doesn't give us a whole lot of time," Granny Taylor observed. "Are you sure you want to choose a husband this way?"

"It wasn't my idea. Da won't let me stay if I'm not married."

Marybeth had been frowning since Melody first told them of the situation. "Maybe Edward can speak to him."

"My Jed could do the same." Granny Taylor picked up her knitting. "I can't abide for you to marry without love."

"Nor I. The very thought is abominable," Marybeth added. "You deserve love, Melody. You above all people."

The latter comment made Melody laugh. "Why me above all? I'm nothing special."

"But of course you are," Granny Taylor replied. "You are God's own child, and your heart is one of the kindest and most loving. You deserve a husband who will adore you—love you and make you happy."

"I won't marry a man unless I think I can love him in time." To be honest, Melody had been somewhat concerned about this very issue. She could always refuse to marry any of the men her father chose. It wouldn't be the end of the world if she had to push on with Da. She could always make her way back to Cheyenne. Still, the thought of leaving the friends she'd made nearly broke her heart.

"But I want more for you. I want passion and romance," Marybeth said, sounding as if she might soon be moved to tears.

"Marybeth, you married to save your little sister from being taken away from you. You married a man for convenience."

"Yes, but I loved him. I didn't realize just how much, but I knew that I loved him at least as a friend."

"Love is important, Melody. Isn't there anyone who has

caught your eye? Made you think he might be the one?" Granny asked.

Melody thought about it for a long quiet moment. "No, there's no one. I know we live in a town where the men probably outnumber the women forty to one, but I've honestly not found myself thinking that way about anyone. You forget, I've been with Da all along the way on building this railroad. I've seen the antics of the men working the line. I know a lot of them, but they're like brothers or wayward relatives." She laughed. "Definitely not men I would consider as a husband."

"We need to get to praying about it, then," Granny said, once again setting her knitting aside.

She'd picked it up and put it down so many times that Melody thought it a wonder she ever got anything accomplished. Still, she was right about praying. Prayer was the answer for getting answers, as Granny Taylor was always saying.

"I hadn't even thought to pray yet." Melody smiled and folded her hands. "That's why I come to you, Granny. You always know the right way to handle a matter."

"Not only do we need to pray, but we need to be keeping our eyes open. I'm sure Jed might know a fella or two who would make a decent husband."

"I can also ask Edward. He spent most of his time with Fred Henderson. . . ." Marybeth's words faded.

"We all miss Fred, to be sure," Granny Taylor said. "And we'll miss Eve and the young'uns."

Fred had worked with the town marshal's office and had hired Marybeth's husband, Edward, to be a deputy in Cheyenne. Unfortunately, Fred had been shot and killed not even two weeks back, and his sweet wife had fled the town she hated. The loss was still keen, and none of the women had quite been able to move on.

"I find myself still expecting Eve to come through the door since it was her house to begin with," Marybeth admitted. "She was such a dear friend."

"You can't blame her for leaving. This town would only serve to remind her of what she lost." Granny shook her head. "I am heartily sorry for that woman. Left with two little boys and a babe soon to be born."

"She's got a good family," Marybeth threw in. "They love her most dearly and will see to it that she has everything she needs. They're quite wealthy."

Granny gave a sigh. "But money can't bring back the one thing she truly longs for. We need to remember her in prayer as well."

The women were used to getting together to pray on a regular basis. Often they would talk with one another for an hour or more before speaking to the Lord, so Granny's comment was expected.

"Yes, and we should pray for my da," Melody requested. "His back is hurting him something fierce. He doesn't say much about it, but I know he's in pain."

"And pray for my Jed. His arthritis is causing him grief in his hands. A mechanic with bad hands won't be much use to the railroad. And while we've saved a good bit of money, it won't last that long if he finds himself out of work. Of course, we could go live with one of the children and make ourselves useful to them."

"I'd hate to see you leave Cheyenne." Having Granny Taylor here was one of the reasons Melody wanted to stay. She was a sort of mother figure to the younger woman, and after so many years without her own mother, Melody cherished Granny's advice.

"Say, don't you have a birthday coming in a few days? The thirteenth, isn't it?" Granny asked.

"Yes, I'll be twenty-six." Melody hadn't been overly concerned about it. Her father always remembered and took her out to dinner for the event. And he always had a gift for her. His gifts weren't bought without thought either. He was most meticulous in what he gave her.

Granny laughed. "Just a youngster. Well, we should plan a party."

"I don't need a party, Granny."

Marybeth's frown finally left her face, and she offered a grin. "No, she needs a husband. Maybe we could have a birthday party and invite all the eligible bachelors in town."

Melody chuckled. "That would save Da the time and trouble of running them down for himself."

"Maybe he could just take out an ad in the paper," Marybeth suggested.

"Or announce it from the pulpit at church," Granny countered, more than a little amused by the entire matter. "Goodness, perhaps we could just put up an auction block in the middle of town."

Melody laughed but wasn't all that certain her father wouldn't jump at the opportunity to try any of their suggestions. What exactly had she agreed to? The thought of marrying a stranger was starting to sink in. What would the rest of Cheyenne think when they learned the truth? And what would the men of Cheyenne think? Would they think her wanton? Or perhaps unreasonable and difficult since she hadn't been able to find a man on her own?

Things were about to get very interesting in the Doyle world. No doubt about it.

2

*C*harles, banking is in the Decker blood. You have your Dutch ancestors to thank for that.*" His father had pointed this out on more than one occasion for the youngest of his three sons.

If banking truly ran in the Decker blood, then Charlie was certain he'd been adopted. Even now, as he reviewed the small Cheyenne Savings and Loan his brother Jacob had started the year before, Charlie couldn't find a single thing that held his interest.

"I didn't expect you to come until summer." This came from the bank's assistant manager and teller, Jefferson Lane. At twenty-eight, the man was eight years Charlie's junior. He was the epitome of what Charlie's father would have expected in a banker. Jefferson was neatly groomed and wore a stylish suit. His black hair was cut close and parted on the right side, and his face was clean-shaven. He carried himself like a man who'd been raised in high society. Shoulders back, chest out, and he wasn't afraid to look you in the eye.

"Yes, well, there was a change of plans. Father felt it was important to have me here now. I got into town two days ago but wanted to settle in before coming here." Charles smiled. "I can see he had nothing to fear, however. The place seems to be in order. Have you been in banking long, Mr. Lane?"

"Call me Jefferson or Jeff." Jefferson smiled.

"And you should call me Charlie." He immediately regretted it and spoke again. "Actually, Mr. Decker is probably best. That way when my brother returns you won't have to change names again." He hoped that would sound reasonable to Lane. He didn't want to come across as snobbish. Truth was, he could use a friend, but Father always maintained you didn't befriend your employees.

Jefferson nodded. "When does your brother plan to return?"

"I'm not sure, but I do know this arrangement is only temporary."

"I see." Jefferson gave a slight shrug. "As for your question, I've been working in banks since I graduated from college. Working my way up, you might say. I hope one day to own my own bank, but for now I'd settle for just managing one."

"I wonder why my father didn't just put everything in your hands once Jacob felt the need to leave."

"How is Mr. Decker doing? I knew he was having a terrible time of it here. He was always having headaches and nosebleeds. I do hope the doctor has found a cure for what ails him."

"The doctor felt my brother just needed a rest, though he suggested it could be the altitude." Charlie shrugged. "I don't seem to notice it."

"I hailed from St. Louis and later from Denver. I've spent a good deal of time in the mountains over the last few years. The altitude doesn't seem to bother me either."

"I'm glad to know that. We'll no doubt have plenty of work

to do to continue building the business, and I wouldn't want you going the same way as Jacob."

"No worries about that," Jefferson replied. "I'm in perfect health."

Charlie noted that the man did seem strong and capable. He could only pray that Jacob would heal and return soon. He looked back at his brother's small office. "I take it that you usually work out here in the teller's cage?"

Jefferson nodded and moved to stand behind the teller counter. "I manage the day-to-day transactions. You will handle all of the requests for loans, of course. I will make sure you get introduced to everyone as they come in. Most are just private citizens with nominal savings. We hold quite a few home and several dozen business loans. The newest business being a freight company who intends to expand as soon as the first loan is paid in full. That should happen later this summer. They've been quite devoted to getting the loan paid off."

"I can't blame them. I'm against carrying debt myself." Charlie chuckled. "I suppose that seems strange for a banker whose bank name includes *loan*, but I've always been careful to save and pay for things in cash."

"I agree with that philosophy," Jefferson replied. "A man should never be burdened with debt. It's a frightening thing."

Charlie picked up one of the ledgers. "There are quite a few healthy savings accounts. Nothing too grand."

"We have a few customers who are better off than others. There are men in this town who wield the power, and they are men of means. Some of them were good friends with your brother and trusted their savings to us. They intend to do more business with this bank in the future as well. I'm sure they'll come by soon to introduce themselves."

"That's good to hear." Charlie looked down a list of figures. "Jacob said that our species . . . that is, our gold and silver reserves are held in my father's bank in Chicago."

"Yes. This is the Wild West, and marauders are known to cause problems, although I cannot imagine anyone coming into our bank to rob it. But it is possible. Look at the havoc wreaked by Jesse James and his gang. They could come this far west."

"They'd have a lot of empty territory to cover to get here," Charlie said, thinking it very unlikely.

"True enough, and there is our vigilante committee to deal with when the law is broken, as well as our marshal and deputies. And don't forget the army. For miles around us, there is nothing to escape to, and it would be sheer madness to attempt theft. Still, your brother said it was wiser to leave that much gold and silver in Chicago."

"I'm sure my father knows best." Charles began to relax a bit. "So we have some wealthier clients who have put their money here. What about the loans? I know my father has never been one to lend on living collateral, such as crops and livestock. I'm not at all sure why he agreed to start this savings and loan, given his attitude, since most of the men who will need loans will be ranchers and farmers."

"We can loan on the value of the land, your brother maintained. That is something tangible and credible. Values here have risen dramatically just since last year. At one time a lot was valued at one hundred fifty dollars. Now that same piece of land can sell for fifteen hundred. Land is a solid investment."

"That is an impressive jump in value." Charlie shut the book. "Well, I suppose it's time to close things up. I need to make my way to the boardinghouse where I'm staying."

"With the Coopers at Nineteenth and Hill, correct?" Jefferson asked.

"Good memory. Yes, that's where I'll be. A short walk and a very comfortable household. Mrs. Cooper is quite the cook."

"I'll be sure and remember that should any of my family need a place to stay when visiting. She does do short term, doesn't she?"

Charlie shrugged. "I have no idea. I'll have to ask." He went to his office. "Is there anything more you want to put away in the large safe? I'm going to lock it now."

"No, I've returned all that goes there."

Charlie secured the safe and grabbed his hat. "Then make sure you secure the small safe and teller's cage before you go. I'll see you in the morning at nine."

Jefferson held the door open for him. "Safe is secured, and teller's drawer is emptied of cash and locked. The back door is locked, and I will lock the front as soon as we leave."

Charlie stepped onto the boardwalk and waited while Jefferson locked the door.

"Good evening." Charlie snugged down his hat against the stiff breeze and headed for his new home. Jefferson took off in the opposite direction. He seemed an amiable enough young man, but there was an air about him that reminded Charlie too much of friends he'd known growing up. Men who had been taught from boyhood that they were better than everyone else.

The Coopers were a nice Christian couple who lived just a short distance away. They had a large two-story house where they boarded six gentlemen of varying ages. Mrs. Cooper was in her fifties and talked with loving affection of the six children she'd left behind in Kansas. All were grown and married, but she spoke of them as though they were still tugging on her apron and in need of her guidance. Mr. Cooper had brought her to Cheyenne when he'd heard the Union Pacific was making the end-of-the-tracks town a regional headquarters. He had great aspirations of making a name for himself in real estate. He had taken an inheritance and purchased ten separate lots when they were inexpensive and sold off half of them in just the past month. He intended to keep the others and build houses on them to either sell or rent. Already, he told Charlie, he had made more money than he'd anticipated.

The gentle couple had a list of five rules that were posted by the front door. Charlie adhered to all of them with more than a nod.

1. *God is revered and honored in this house. There will be no taking of His name in vain, nor swearing of any sort.*
2. *Church attendance is required every Sunday—unless you are sick in bed.*
3. *Drinking of alcoholic beverages is prohibited at all times.*
4. *Smoking will be contained to the front porch or yard in warmer months and the smoking room in winter.*
5. *No women are allowed on the second floor at any time.*

Breaking these rules will be grounds for immediate removal from this house.

For Charlie, the rules weren't difficult. He didn't drink. He didn't smoke. He didn't swear, nor would he ever dishonor

God by taking His name in vain. Church was a pleasure to him, not a chore, and he would never dishonor a woman by compromising her reputation. They were easy rules to abide by, and it appeared that the other men felt the same way.

In return, Charlie had a pleasantly appointed room with a large single bed, a dresser, and a desk and chair. There was a small open closet where he could hang his clothes, and down the hall was a shared bathroom. Mr. Cooper saw to it that there was water for washing up, and for fifty cents more, he would heat enough water for a bath and dispose of the dirty water afterward.

Mrs. Cooper provided most of the benefits Charlie enjoyed. She cooked amazing meals for breakfast and dinner. The noon meal was something the men were expected to see to themselves, although for an extra fee Mrs. Cooper would provide a lunch there at the house or pack a few things the men could take with them to work. Mrs. Cooper would also wash clothes and provide ironing services for a small charge and cleaned the rooms once a week as part of the boarding fee.

Charlie felt he couldn't have found a better place. The porch was lined with chairs for evening enjoyment during the warmer weather, and there was a large parlor for reading and discussions in the evening. In the winter, a smaller closed-off parlor was billed as "the smoking room," and the gentlemen were allowed to smoke there in the evenings between the hours of six and nine. Since it was spring and the long sunlit hours of summer stretched out before them, it would be some time before the smoking room was needed. Even in downpours, Mr. Cooper assured the men they would stay quite dry on the porch, unless, of course, the wind was blowing hard.

The Coopers were good to their guests, offering sage advice, directions to a variety of locations, and evening snacks. Mrs. Cooper said the men were to be treated as family so long as they behaved themselves. And if they didn't behave, even then they'd be treated like family and forced to make amends or go. Charlie found their honesty and fairness to be just, and their sense of humor and charm a delight.

"Well, Charlie Decker, you look plumb worn out," Mrs. Cooper said in greeting as he came to the supper table at exactly five thirty.

"I have to admit that I am rather done in." He smiled and reached out to take the large platter of fried chicken she carried.

"Thank you, Charlie." She glanced down the table as the other men gathered. Seeing that everyone had arrived on time, as was required, she took her place at the foot of the table. Only after she was seated with help from Mr. Cooper did the other men take their seats.

Charlie was still learning the names of his fellow roomers. There was Stuart Johnson, who worked for the railroad as a comptroller. Bryce Clemmons, who also worked for the Union Pacific. A newly arrived pastor, Wilson Porter, who appeared to be around Charlie's age. Gary Newman—no, it was Nyman—was employed with a freighting company that hauled goods back and forth to Denver, and the rather stocky man seated beside Charlie had come west to Cheyenne to start a newspaper only to realize there were already five other publishers. Charlie couldn't remember his name but knew it would come out in the course of conversation.

"Let us say grace," Mr. Cooper said and bowed his head. "Father, for this food we are about to receive, we thank You and ask Your blessing. Thank You for yet another good day and for the guidance You offered each of us. In Jesus's name, amen."

"Amen," the men murmured along with Mrs. Cooper.

"Charlie, how was your day?" Mrs. Cooper asked as the food began to be passed around the table.

"It was a good day, Mrs. Cooper. I'm slowly getting used to finding my way around. I think I'm going to like it here."

She smiled and handed him a basket of homemade rolls. "I'm glad to hear you say that. And your room? Is it to your liking?"

"It is. I slept quite well and have absolutely no complaints."

"Don't forget to have your laundry outside the door by nine tonight. Mr. Cooper will be by to pick it up directly after that."

"Yes, ma'am." He had already told her he would need her skills for his upkeep. He'd much rather pay her to see to his things than take them elsewhere. There were quite a few Chinese immigrants running laundries on the west side of town, but Charlie had heard that most of them were heading west with the railroad workers.

Charlie passed the rolls to his right and received the platter of chicken from the man across the table. He held it while Mrs. Cooper chose a thigh for herself, then he grabbed a breast for himself and moved the dish down the line. This went on with all of the food until everyone had been served. Then, as if on cue, everyone picked up their forks and began to eat.

The food was some of the best Charlie had had since leaving home. His mother's cook did a wonderful job, but his dishes were often quite rich and sometimes exotic. Charlie preferred the simpler fare he enjoyed at the Coopers' house. And if there was a need to add to the richness, Mrs. Cooper generally had cream gravy and freshly churned butter that could be incorporated into just about anything a man wanted to add it to. Charlie was just as happy to eat his meal the way Mrs. Cooper served it.

"Boys, you needn't use a knife with your chicken," Mr. Cooper announced from the far end of the table. "Never was able to master it that way. Use your hands if you're inclined. You'll get no reprimand from me. Just don't wipe your hands on Mrs. Cooper's tablecloth. You have napkins for that."

Charlie nearly laughed out loud at the look on the newspaperman's reddened face. He had only been in the house a couple of days longer than Charlie and looked as if there had been some other incident that brought about this warning. The man hurriedly tucked his head and focused on buttering his roll.

There was all manner of chatter at the table. The railroad men shared information about the line moving west. Some of the workers had been clearing land and laying tracks, and others were loading up train cars with supplies from the stores of goods laid up all winter in the warehouse.

Mr. Nyman told about the argument of whether to use mules or oxen to haul the heaviest loads bound for Denver. He was a mule man himself and despised oxen. Thought them sluggish creatures who suffered far too many hoof problems.

"Mr. Jackson, how goes plans for your newspaper?" Mr. Cooper asked.

Jackson. Otis Jackson. Charlie smiled as the man's name came to mind.

"I had a discussion with the young man who runs the *Daily Leader*."

"Oh, Nathan Baker. Yes, he is a dear," Mrs. Cooper commented. "He has a wife and little boy."

"He's but a child himself," Mr. Jackson countered.

"Folks start young around here. Our butcher isn't yet eighteen, but he knows his business," the woman replied.

"Yes, well, it seems there are numerous newspapers in the city, but most are weekly or even monthly. The *Leader* is the only daily paper."

"With the exception of Sunday. Baker chose to follow God's example and rest on the Sabbath," Mr. Cooper chimed in.

"Yes, well, the news should be told on Sunday as well as weekdays. Oftentimes, a great many important things happen on the weekend, and the public has a right to know."

The other men began discussing the virtues and foibles of having businesses operate on Sunday, while Charlie focused on his meal. Banking business wasn't done on Sunday and probably never would be.

"Charlie, you said that you have family back in Illinois, I believe."

He smiled at Mrs. Cooper. "I do. They live in Chicago. My father and mother and my two older brothers. Both of whom are married."

"But not you? Why is it that you're still single?"

Charlie shrugged and picked up his dinner roll. "I guess the Lord just hasn't sent me the right young woman."

"And He won't send her here in Cheyenne neither." This came from Bryce, who sat across the table to Charlie's right. The two exchanged a nod. "I've been looking for the last six months," Bryce continued. "Women—good women—are hard to find in these parts."

"But in time they will come. Once this town settles down, families will feel safe to settle here, and those families will have daughters. Single daughters. I'm hoping my own brother will move his wife and daughters out here." Mrs. Cooper picked up the bowl of mashed potatoes. "Charlie, looks like you could use some more of these."

Charlie didn't want to say no and took the bowl. He spooned out a little bit more of the potatoes onto his plate, then extended the bowl toward Bryce. "What about you?"

To his surprise, it was Mr. Jackson who grabbed hold. "I'd like some more myself."

"Oh, I read in the *Leader* that the fire ladder was returned. Seemed some rowdy boys stole it as a prank. The sheriff threatened to lock them up but showed leniency," Mrs. Cooper declared. "The children here have run positively wild, but with the public school operating and more private schools opening, they will hopefully receive a little more structure and discipline."

The conversation turned to other things, and the food was passed once again until most every dish was emptied of its contents. Charlie couldn't help but reflect on the topic of schools and education. Teaching was his passion. A passion his father seemed to have little respect for, but nevertheless Charlie found most fulfilling. More than once his professor had asked him to help with tutoring other college students. He had also taught Sunday school for younger boys.

Charlie had hoped to talk to his father about his leaving banking for the world of education. In fact, with the inheritance Charlie had received from his grandfather, he had contemplated creating his own small school. From the comments around the table, and elsewhere in town, it seemed private schools were most welcome. Perhaps Jefferson Lane could run the bank, as he longed to do, and Charlie could just check in with him from time to time, while teaching school elsewhere. The idea intrigued him.

3

elody made her way into the Cheyenne Savings and Loan, where her father had arranged a joint account. Since he wasn't able to work, they were pulling out a little of their savings each week to pay rent and buy food.

"Good morning, Jefferson," she said, greeting the teller. "I've come for our weekly stipend." She pushed a piece of paper across the counter to the smiling man. She'd always thought Jefferson handsome. Unfortunately, he knew he was good-looking and was rather full of himself to boot.

"Miss Melody Doyle, aren't you a ray of sunlight." He gave her a lingering gaze. "I haven't seen anyone half as pretty as you all morning."

She laughed. "Well, the day is early."

To her left, someone cleared their throat. She looked over and found a tall man with brilliant blue eyes and dark brown hair. His hair was combed back off his forehead, and he was clean-shaven—something Melody preferred. He was impeccably dressed, but there was still something almost casual about him. He gave her a smile that seemed to light up his eyes.

"Jefferson, are you going to introduce me to our customer?"

Melody didn't wait for Jefferson but stepped to where the man stood. "I'm Melody Doyle. My father and I have an account here. And you are?"

"I'm Charles Decker. This is my father's bank, and I've come to take over for my brother Jacob until he can return."

"That's right, I heard from Jefferson that he was ill. I do hope he's doing better."

Mr. Decker's gaze never left hers. "He is, thank you."

"I'm so glad," Melody replied. "He is such a nice man, and I enjoyed hearing about his family."

"Jacob told you about his family?"

His question took Melody aback. "Why yes. He was quite sad to have left them behind in Chicago, but he said his wife was fearful of bringing the children west, where wild Indians were still known to raid. He seemed to miss them a great deal."

"Jacob has always been very private. I'm just surprised that he would say a word about his family."

"Melody has a way about getting folks to talk," Jefferson interjected. "It's her pretty face and kind spirit."

"I can see that possibility."

"So, Mr. Decker," Melody began, only to be interrupted.

"Call me Charlie. All my friends do."

Charlie was a much friendlier name than Charles and far less formal than Mr. Decker. "Charlie, I'm very glad to meet you. I hope you'll enjoy Cheyenne and stay for a good long time."

"I hope so too. I find the location quite beautiful and the people very friendly, Miss Doyle."

"Melody. Like a song. That's my name," she said, laughing.

"Things are calming down now that the railroad is moving out. You will still need to watch out for undesirable characters, however. Cheyenne seems likely to always contend with a few hoodlums," Jefferson said. "Miss Doyle, I have your money all counted out."

She glanced over at him and found his expression a bit pinched. "Are you having a bad day, Jefferson?"

His frown deepened. "Why do you ask?"

"You look a tad miserable. I just wondered if there was something I could pray about on your behalf."

Jefferson shook his head. "No, I'm just preoccupied with business."

Melody looked back at Charlie. "You have a very dedicated associate, Charlie."

"I have heard as much and am just now learning that for myself. He was here this morning seeing to bank operations before I even arrived."

"Are you planning to make Cheyenne your home, Charlie, or are you just here temporarily?" Melody went to the teller's window, where Jefferson stood waiting. She reached out to take the money, but Jefferson pulled it back.

"I have to count it out to you," he snapped.

"Of course. Go ahead." She held out her hand again but glanced back at Charlie. "All the regulations must be a hardship at times."

"Yes, but adhering to them, just as with keeping God's commandments, offers better benefits than ignoring them. Oh, and the answer is yes. If there's a reason to stick around. I've long been ready for a change, and I've been seeking God to show me the direction He'd like me to go."

Melody smiled. "So you're a man of God, Charlie?"

"I am. And you? I mean, are you a woman of God?"

"Of course. God has seen me through so many bad times that I would have to be completely ignorant to ignore Him now. He is my mainstay."

"Melody, I need you to pay attention," Jefferson protested.

She turned back to him. "Go ahead."

He counted out the money to her and had her sign a slip of paper. "Are you satisfied with your transaction? Is there anything else I might do for you today?"

"I'm completely satisfied, Jefferson, and I don't need anything else."

She put the money in her little purse and turned back to Charlie. "Do you have a church yet? If not, I would love to extend the invitation for you to come and join the Methodist services. We meet at the public school since we don't yet have a building of our own. The services are at seven in the evening because another congregation uses it in the morning."

"Mrs. Cooper invited me to the Methodist services as well. I intend to be there on Sunday. Perhaps I'll see you. Unless, of course, there is more than one Methodist church in Cheyenne."

"No, it's the same one. I know the Coopers well. It will be nice to see you there. We have a wonderful service. Dr. Scott is our fearless leader, and he's so knowledgeable about the Bible, as well as being a talented physician. I must say I've learned a great deal under his instruction."

"I shall look forward to seeing you there."

"How come you've never invited me to church, Melody?" Jefferson asked.

She looked back at him. "I could have sworn I had . . . back last year. I do apologize if I was remiss. Of course you are welcome to join us. Speaking of the school, have you heard that the school board is already looking to expand and trying to figure out how to accommodate the ever-growing number of children? I heard that no fewer than ten private schools have been formed."

"Ten?" Charlie asked.

Melody nodded. "Apparently with all of the new families arriving, the school is overflowing. At last count, there were nearly one hundred thirty children who wished to attend but hardly the room for half that many."

"What are the requirements for opening a private school?" Charlie seemed quite interested in the topic.

"I have no idea," Melody replied. "I can't imagine it's much more difficult than to just announce that you're willing to teach and have a location. One young lady in our church has opened a private school in her parents' house on O'Neill Street. I believe her students are all quite young, but of school age."

"Fascinating." Charlie rubbed his chin. "Teaching was always my first love."

"And yet you're here."

"My father and grandfather were bankers. They felt it was a family duty to continue. My brothers took right to it, but I . . . well, not so much." His eyes seemed to twinkle. "Yet here I am, as you pointed out."

"There's always the opportunity to change directions, Charlie." She glanced over at Jefferson. "And never too late to join us at our church. I shall see you gentlemen next week, if not sooner at services."

She headed outside. She rather liked Mr. Decker. He was nothing like his stuffy older brother. That man was most serious, and rarely had she seen him so much as crack a smile. Melody shrugged. She supposed happiness came in different forms for different folks.

"Miss Doyle is quite a pleasant young lady," Charlie told Jefferson after she'd gone.

"Yes, she is. I've long thought of asking to court her." Jefferson didn't particularly care for the sappy smile on his employer's face. "Her father works for the railroad. He was injured in an accident at the warehouse and is still on the mend. Soon, however, I'm sure they'll be leaving us. Folks go just as quickly as they come, it seems."

"What about you, Jefferson? Will you go as quickly as you came?"

Jefferson had stopped in Cheyenne after leaving his parents' home in Denver. Completely by chance, he had managed to intercede on Jacob Decker's behalf when a freight wagon nearly knocked him down in the middle of the street. Cheyenne was well-known for its dangerous roads.

Lady Luck had smiled upon him, and Jacob had been so grateful that he'd hired Jefferson on the spot to come work at the new savings and loan. Now, however, he had to work with Jacob's younger brother, and the man wasn't nearly as easy to manage.

Having heard so much about the new end-of-the-tracks town to the north of his parents' home, Jefferson had decided to make his way there, hoping for a chance to make his fortune. The only other place that held any interest was California, and that seemed much too far away. But he wasn't about to share his plans with Charlie.

"I don't intend to go anywhere. My parents are in Denver, and Cheyenne gives me just the right distance to be on my own yet know they're nearby. I'm on a mission to make my fortune and prove myself a capable man."

"I suppose in one way or another, we're all doing that." Charlie started for his office, then turned back around. "Do you really think starting up a school is as easy as Miss Doyle made it sound?"

He shrugged. "Cheyenne seems content to set the rules as it goes. The school is, as Melody said, overflowing. The school board has decided to build a large addition onto their new building. They're going to charge a fee per student to raise the money. They are asking for folks to volunteer time and materials to build it. Perhaps they'll hire more teachers, and you could apply."

"No, my desire is to have my own school so that I can teach from a faith-based perspective. I want my pupils to have the Bible as the foundation of their education."

"I'm sure there are enough religious folks around here to accommodate your desires, Mr. Decker."

Charlie smiled. "The possibilities seem endless. And Miss Doyle brightens thoughts of staying here in Cheyenne even more. Do you know her well?"

"Well enough."

"Is she promised to anyone?"

"Not that I know of. Of course, her father is quite the force to be reckoned with. He gets into fights all the time, and many of them are regarding Melody. I'd tread lightly."

Charlie laughed and headed once again for his office. "A beautiful and godly young woman is worth any effort to woo."

Jefferson shook his head as he glanced toward the ceiling. It sounded like Charles Decker might become a rival for Melody Doyle's affections, and that was the last thing Jefferson wanted to have to contend with. He'd long had his eye on Melody. She was a beautiful woman. Tiny and slender. He guessed he could span her waist with his hands. Her blue eyes were huge, and her sandy-brown hair, almost always plaited in a single braid, reached her waist. Jefferson liked to imagine it flowing free in the wind. And even better still, her father had a healthy balance in his savings account.

No, he didn't want to deal with Charles as a rival. Already he was trying to figure out a way to keep the two separated. He supposed he'd have to start attending church services since it seemed likely that Charles would. Decker had already mentioned that it was a requirement of living at the Coopers' boardinghouse. Imagine forcing people to attend church.

Still, he knew religion was important to Melody, and if Jefferson was to have a chance with her, he'd need to at least pretend interest in God. It shouldn't be that difficult. He had grown up going to church with his parents. His father insisted that men of importance should be a part of as many prominent social organizations as possible. Church was merely one of those. The idea of boring sermons about ancient patriarchs of the Bible, however, did not interest Jefferson in the least, especially when contrasted to sleeping in on Sunday morning. However, Melody's church did meet at night. It wouldn't be that hard to participate.

And he was determined to impress his father. *"When you've made your first thousand,"* his father had told him, *"bring proof to me, and I'll double it."* That was just the first step in a line of conditional promises, and Jefferson intended to meet each and every one.

Jefferson went to where he had put a stack of loans whose payments were due in the next few days. He started thumbing through to put them in date order. There was also a stack of loan requests that were now Charles Decker's problem. He gathered them and took them to the older man's office.

"I have several loan application requests for you to consider. However, two of them have no collateral to back up their requests, and I know nothing about the men and have not been able to secure references."

Charlie looked up from his desk, where he was studying one of the bankbooks from last year. "Leave them here with me, and I'll see what I think. Do you know when the customers intend to return for an answer?"

"Most will be here Friday. That's when your brother usually met with folks. That way if his answer was no, he wouldn't have to worry about seeing them again until Monday because the bank would be closed. Sometimes applicants would return to beg. If it was yes, well, then it didn't matter because they weren't complaining." Jefferson left Decker's office and glanced at the clock. It was almost eleven, and he was starving.

He stopped and headed back to Charlie's office. "If you don't mind, I'd like to take an early lunch and go now."

"Of course. That's more than fine. I've got plenty of work to keep me busy."

Jefferson couldn't imagine what was so urgent. Jacob Decker had put things in order before going, and quarterly reconciles weren't due until the end of the month. It didn't matter. As long as Jefferson could leave and maybe catch up to Melody.

He took up his hat and headed outside. The day was a bit chilly, but the sun shone without a single cloud to block its rays. When Jefferson lifted his face, he relished the warmth. It seemed like a good omen of things to come. Things that might include Miss Melody Doyle.

Charlie stretched and glanced at the clock. It was nearly noon. Surely Jefferson was due back before long. Generally, they didn't take hour-long lunches. Although, he had been here less than a week, and who could say what his employee's regular schedule was. Jacob had headed back to Chicago in early March, so Jefferson had been running things for a little less than a month. He might have gotten lax in his routine.

They would have to speak about the schedule in more detail and make certain that it was well understood. Charlie didn't mind a little late return now and then, but he definitely needed to establish himself as the one in charge. He didn't want Jefferson thinking that since he'd been in charge the last month he could do as he pleased.

Melody Doyle came to mind once again, pushing aside any worries about Jefferson. Charlie felt quite smitten. She was beautiful, to be sure, but her heart for God was even more appealing. She had invited Charlie to church without any hesitation at all, had even asked if he was a man of God. She wasn't the least bit pretentious and didn't flirt or put on airs. She fit many of Charlie's criteria for a wife on those counts. Perhaps as they got to know each other through church and banking business, Charlie could get to know her better personally.

The door opened just then, and Jefferson strolled in as if he owned the place. He had a general sense about him that seemed to suggest he was used to being in control. Perhaps Jacob had been sicker than he'd let on. Had his brother been so often out of the office that Jefferson could do as he liked?

"Glad you're back. I was beginning to worry."

Jefferson gave a look that seemed to be a cross between a smirk and annoyance. "Sorry about that."

He didn't sound that sincere. Charlie gave a nod. "Well, we need to be on top of things here."

The younger man seemed to consider Charlie for a moment, then nodded. "I lost track of time. It won't happen again."

Charlie thought about inquiring as to what he'd been doing but decided against it. Jefferson hadn't really done anything wrong.

"When do you usually take your lunch, Jefferson?"

The man shrugged, as seemed to be his common habit. "Your brother and I didn't stand on the formalities of a schedule."

"Well, I think it best if we do. I suggest that if you're given to early lunches, then perhaps you would like to take your lunch from noon to twelve thirty. I'll take mine from twelve thirty to one."

"Just a half hour?"

"Yes, unless there's something special that you must attend to. We can always make an exception. The bank will be open from nine in the morning until five in the evening. That should allow for everyone's banking needs, don't you think?"

"That has been our normal practice, but your brother liked to have a full hour for lunch."

Charlie considered that a moment. "As I said, on occasion I think that would be just fine, but let's just do a half hour lunch for now."

The door opened to admit a young cowboy, and Charlie turned his attention to him. "Welcome to Cheyenne Savings and Loan. How may I help you today?"

"Name's Bruce Cadot. Came to discuss a loan." The man took off his hat and gave Charlie a nod. "Put in my application last week."

"We don't review applications until Friday," Jefferson said, coming forward.

Charlie smiled. "That's all right, Jefferson. I like to do things my own way. Why don't you step into my office, Mr. Cadot, and we'll see what we can do."

"Yes, sir."

Charlie held out his hand to the man. "The name is Charles Decker."

"He's quite a looker," Melody said as she shared tea with Marybeth Vogel.

"Who? The new banker?"

"Yes. Who else would I be talking about?"

"I thought perhaps you were speaking of Jefferson. Since you're of a mind to find a husband, I thought maybe there was something there that had caught your attention."

"Not really. I suppose Jefferson could be a possibility. He compliments me often and always wants to discuss any variety of topics. Still, I just don't feel any connection to him. He . . . well, frankly, he bores me, and there's something about him that doesn't quite seem sincere. I imagine him as the kind of guy who spends a lot of time in front of the mirror."

Marybeth nodded. "You said that your father has a gift of discernment where people are concerned. No doubt he could figure out if Jefferson is sincere. We'll keep thinking about it. What about the banker?"

"Mr. Decker could be a possibility, I suppose. Obviously, I don't know him well enough to judge his character."

Melody took a sip of her tea and pondered the man. He did seem amiable and pleasant. He was handsome, and she was very drawn to his blue eyes. Was that enough on which to base the start of a romance?

"This entire matter is so unexpected. I truly thought Da would let me stay, given you and Edward offered to let me live on your property. He's determined, however, to see me married. I suppose it has something to do with the old traditions and his desire to have some sort of hand in my courtship. Da has never been overbearing about it, though."

"My father always believed that when I found a good man, I would know if he was the right one."

"I don't know if Da believes that or not, but I know he wants to be a part of the choosing, and I won't dishonor him. His ability to figure out a man's character has always been impressive to me, and if he wants to filter through the men who are interested in me, then I support him. I feel better knowing they've passed Da's scrutiny."

"But he will let you have the final decision, won't he?" Marybeth looked more than a little worried.

"I believe he will. Da is a bit of a romantic at heart," Melody assured. "He'd never impose a husband on me."

Marybeth's expression relaxed. She poured Melody more tea, then added some to her own cup. "No matter what, I think your father has your best interests in mind. I'm sure it's worrisome to him to think of leaving you behind in a town known for its wild and reckless ways."

"But he knows from experience that sounder heads will prevail once the railroad continues west. We've seen that over and over in building the UP. Da's seen it elsewhere as well. Some of the smaller towns disappear altogether, but that won't happen to Cheyenne. Da says the Union Pacific will see to that."

"Edward says the same thing. He feels confident that Cheyenne will thrive."

"Oh goodness, just look at the time. It's gotten the best of me once again. I need to head home and see to supper. I haven't even thought about what to make."

"Why don't you and your father have supper here tonight? I've made a large pot of chicken and dumplings and have an apple pie for dessert. I know Edward would love to have the chance to play a game of checkers with him."

"Da's been hurting in a bad way. I think that fall was harder on him than he lets on. The doctor says very little about it, but I don't see Da getting any better. At least not as quickly as he used to."

Marybeth was undeterred. "Go home, then, and check on him. Ask if he'd like to come, and if not, why don't you come back with a large bowl and a plate, and I'll send some food home with you?"

"Thanks, Marybeth. That would be wonderful. It would be great not to have to worry about cooking. Maybe I'll have a chance to check on the garden plot. Those of us in the tent community had a bit of the land plowed up for planting. It's really too early for anything to be growing, but I like to check just the same."

"We've had our garden plowed as well." Marybeth put her teacup aside. "We made it quite large, and I'm excited to get it planted with all sorts of wonderful vegetables. Edward even talked about us buying some chickens. I think I'd like that a lot. You can't beat having your own eggs."

"Someday, Marybeth. Someday." Melody finished her tea and got to her feet. "I'm going to have it all someday. My own house. My own garden and even the chickens." She laughed and grabbed her shawl. "I'll be back shortly and let you know what Da says."

"Try not to despair, my friend. I know God is watching over you in all of this. He has a journey figured out for you and just the right man for you to take it with. You'll soon be just as happy as I am."

4

I can't believe you're going to loan Cadot money. His ranch is already being used as collateral." Jefferson paced back and forth.

"The cattle themselves are of value, and the ranch hasn't been reassessed since the improvements Cadot made over the winter," Charlie told Jefferson. "I think there's more than enough equity to support the additional loan. Besides, he's getting a really good deal. Those Texas boys are desperate to get rid of their herd, and the price is a good one. Cadot is only paying ten dollars a head and will sell them in the fall for triple that or more. The army has already arranged to buy whatever animals he wants to sell. He plans to use the profits to pay off the loan and still have enough to bring in new stock. He has a reasonable plan."

"What do you know about raising cattle?" Jefferson asked. The smirk had returned to his face.

"Not that much, but I'm not afraid to learn."

"What about your father's advice not to use animals as collateral? Anything living can die."

"Like I said, the ranch is worth more now than when he

borrowed the money against it last summer." Charlie frowned. He didn't like that a subordinate would give him such a difficult time. "Now, the matter is settled, and I'd appreciate it if you'd get back to your own job so that I can do mine."

The front door opened, and Charlie recognized Wilson Porter from the boardinghouse. "Pastor Porter. How can I help you?" He went to the man and extended his hand.

The man shook hands with Charlie. "Thought I'd come set up an account. Mrs. Cooper told me how to find you."

"Come into my office, and we'll talk."

Wilson followed him and took the leather-bound chair Charlie offered. Charlie had hoped to get to know the man better; after all, they were about the same age and neither had family in the area.

"If I heard you correctly the other night, you're out here to minister to the Indians."

Wilson nodded. "I am. I felt God called me west, so after the war, I attended seminary and then talked my local church into sponsoring me."

Charlie felt obliged to share a bit of his own life. "I'm from Chicago. Served in the war and came back home to continue with the family business of banking. Although, it's not exactly how I'd like to spend the rest of my life."

Wilson eased back in the chair. "I remember hearing you say over supper that you were interested in teaching."

"Yes, I truly feel it's my calling."

"So God called you to teach, but you chose banking instead?"

Charlie laughed. "Well, Pastor Porter, I guess that's one way to put it. Frankly, I was trying to honor my father. He wanted all three of his sons to follow his example and be bankers."

"You can call me Will. Never did take to titles."

"Will it is. Now, you mentioned something about wanting to open an account."

Just then, Jefferson appeared at the open door. He paused to knock, and Charlie waved him in. He put two ledgers on Charlie's desk and turned to go without a word. The expression on his face, however, left Charlie little doubt he was most perturbed.

"Jefferson, wait just a minute."

The younger man turned, not even trying to hide his annoyance. Charlie just smiled. "I'd like you to meet a new customer of ours. Pastor Wilson Porter." He figured using the title was appropriate given the situation. "And Pastor Porter, this is my assistant, Jefferson Lane."

"Pastor Porter," Jefferson said in a clipped tone. He didn't so much as smile.

"Mr. Lane." Will gave a nod. "Very nice to meet you."

Charlie didn't care for Jefferson's stiff and unfriendly manner but said nothing. He supposed this was just going to be the way of things until Jefferson realized Charlie was going to do things his own way.

"So, Will," Charlie began after Jefferson had gone, "where are you from?"

"Ohio. Outside of Cincinnati and later in the city of Salem. As you come from a family lineage of bankers, I come from a long line of preachers."

"Do you still have family in Ohio?"

"My mother and sister sold the house after Father's death and went to Mississippi to stay a time with my aunt. My mother's older widowed sister."

"I'm sorry to hear of your loss."

"It was a great loss, to be sure. I'm trying to convince my

mother to move here. I hope to be working closer to Fort Bridger, but Cheyenne would put them so much closer to me."

"We've both been here such a short time, but I hear the town is still pretty unsettled. They keep telling me things are better than it used to be and will continue to improve as the railroad moves west, but it might be dangerous for two women who have no man to watch over them. Something to think about, anyway. Now, what about your work? Do you have a specific tribe you'll be working with?"

"I've been corresponding with the Indian Affairs offices in Washington. They are working with the Shoshone to finalize additions to a treaty written in 1863. Once that is complete, I hope to go to Fort Bridger to meet with the Indian agent Mr. Blevins and begin working with the Shoshone."

"I admire you for that." Charlie found the man's willingness to lay his life on the line and move to regions of unrest to be quite commendable. "Do any of the Shoshone speak English, or will you have to learn the language?"

"There are some who speak English, but not many. As I understand it, the Indian agents have been working with them, and this new addendum that is being written will require the children be educated. That, of course, will mean teaching them English."

"So they'll need teachers?"

Will shrugged. "I would imagine so."

"That's very interesting." Charlie couldn't keep from picturing himself teaching to the native children. Wouldn't that be something?

"Well, if you don't mind, I should probably finish up my business here," Will declared. "I promised I'd meet Dr. Scott in about half an hour."

"Of course." Charlie smiled. "Let's get your account set up."

~ ⌒ ~

The afternoon wore on, and each time Jefferson came to the office to bring something, Charlie noted his sour expression and minimal words. He was more than a little unhappy with Charlie's choices, and yet he had no right to be. It wasn't his money.

"Is there something you need to say?" Charlie asked after Jefferson's third trip to his office.

Jefferson looked as if he might say something, but then he turned to go back to his teller's cage. "Just wanted you to have the information you asked for," he said over his shoulder.

Charlie was starting to wonder why Jacob had ever hired him. Jacob would never have allowed Jefferson to question his choices. Charlie didn't want to have to get firm with the younger man, but he had learned from his father that authority had to be established early on. If not, employees would take advantage of the situation. The same was true in the classroom, which was where Charlie really wanted to be. However, since the bank was his assignment, he had no other choice.

I guess I'll have to put my foot down.

Charlie looked at the clock. It was nearly five. He might as well say something to Jefferson now, and then they could close for the day and be done with it.

He drew a deep breath and got to his feet. He had never wanted to be an employer with people to boss around. His father had pushed him into the world of banking, and Charlie could hear him even now, hundreds of miles away in Chicago.

"I have plans for you, Charles," his father had declared. *"You*

have finished your education and served your country. Now it's time to settle down and take over your part of the family business. Your brothers have done well, and I've no reason to doubt you'll do the same."

But that wasn't what Charlie had wanted to do with his life. It still wasn't, and now he had to face reprimanding an employee. His heart just wasn't in this.

He locked his office door and turned to find Jefferson already standing at the front door. He could see the look of irritation on the young man's face. Maybe their talk could wait for the morning. No, if Jefferson took on an even worse attitude, then Charlie would have to deal with it all day.

"You know, Jefferson, it's good for a man to know his mind and to hold his own opinions," Charlie began as he crossed the room. "But as my employee, it might be best for you to hold that opinion to yourself unless I ask for you to make it vocal. I will fall or rise on my own merits, and you won't be the one who must account for the results."

Jefferson straightened and looked Charlie in the eye. "I understand, sir." He emphasized the latter word.

Charlie smiled. "Good. I appreciate that you do."

There, surely that would be enough to put the man in his place and let him know that Charlie was in charge and ready to defend his position. And his choices.

Jefferson opened the door for him. "Have a good evening . . . sir."

Charlie thought to stop him from the formal address, then decided against it. If that was how Jefferson needed things to be to remind him of his place, then so be it. Charlie refused to be offended by his tone or his choice of words.

He waited as Jefferson finished locking up. "I'll see you in the morning."

Jefferson nodded but said nothing more. He turned and walked in the opposite direction that Charlie planned to go, and for a minute Charlie just watched him. Jefferson struck him again as a man who intended to go places, to be important, to be in charge. He didn't seem like the type to allow anything to stand in his way.

Charlie hadn't checked to see whether Jefferson had an account with the bank but presumed he must. It might be interesting to see what kind of wealth he had set aside for himself since he'd started working for the savings and loan the year before. The bank wasn't quite a year old, but Charlie knew from what Father and Jacob had said that Jefferson had been on board since the start.

Heading toward the boardinghouse, Charlie couldn't help but wonder what the future would hold with Jefferson Lane. The man wasn't at all happy with following orders. Jacob had never been one to tolerate insubordination. Had his health issues caused him to give the younger man free rein? Maybe Jefferson didn't treat Jacob the same way he did Charlie. Jacob was older and better established in being a man in charge. He had no doubt set boundaries in place even before hiring Jefferson. Charlie remembered his father's words.

"There must be a division between the worker and the one in charge, Charles. This is most critical. A man needs to know his place, and it is the responsibility of the man in charge to put him in that place from the beginning. Anytime he tries to venture from that position, a supervisor must be ready to reassert authority and put him back into it. Otherwise, you'll have utter chaos."

Those words, and so many others, echoed in Charlie's head. His father had always been stern and commanding.

He'd never once asked Charlie for an opinion but had instead told him what to think and do. The only time Charlie had gone against his father's wishes was when he'd enlisted to fight in the war. Even then, however, Bertram Decker had had the upper hand. He'd quickly arranged for his son to be the aide for a high-ranking officer who preferred making battle plans to fighting. Charlie had seen less than two major battles, and those he'd seen only from the far rear echelons, where it was somewhat safe. At least as safe as any battlefield could be. Still, he'd hated his position of privilege when he knew his friends were laying their lives on the line. But at least he had been able to serve.

The opportunity to take over for Jacob at the savings and loan had come as a welcome change to Charlie. Not because he wanted to continue his hand at banking. Not even for the ability to be in charge. No, leaving for Cheyenne gave Charlie a chance to escape the men in his family . . . as well as their scrutiny and criticism.

Charlie had tried numerous times to discuss his desire to teach and, perhaps, to build his own school, but no one cared enough to listen. He was always silenced with talk of new business opportunities and the state of national finance.

Coming to Cheyenne at least allowed him the freedom to make his own choices. To a degree. His father still expected to hear updates on Charlie's state of affairs, and, of course, there were the quarterly reports that had to go in. Not to mention that Father expected to have monthly letters explaining the general conditions of Cheyenne and Charlie's opinion of opportunities for growth. Not that his father would really consider Charlie's opinion. He still treated Charlie as though he were ten instead of a man in his thirties.

Maybe that was due in part to wanting to be called Charlie instead of Charles. Or maybe it was due to Charlie's carefree spirit and general positivity toward life. Mother always said he was the happiest of all her children.

Charlie credited his spiritual walk for that happiness. Mother had helped him to understand the need for God's guidance and direction from an early age, and in seeking to know God better, Charlie had learned a contentment that seemed to elude his brothers and father.

He cast a glance around the growing town and smiled. He could see being happy here. He could imagine himself building a school for boys and finding a young woman to marry. Melody Doyle came to mind as a possibility. She was quite pretty and so kind in her nature. Of course, Jefferson had voiced interest in the young woman. But if she was the one God had for him, Charlie knew God would arrange it in time. Charlie just needed to be obedient and mindful of what God wanted him to do, and right now it seemed banking was a part of the plan.

"Are you sure you want to take on a job?" Faith Cooper asked Melody as they made their way to the Coopers' house. Melody had run into Mrs. Cooper on her way back to get food from Marybeth, and the conversation had led to Faith explaining that she needed to hire someone to help her with the boardinghouse.

"I'd love it. Da's able to do for himself, even if the railroad won't let him come back to work just yet. That in and of itself is a puzzlement. I've never known the railroad to turn down a hard worker like Da, but the doctor says he's just not up to it, leastwise that's what Da told me. Anyway, he doesn't need me at home all the time, and helping you would allow us to bring in a little money."

"Are you in need?" Mrs. Cooper asked in a serious tone.

Melody moved the basket she carried from one arm to the other. "No, not at all. Da saved a good amount of money before he got hurt. We've been using the savings, but if I were to work, we could use my money instead."

"Well, as far as I'm concerned you can start on Monday. I'll need you there by five thirty to help with breakfast." They'd reached the Coopers', and she motioned Melody to follow her into the house. "You can see for yourself the dining room is just through there, and beyond is the kitchen. I'll have plenty for you to do in the mornings just feeding this bunch."

"That won't be a problem," Melody assured the older woman.

"And I'll need help with the garden. My knees are so bad it's hard for me to get down and plant. Do you think you'd be able to manage that as well?"

"Of course. I love to garden."

"Then we have laundry. So much laundry. Most of the men want me to manage it for them, and that takes quite a bit of time. Not only that, but I change the bedding once a week and wash the blankets every month. Gerald is going to string me two more lines for drying clothes."

"I can help with it all. When the vegetables start coming in, I can even help you to can and preserve them. Of course, by then I'll probably be married off to someone, and they might have something to say about me working. Or I'll be on down the track with Da."

"Is your father really determined to find you a husband?"

Melody nodded. "He is, and if he doesn't, I'll have to leave

Cheyenne and continue west with him." The thought wearied her to the bone. "I'm hopeful, however. I really believe God would have me stay here in Cheyenne."

"I hope so. I've come to enjoy our friendship."

"Well, now you can enjoy me as your housemaid too." Melody smiled and held up her basket. "I'd best go now. Marybeth Vogel is waiting on me."

"I'll walk you out."

Melody hurried to leave the house, exiting out the front door. She paid no attention to where she was going and nearly ran into one of the boarders.

"I'm so sorry," she said, putting her hands out to steady herself. Only after doing it did she realize she'd planted them in the middle of the handsome brown-eyed man.

"Forgive me again," she said, pulling away.

"That's quite all right. No harm done."

"Melody, this is Wilson Porter. He's a pastor newly arrived in Cheyenne. He's hoping to set up a ministry with the Indians."

"It's very nice to meet you. I'm Melody Doyle."

"Melody is going to be working here at the boardinghouse and helping me with a variety of things," Mrs. Cooper offered.

"I'm glad to meet you, Miss Doyle. Now, if you'll excuse me, I have some things to attend to."

Melody nodded as the man hurried by and headed upstairs. Faith chuckled, causing Melody to look at her in question.

"I was just thinking of your father's bargain. Maybe you should consider becoming a pastor's wife."

Melody laughed and headed down the street. There really didn't seem to be any problem finding single men, but finding one her father approved of was an entirely different story.

Still, the day was going quite well, and Melody wasn't going to worry about her need for suitors.

It had been her good fortune to run into Mrs. Cooper. She wasn't sure what Da would think of her taking a regular job, but maybe if he saw that Melody could support herself and had a place to live, he wouldn't worry so much about her finding a husband. Not that she minded the idea of finding a man of her own. But she preferred to fall in love with someone rather than marry for convenience. She had been certain that Da would rather she do that as well, but he didn't seem to think it a problem to interview men for her to go out with. The entire matter was something of a curiosity, and the more she talked about it with her friends, the more it caused Melody to wonder if she was making the right decision.

After seeing Marybeth, Melody headed back to the tent. Children played outside, enjoying the closing of the day. It had been a clear day, and while a cloudbank had formed in the west, there wasn't yet any real threat of rain.

"Da?" Melody said as she walked into the open tent. Her father had tied back the flaps to let in the fresh air.

He came from around the curtain they used to divide the living area from the sleeping space. "I'm here."

"I've brought our supper. Let's eat while it's still hot." She set the basket down and drew out the bowl of chicken and dumplings.

Melody placed the bowl on their tiny table, then retrieved the plate. Marybeth had cut two large pieces of apple pie, and Melody knew her father would enjoy the treat. She'd give him one now and save the other for tomorrow.

"I have some news," she said, putting the pie on the table.

She hurried to retrieve bowls and spoons. "Do you want me to make coffee?"

"I just made a pot. That on the stove is fresh."

"Wonderful." Melody found his coffee mug and filled it. "Ready?" she asked, placing the cup beside his bowl.

"I am."

Da prayed a blessing over the meal and then waited while Melody dished up the food. "Smells mighty fine," he said. "Sorry I wasn't up to going to the Vogels' for a visit." His Irish brogue sounded all the thicker when he was tired.

"Oh, they completely understand. Edward was just waking up for his evening shift when I was ready to leave. He said that he hopes you'll be feeling better soon and that he'll come by another day to check up on you and maybe get that game of checkers." She paused and gave him a long look. "Da, you look tired. Did you not rest while I was gone?"

"Oh, to be sure, I did. I'm fine." He smiled. "Ya worry over me like yar ma used to. Now tell me about Marybeth's little one. How was she doin'?"

"Growing like a weed. Marybeth said that Carrie has shot up at least two inches in the last couple of months." Carrie was being raised as Marybeth and Edward's daughter, even though she was actually the woman's little sister. Carrie's mother had died shortly after giving her life, and both girls had lost their father the previous year.

"She's a precious one, to be sure. One day ya'll be havin' a houseful of your own young'uns."

Melody chuckled and finished serving the food. As an afterthought, she went to the bread box and brought the bread and butter to the table. Taking her own seat, she gave her father a nod. "And you'll be teachin' them all to play checkers and shoot marbles."

"And what would be wrong with that?" Da's eyes twinkled with delight. "I'm thinkin' it would be a fine thing for a grandda to do."

She nodded. "It would be, at that." She picked up her spoon. "Oh, as I said, I have news."

"Well, get on with it, then."

"I met Mrs. Cooper on the street, and she told me their house is now full with six full-time boarders, and she needs help to keep up with the work. I told her I would love to come and ease her burden. I hope you don't mind."

"Not at all. What will ya be doin'?"

"Washing up and cooking, a little gardening and such. I'll head over about five thirty and help get the breakfast on and go from there. I thought if you wanted, I could fix you something first and leave it warming on the stove if you weren't of a mind to get up early."

"I can be fixin' me own breakfast. Ya'll have enough to worry with. I'll get up in the mornin' and walk ya over. It's not that far, but it's still dark in the wee hours. I'll feel better goin' with ya."

"That's kind of you, Da. I'll feel better having you along too. Things are already calming down, but there's no sense taking foolish chances."

"To be sure." He pointed to the bowl. "This is a mighty fine bowl of soup. Marybeth makes a dumplin' as light as yar mother's."

"She's a good cook, to be sure."

"And we're blessed that she takes pity on her busy friends."

Melody knew that she was about to get all the busier and didn't want Da to worry. "I'll make sure to see you fed, Da. Never worry. Mrs. Cooper said I can figure out the hours that work best for me. I can even come home during the day and take care of business here, then return to their house."

"I wasn't worried about it, my dear. Ya've never failed me, and I don't believe ya'll start now."

5

Charlie had never been so full in his life. He figured most of the men around the table probably felt as stuffed as he did. Mrs. Cooper had put on an amazing Easter luncheon, and none had been shy about eating.

"Mrs. Cooper, I am amazed at all that you prepared for us," Charlie said, shaking his head, "and it was so very good."

"It was indeed," Otis Jackson replied. "Had my newspaper been up and running, I would've devoted an entire article to you, ma'am."

The older woman laughed. "You boys are too kind. Most of it's just simple fare that my ma and granny taught me. I'm glad you've enjoyed it."

"It's a pity Mr. Nyman had to miss this," Otis continued. "I'm sure whatever he's managed to eat in Denver isn't nearly as good."

"Mr. Nyman told me he has an elderly aunt in Denver, so perhaps they've partnered together to share an Easter meal," Mrs. Cooper explained.

Charlie knew from a discussion with Nyman that he had bought into a new freighting business that made regular runs between Denver and Cheyenne. It worked well for the man because his aunt allowed him to have a room in her small house so that he didn't need to keep two residences. Still, Charlie figured Nyman got the worse of the deal in missing out on Faith Cooper's Easter feast.

The conversation changed several times, finally landing on cattle and the great number of herds that were forming up around the growing town. Charlie listened with great interest as the railroad men, who seemed to have some knowledge of cattle, discussed the necessary needs that the ranchers would have.

"So long as the grass and water are good, they'll be in great shape," Bryce declared, nodding when Mrs. Cooper offered him another cup of coffee.

"A couple of our boys raise cattle in Kansas," she said before moving on to the next boarder to fill his cup.

"The real problem will come in the winter months," Stuart Johnson piped up. "You have to be ready to supplement their feed and bring them into safety up here. Blizzards can be fierce, especially when they last for days."

"Yes, but the newspaper ran an article earlier this month about Seth Wood. He left his cattle out to range all winter and did just fine. Hardly lost any at all."

"I heard the same for a couple of other herds. Most got through just fine," Otis said, helping himself to another dinner roll.

"Most, but not all."

Charlie listened as they discussed the various farms and ranches in the area and how well or poorly they'd done. Seemed sheep were also taking to the land around Cheyenne. There was talk of the small temporary slaughterhouse becoming permanent and expanding.

"Once they make up their minds about running trains up from Denver, this place is going to be busier than ever before," Mr. Cooper declared. "We'll need that slaughterhouse running full time. I'll bet our population will triple. Maybe even quadruple."

"Quadruple. What a word," Mrs. Cooper said, shaking her head.

Once dinner was over, Charlie offered to help wash up. Mrs. Cooper was more than happy to accept his offer. "We're bringing some help in, starting in the morning," she told Charlie. "A young lady who goes to our church, Melody Doyle."

"I met her at the bank." Charlie easily remembered her sweet smile and pretty face.

"She looks as delicate as a china doll, but I've seen that girl hoist a fifty-pound sack of flour over her shoulder. She's got muscle aplenty on that petite frame."

Charlie laughed and took up a dish towel to dry the plates that Mrs. Cooper had just washed. "She seemed capable of handling herself, and she invited me to church tonight."

"She's a good Christian girl. Her pa is a godly man. He works for the railroad but had an accident a few months back, so he's healing up right now. I reckon once he's well, he'll be heading on west with the railroad."

"Town seems a little emptier every day. I haven't even been here that long, and I have certainly noticed."

Mrs. Cooper handed him one of the plain white plates. "It was a terrible place last winter. Fighting and murdering. Thieves everywhere. A woman couldn't walk alone in town. Not even in the better part. It just wasn't safe."

"And is it now?"

"It's a whole sight better," she replied, ready with another plate. "The railroad is already fifty miles to the west, and they've set up another town. Soon the workers won't be flocking back here for much of anything."

Charlie hurried to dry the dish he held, then set it aside so that he could take the next one Mrs. Cooper offered. He was glad to hear another person confirm that the town was in better shape than it had been. He didn't like the idea of living in a lawless society. His father would never have started a bank in Cheyenne if he'd known just how bad things were to begin with. Jacob had written home about some of the lawlessness but hadn't fully described the danger. If he had, Father would no doubt have put an end to the venture.

"The vigilante committee and town marshal's office have done a good job cleaning things up. Mr. Cooper told me the committee has been needed less and less, and we're all glad about that."

"Were they pretty ruthless?" Charlie had never lived anywhere that boasted a vigilante committee before.

"They were just. And they saved the town a lot of court costs. Still, I like the idea of law and order by the book." She handed off another plate.

Charlie nodded. "So do I. Vigilantes make me think of a lack of civilization."

"Well, that for sure was Cheyenne a few months ago, but it's settling down day by day. I think we're going to be a great town now. We still have some lesser-desired characters, and of course there are still the saloons and gambling halls." She glanced around before meeting Charlie's gaze. "Not to mention those places where certain women . . . make a living."

"Of course. Hopefully that will be cleaned up in time."

"I do hope so, although I suppose sin is sin and will always be with us."

⁓

"It's mighty nice to have everyone gathered for Easter services," Dr. Scott said from the front of the room. "As we celebrate the resurrection of our Lord and Savior Jesus Christ, it's good to remember His sacrifice for us."

Charlie fingered the leather spine of his Bible as the man continued to speak of God loving the world enough to send Jesus. Easter always brought to mind the hopelessness of the world without a Savior.

"Most of us have seen this town at its worst," Dr. Scott said, and many of the people around Charlie nodded or made some comment. "We've borne the brunt of terrible men who've done terrible things. A few women as well. Sin abounded, as it always seems to do, but as God's people have come together in prayer and worship, we have seen God change hearts and minds."

Charlie glanced to the right, where he'd seen Melody Doyle and an older man take their seats. He presumed the man was her father. Next to them was a young couple with a little girl, and just ahead of them, an older woman and man. Charlie could hardly wait to get to know everyone.

"We are glad to see Cheyenne take on the refinement of law and order, just as we rejoice when a lost sinner comes home to accept Jesus as Savior. Cleaning up the foul and dirty brings a light and joy to those who experience it. The people who turn themselves over to Jesus rise up from the grave of sin and sorrow to a new life eternal. And the process is as simple as believing and accepting."

Charlie had heard the salvation message preached many times, but on Easter the message always held special meaning to him. He thrilled as a boy to hear the story of Peter and

John racing to the tomb to find it empty. He tried to imagine himself there as one of the disciples learning that his Lord was no longer in the grave. He could picture the group gathered later to discuss the matter and Jesus appearing before them. Were they terrified? Were they completely awestruck when they realized that Jesus was alive?

"If you don't know the Lord," Dr. Scott preached, "then you don't know peace of mind and soul. Jesus welcomes all to come. He tells us in the book of John that He is the way to God the Father—that there is no other. Not even one option. Salvation is through Christ alone. And it's not hard to obtain. We don't have to do anything special. No tricks. No cost to us, because Jesus already paid the cost. We just have to believe and confess."

Mother had once told Charlie the same thing, adding that far too often people tried to make it much harder. They couldn't believe that something so important should be so easy . . . but it was.

It wasn't long before they were singing the closing hymn and prayer was offered to end the service. Charlie felt a sense of joy in having joined this congregation to celebrate the resurrection. They had welcomed him as if he were already a member, a part of the family.

"Before we leave this evening," Dr. Scott said, holding up his hands, "I'd like to ask you to retake your seats for just a moment. Clancy Doyle has asked to address the congregation."

Charlie watched as the older man with Melody moved past her into the aisle and headed to the front of the room. Charlie and the others sat down to hear what the man had to say.

"Most of ya would be knowin' me, but for those who don't, I'm Clancy Doyle." His brogue betrayed his Irish heritage.

"I work for the UP, and me daughter, Melody, is just over there." She gave a little wave, looking almost embarrassed.

"It's on account of Melody that I asked to be speakin' to ya now. The fact is, she would be likin' to settle down here in Cheyenne, and since the railroad is soon to be movin' me westward, I find meself in a bit of a fix." He took hold of the lapels of his coat and smiled. "I need to be findin' a husband for me daughter."

Charlie's eyes widened. He was begging for a husband for his beautiful daughter? Grief, but the woman could surely have a dozen suitors if she wanted them.

"Now, if ya know me," the older man continued, "then ya'd be knowin' I'm mighty particular about who comes courtin'." There was laughter from around the room. Most of it from the men. "But I'll be entertainin' any man who cares to come and speak to me about Melody. He must be a God-fearin' man with a good job and decent place to live. He must talk to me first before he goes talkin' to Melody about courtin'. That's me first and most important rule. She's a good woman with a kind heart. She loves the Lord and keeps our house well and cooks meals that melt in yar mouth. She'll make a fine wife for someone, but first they must come speak to me."

Charlie glanced over at Melody, who looked to have slidden down a bit in her chair. Poor woman. Her father wasn't making this easy. For all purposes, she was on the auction block with her father esteeming her virtues.

"Well, that's me piece," Clancy finished with a nod. "May the good Lord lay His blessin's upon ya."

Immediately folks started talking around him, but Charlie was far more interested in the men who approached Clancy Doyle as if his announcement were the most natural thing in the world. The older and married men seemed to clump together, while several women went to Melody's side.

He wasn't at all sure what to do. He'd wanted to say hello to Melody, but now it seemed as if that might not be the best idea. He didn't want her father to think he was disrespecting his command to talk to him first. But on the other hand, Charlie wasn't truly seeking a wife yet. Was he? God knew he prayed about it nearly every day. He often imagined settling down and having a family, and he even liked the idea of staying in Cheyenne permanently.

"I'm Edward Vogel," a man announced.

Charlie looked to his side. It was the man who'd sat near the Doyles. "Pleased to meet you. I'm Charles Decker, president of the Cheyenne Savings and Loan."

"Good to meet you. I figured you were new to town. I'm one of Cheyenne's deputy marshals. I usually work evenings, but Sunday's a day of rest for me."

Charlie shook the man's hand. "Good to meet you, Mr. Vogel. Or should I call you Deputy Vogel?"

"Call me Edward."

"I'd like that. You can call me Charlie."

"Are you related to Jacob Decker, then?" Edward asked.

"Yes, he's my brother. He fell ill and moved back to Chicago. Our father sent me here to take his place, at least temporarily. We're hoping Jacob will recover and be able to return. Starting a bank on the frontier was his idea."

"Kind of like coming to the ends of the world after living in Chicago, eh?" Edward smiled. "I haven't lived here all that long myself, but I know it was quite a lot to take in when we arrived at the end of last year. We hail from Indiana."

"Then we were neighbors," Charlie replied.

"Well, except you were at the top of your state, and we

were at the bottom of ours. But close enough. Glad you could join us here today."

"Edward, I see you've met Charlie," Melody Doyle said, coming to join them. Beside her stood the woman and little girl who'd sat next to her in church. "Charlie, this is Edward's wife, Marybeth, and their daughter, Carrie."

Charlie gave a slight bow of his head. "Good to meet you." He locked eyes with the little girl, who was reaching out to him.

"When she takes to someone, she immediately believes they should accommodate her," her mother said. "Carrie, the man doesn't need to hold you."

"I don't mind." Charlie laughed. "It has been ages since there were any youngsters around to hold."

The little girl dove from her mother's arms, and Charlie had no choice but to catch her. "Hello there. I'm Charlie."

"Chawie," she said and patted his face with both hands.

"I feel like I should go around and apologize to everyone for Da's announcement, but especially to you, Charlie." Melody's cheeks were flushed as she met his eyes. "Here it is your first Sunday with our church, and you're forced to experience my father's outspoken ways." She gave a nervous laugh. "But Da is determined."

"To find you a husband?" Charlie asked.

"Yes."

Carrie held out her arms to her father. Edward took his daughter and smiled at Charlie. "Carrie seems to approve of you, but then, she approves of most everybody. We'll have you over to the house some Sunday."

"I'd like that." Almost immediately they were surrounded by others in the congregation who wanted to welcome Charlie. He tried for a time to keep a side glance on Melody, but she was soon swept up in a circle of women who seemed to want to discuss the new turn of events.

Charlie chuckled to himself. Cheyenne was looking better all the time.

⌒

Melody stretched out on her cot and nestled down into the beautiful quilt Granny Taylor had given her that evening for her birthday.

"I wasn't sure if we'd have a chance to see each other tomorrow, so I wanted you to have it tonight," the older woman had said as they left church.

"Oh, Granny, this is such a surprise." Melody had taken the quilt and hugged it close. Just as she did now.

"You're a dear girl, and it does me good to bless you with this gift. I hope you enjoy it for many years. The double star pattern is my favorite."

Melody knew it would be her favorite as well. She loved Granny Taylor and sought her advice and counsel as she might have her own grandmother, if she were alive. Granny and her husband, Jedediah, had been a part of Melody's life since Omaha. Jed had put in to stay in Cheyenne when the railroad continued west, and that was part of the reason Melody had desired to stay as well. Knowing he and Granny would be close by would be almost as good as having Da with her.

Still, it was hard to imagine life without Da there day-to-day. He always made Melody feel that she was loved and cared for. Despite his rough-around-the-edges personality and readiness for a fight, Da was the gentlest of men when it came to dealing with his daughter.

"Ya still awake?" her father asked from the other side of the curtain.

"I am, Da. Do you need something?"

"No, just wanted to be sayin' happy birthday to ya. Me watch shows midnight."

Melody smiled to herself. "Thanks, Da. I was just enjoying my new quilt. It's nice and warm and so pretty. Not that I can see it all that well." The glow from the lantern on Da's side of the curtain didn't afford much light.

"Well, I was just puttin' out the light. There'll be time enough to see it tomorrow."

The tent went black, and Melody closed her eyes. "Good night, Da."

"I thought we might be takin' our supper at Belham's to celebrate your day."

"That sounds fine, Da." She sighed in the darkness. Her father was always so good to make sure she felt special on her birthday.

"I have a gift for ya, but of course ya'll have to be waitin'." He sounded so tired.

"I'm sure it will be wonderful, Da. We should go to sleep. I love you."

For a moment her father said nothing, and Melody wondered if he'd nodded off. Then he cleared his throat. "I've only loved one other woman more than I would be lovin' me darlin' daughter, and that was yar ma." He gave a long pause. "I love ya, Melody. I've always been blessed to be yar da."

Tears came to her eyes. "I'm the blessed one, Da. You've always been there for me, and I know you always will be."

6

It was still dark outside as Melody and her father made their way to the Coopers' house. The sun wouldn't be up for nearly an hour, yet the town was already coming to life. Melody was grateful for Da walking her over since she noted a few odd characters milling about.

"Are you sure you're going to be all right without me there to watch over you?" Melody asked her father. "I know your back is still bothering you, and you admitted you didn't sleep well last night."

"Me back is just fine. Gives me grief now and then, but it's of no bother. I'll catch me a nap later on."

Melody nodded and continued walking. "I heard at church that most of the undesirables are heading west today. The railroad is giving them free rides to the next camp and hauling over their temporary buildings and tents at a discount."

"Probably won't charge 'em a cent," Da replied. "The UP likes keepin' the workers close to home. If they had to take the train back here on payday in order to be spendin' their money, they might not be makin' it back to work. You know how it's been all along."

"Yes, and I'll be glad to see them all go. It's been a relief to know they'll soon be gone. Although I also heard some of the brothels are staying, along with some saloons and gambling houses. I suppose it would be too much to hope they'd all leave."

"Don't be frettin' too much," her father said, waiting to cross the street until a six-horse team pulling a large freight wagon passed them. "The men in charge of Cheyenne have made some of that business illegal. They'll be clearin' 'em out and makin' life difficult for them that stay, chargin' 'em license fees with fines and jail time. I've seen it happen before. Only the most stalwart will remain. The rest will be goin' elsewhere, seekin' a place where no one cares what they do."

"Do you really suppose Cheyenne will grow to be a big and civilized city?" she asked, trying to imagine it all.

"I do. The railroad will be seein' to that growth continuin'. Railroads hold a lot of power back east, and it won't be long before the West is crisscrossed with iron rails. It'll no doubt be a sight to behold."

"Well, here we are." Melody turned. "Thanks again for walking with me. I've enjoyed our time together with everything still quiet. I love this time of morning." She kissed Da on the cheek. "I'll see you this afternoon. Maybe sooner. Mrs. Cooper said I could come home and tend to my own chores in between meals if there wasn't anything else to do. Don't forget to keep the fire in the stove going. Otherwise, the roast won't get done."

"I'll see to it, but ya shouldn't have worried about it since we're going out to eat tonight."

"That's quite all right. It will be ready for us to eat tomorrow."

She headed up the front porch steps and turned at the

top to wave good-bye. Da had already headed back toward home. Melody watched him for a moment. His stride bore evidence of the pain he tried to hide. She would have to check in with his doctor and see if there was something he could take for the pain.

She turned back to the house and knocked at the front door. In a moment, Faith Cooper opened it and welcomed her inside.

"I was just putting on my apron, glad to see you're here. I hate that you must come in the dark."

"It's fine, really. Da walked me over. Soon enough it will be light earlier, and we'll have no worries."

Mrs. Cooper showed her where to hang her shawl, then handed her an apron. "We're having biscuits and gravy for breakfast. How are you with making lard biscuits?"

Melody smiled. "Da says mine are light as fairies' dust. I'm quite at home making them."

"Good. I'll let you get started on that. There are eight of us to eat. No, nine counting you. I usually figure on four for the men, and there are seven of them. So with you and me, I'd say make three dozen. No, go ahead and make four dozen, and that way we'll have some left over for lunch."

"Sounds good." Melody went to work.

Mrs. Cooper had a well-ordered kitchen, and Melody found it easy to find everything she needed. Within a very short time she had her first two trays in the oven. While the biscuits baked, Melody prepared the next batch. She mixed the dry ingredients and cut in the cold lard. Last, she put in the milk. Mrs. Cooper hadn't any buttermilk, so Melody added white vinegar to the milk before putting it into the rest of the mixture. When the ingredients were combined and the dough sufficiently worked, it was time to check the oven.

While Melody did this, Mrs. Cooper very expertly fried up sausage, then added flour, salt, and milk to the pan. The aroma of breakfast filled the air along with the coffee that had been put on before Melody arrived.

"We work so well together," Mrs. Cooper declared, "you would have thought we'd done it all of our lives."

Melody chuckled. "I was thinking the same. You've a beautiful kitchen with all the necessary ingredients, and they're easy to find. I couldn't have ordered it better myself."

By six thirty the food was on the table, and the men were seated, awaiting their meal. Mr. Cooper offered grace, and then the meal was quickly passed around the table until each man had what he wanted. Melody poured the coffee while Mrs. Cooper introduced her to the men.

"This is Melody Doyle. Some of you might already know her."

Melody glanced at Charlie and smiled. She wasn't familiar with the other men, with the exception of her brief introduction to Will Porter. Charlie smiled back at her, then turned his attention to the large bowl of gravy coming his way.

"Melody will be helping fix meals, do laundry, and clean. She'll also help with the garden and other odd jobs. You will treat her with respect. I'll not have her molested in any way," Mrs. Cooper admonished. "Not that we really need to tell you that. You seem reliable and honest men."

Mr. Cooper added his own thoughts on the matter. "Still, it doesn't hurt to stress the point. Miss Doyle is a fine young lady with an impeccable reputation, and we won't have it damaged by any nonsense. Understand?"

"Yes, sir," Charlie replied loud and clear. This prompted the others to murmur their assurances as well.

Melody brought the coffee to Charlie and poured the

steaming liquid without a word. He glanced up and once again offered her a smile. "I'm glad you could come to help. Mrs. Cooper has more than her share to do."

"I'm glad to be here. Mr. and Mrs. Cooper are dear friends of mine. It's nice to be useful to them."

"We will certainly appreciate your work, Melody," Mrs. Cooper added.

Mr. Cooper went around the table and introduced Melody to each man, adding what he did for a living and which room was his upstairs.

"We're only upstairs one day a week," Mrs. Cooper told her later as they did up the breakfast dishes. "We women do not go upstairs otherwise, nor are they allowed to have women on the second floor."

"Seems like a good rule." Melody finished with the drying and began to put away the dishes.

"We'll clean each room and change the bedding on Wednesdays. We'll also attend to the bathroom and put in new towels. Mr. Cooper takes care of the outhouse and its needs. He also gathers up the laundry for me and brings it down to the back porch."

"So, with breakfast cleaned up, do we immediately start working on supper?"

"I generally do. Especially if I'm putting in a roast or making pies and bread."

"And what would you like me to do?"

Mrs. Cooper smiled. "I'd just as soon you get to work on the laundry. There's a cauldron of hot water that Mr. Cooper prepared for us before breakfast. The water should be perfect to work with. I'll show you around the back porch so you can see how I have things set up."

By lunchtime, Melody had filled the lines, including the

two new ones, with a variety of clothes and kitchen towels. Once these were dry in the afternoon, she would iron what needed to be ironed and fold up the rest. For the time being, however, she made a quick trip home to see how her father was doing.

She was surprised to find him sleeping quite soundly. He didn't even stir when she came in. The poor man had been so restless through the night that his movements had woken Melody more than once. She decided against waking him. Instead, she checked on the roast. It looked perfect. She sliced off a piece and sampled it. It was delicious. She closed the oven door and left it to rest there.

Deciding she needed to tell Da not to add any more wood to the fire, Melody went to the table and took up a pencil and piece of paper. She noted an envelope on the table. It was addressed to her father, and the return address was from Ireland. Her uncle David had written. She couldn't help but wonder what had prompted that. Her father's relatives seldom wrote.

She considered reading the letter but decided against it. She wasn't one to pry, and besides, Da would tell her about it if she needed to know what was said. She ignored the letter and jotted a note to her father regarding the roast. She added that she was excited for their night out, then placed the note in plain sight. She took one last longing glance at the letter. What if it was bad news? Maybe some family member had passed away.

"If you need to know, he'll tell you," she whispered to herself. Then, grabbing up her gardening gloves, she hurried out before accidentally waking her father.

Thoughts of her new job quickly replaced the mysterious letter. There was a lot of work to do in keeping up with eight people, but she really didn't mind at all. She thought of Charlie and his sweet smile. He seemed quite at ease with his newfound family. The other men seemed equally content. The Coopers were good at making a home for strangers.

"Are you heading to lunch somewhere?"

She looked up to find Charlie had materialized before her very eyes. "I was just thinking about you," she admitted. Then wished she'd said nothing. How brash that must seem to him.

"You were? Whatever prompted that?" His eyes seemed to twinkle as if genuinely amused at her announcement.

"Uh, well, I was just thinking of my new job and seeing you there. I thought you seemed quite content."

"I am. The Coopers are amazing people. I love that they are devoted to God and each other, as well as their boarders. I feel like part of their family."

"As do I. Mrs. Cooper is quite motherly, and I welcome it. My own mother died years ago."

"I am sorry to hear that." His expression bore compassion, but it was the tenderness in his voice that caught her attention.

"I especially miss her today. She always made me feel so special. Da does as well. In fact, we're going out to eat tonight."

"What's special about today, if I might pry?"

Melody laughed and shook her head. "Sorry, that must have sounded confusing. It's not a pry at all. It's my birthday. I'm twenty-six."

"I thought ladies never admitted their age," he said, raising a brow.

"Well, I certainly have nothing to hide. Goodness, but my father just advertised to get me a husband. I certainly have no pride." She laughed again, but only to cover up her embarrassment at rambling on.

"I like that you're so open about it—your age and the situation created by your father. It's refreshing to find that kind of confidence in a woman. Happy birthday, Melody Doyle."

"Thank you." She glanced to make sure the street was safe to cross. "And now I must get back to work. I have laundry to iron and a garden to plant."

"Perhaps I'll see you later tonight when I get home from work."

"I doubt it. Mrs. Cooper said I won't be needed for supper work. And I'll be wanting to get home so I can clean up for my big night out."

"Of course."

She smiled. "Well, it was very nice running into you, Charlie. I hope you have a blessed day."

"And you as well, Miss Melody."

Charlie watched her cross the street with a spring in her step. The young woman seemed perpetually happy. Every time he encountered her, she was smiling or laughing and never seemed wont to gossip or speak negatively about any topic.

He thought of her father's request for suitors just the night before. It seemed crude and uncalled for. Melody Doyle was quite lovely—beautiful, in fact. Her dark blue eyes and sandy-brown hair were a perfect complement to her peaches-and-cream complexion. Why in the world did she need help finding a mate?

"Charles Decker, how opportune to run into you."

Charlie looked up and found Dr. Scott. "Good to see you

again, sir. I enjoyed all that you had to say at our services last night."

"Thank you. Easter is one of my favorite celebrations. Nothing quite so thrilling as the resurrection of our Lord. Not to mention the benefit given to us in His death."

"Very true. I'm certainly glad that Miss Doyle and Mrs. Cooper invited me to come."

"They are quite vocal in their beliefs. I've never known two women to live their faith more evidently for the world to see. They've both been good to encourage believers to join our ranks, and it won't be long before we have raised enough money to build our own place of worship."

"That will be wonderful for everyone, I'm sure. It feels rather awkward having church services at night in the local school," Charlie admitted.

"Yes, well, at least we have a place where we can come together. Some people of faith are meeting in homes. I suppose we can't all be as industrious and prosperous as the Episcopalians. They have been hard at work to raise the money and build their own house of worship. The UP donated two city lots, and many of the congregants have donated their time and skills. It's said they'll have the church built by August. They're calling it St. Mark's, after their sister church in Philadelphia."

"I had heard that the Union Pacific was generous to donate land to the churches. I suppose it supports and encourages morally sound growth in the community."

"Yes, and they have promised us land as well. We just need to raise more money to build on it. The Episcopalians have Reverend Cook, and he seems to know just what to say to motivate his people. They raised more than five thousand dollars. It will be quite the church once it's completed. They even plan to have a bell tower."

"I'm sure ours will be just as lovely. I might even speak to my father about donating to the cause. I know I will be happy to support the project."

"That's most generous of you, Mr. Decker. The Methodists were the first organized church in Cheyenne, but we're slow to build our own place. I am certain, however, that God is in charge of our plans. We will trust Him to show us when and where to build."

"I'm glad you entrust the project to God, Dr. Scott. I've never had much confidence in projects that came at the sole discretion of man. We always seem to have a way of messing things up."

"True enough," the older man agreed. "We've definitely not accounted in a realistic way for our school system. No sooner is the school in place than it's already bursting at the seams with students. We are going to have to add on to accommodate the one hundred-or-so students. And then there's the need for teachers."

"Teaching is my first passion. My heart has been to open my own school for boys. One based on strong Christian principles."

"We could definitely use men such as yourself in that capacity. Perhaps when your brother recovers and returns to Cheyenne, you could consider taking up that role."

"I used to teach Sunday school back in Chicago and feel positive that I could design an entire curriculum around the Word of God."

"I like the way you think, Charlie. This town could use more men like you."

"I want to do God's will and feel teaching is where God has entrusted me with talent. Banking is not my desire at all."

"God often puts us in positions that we feel are uncomfortable. Yet it has also been my experience that those positions are necessary for some other purpose. They teach us something that has been missing in our life or guide us to learn something we'll need later on down the road. Don't despair, Mr. Decker. In everything, trust it to God and seek His kingdom first, as Luke twelve admonishes. Then all the rest will be added unto you."

"I am, Dr. Scott. I assure you. It's the only way I've continued to stay the course."

"I'm glad to hear it. I hope that God is settling you well enough in our town."

"He is. I have a wonderful place to live for the time being. I'm at the boardinghouse run by the Coopers. They've been so gracious and kind. And Mrs. Cooper is quite the cook."

"Yes, she's known for her kitchen abilities, to be sure. We have bake sales from time to time to raise money for the building fund. Her cakes, pies, doughnuts, and strudels are known far and wide and always bring in the highest price." Dr. Scott leaned closer, as if sharing a secret. "There's an officer at Fort Russell who has a standing order for her apple strudel. He'll pay any price."

"All this talk of food is making me hungry. Would you allow me to buy you lunch?"

"No, I'm afraid not. I have a patient to see. I was just on my way there. If you don't mind, I would enjoy taking you up on the offer another day."

"Of course, Dr. Scott. I'd like that very much."

"Thank you. I'll bid you good day." He tipped his hat, and Charlie did likewise. He liked Dr. Scott very much and appreciated his heart for God.

Thoughts of opening a boys' school came to mind again as Charlie made his way down the street.

Lord, could it be possible that You brought me here for such a thing? Could I ever manage to convince Father that this is my calling?

The tiny ember that had always burned for his dream seemed to flame up momentarily. Dare Charlie allow it to burn—to stir him to action?

"Oh, that was a wonderful meal," Melody told her father as they arrived back at their tent home. "I have to say that I love a good beef steak, and having it on my birthday with my da makes it all the better."

Da lit a match to see his way inside. Melody let her father go into the tent first and waited until he had the lamp lit before pulling the flap down behind her and tying it closed. The night was chilly, so Melody started a fire in the stove.

"Would you like some coffee?"

"No. Just come and sit a moment, and I'll give ya yar birthday present." Da disappeared behind the curtain that separated their living space from the sleeping area.

Melody sat down at their little table and looked around the room. The tent had been home for a long time now. Except for the winter months, Melody spent very little time inside. Da usually pulled the chairs outside to sit and enjoy the close of day. Often they would eat out in the open air and visit with the neighbors.

She had to admit that she was tired of tent living. There was no room for anything that didn't serve a precise and necessary purpose. She had grown so weary of this life. Enough so that it made the prospects of settling down with a stranger sound appealing. She couldn't help but smile. Da would see to it that the man wasn't a stranger. Da had a way of getting every secret and quirk out of a person. She supposed it was the way he put people at ease that caused them to divulge their hidden bits of life.

"Here ya go. I thought long and hard about this gift, and when the opportunity presented itself, I knew it was the right thing." He came to the table and sat down. He placed a large envelope in front of Melody. "And it's not like ya'd be havin' room for much else."

Melody laughed and looked at the strange gift. She opened the envelope and pulled out several pieces of paper. Scanning the first sheet, Melody realized it was a stock certificate for the Union Pacific. She fanned through the other pieces of paper and found them all to be the same.

"To be sure, these will be worth a lot in a few years," Da began. "I'm thinkin' if ya save 'em and add to 'em ya'll have a fortune and never have to struggle as we have in the past."

Melody stacked the papers together. "Oh, Da, you always give such thought to my gifts. Thank you." She got up and kissed his cheek. "This has been a wonderful birthday. My only wish is that you would soon feel completely healed and be free of pain."

"Oh, I'm not doin' that bad, darlin'. Ya needn't worry about me." He gave her a hug. "But I am gonna be headin' to bed. It's been a long day, and ya'll be needin' me in the mornin'."

She hugged him. "Goodnight, Da. I love you."

He smiled back at her. "And I love ya more than life itself, me darlin' girl."

7

On Wednesday, Melody used her midday break to run to the bank for their weekly money. Da said he'd be busy all morning and asked her to take care of going to the bank, as well as stopping by the mercantile on her way home that day. Melody had no idea what was going to occupy him, but he seemed to have his thoughts elsewhere. Perhaps he was interviewing potential suitors. After all, they needed to move quickly. On the other hand, he had still said nothing about the letter from Uncle David.

The bank was unusually quiet when she entered. A quick glance at the large lobby clock revealed five minutes past the noon hour.

"Hello?" She saw nothing of Jefferson, and the door to the president's office was closed. She thought perhaps she'd leave, but then the door opened and two men exited. One was Charlie, and he shook hands with the other.

"I'll look forward to hearing back from you, Mr. Dawes."

"I should have all the information by Friday." With that, the man turned to go. He spied Melody and tipped his hat. "Ma'am."

Melody nodded with a smile and waited for him to leave before approaching Charlie. "I've come to withdraw some money from our savings," she told him.

"How's your father feeling?" Charlie asked as he made his way to the teller's cage.

"He's doing well, thank you for asking." She pushed a slip of paper to him with the amount she needed written down. Charlie glanced at it, then went to work getting the money and noting the withdrawal in the ledger.

"I'm glad to hear it," he said after counting out the money in front of her.

Melody slipped the cash into her little purse. "Da's got a strong constitution and a heart of gold."

"From what little chance I've had to talk to him, I have to say I found him to be quite amiable. His faith is clearly revealed in his actions and speech."

"It wasn't always so. Before Da found the Lord, he was always drinking and fighting. He once told me that people in five counties of Ireland regretted seeing him come their way."

"Well, he certainly changed for the better."

She nodded with a smile. "He did, to be sure. God nearly had to kill him to get his attention, but Da finally learned his lesson and changed his tune. Now he's better than most men. And I don't just say that because he's my da."

"Of course not. I wouldn't say such things about my father, necessarily. He's not a bad man, just very serious and driven in regard to his goals and accomplishments. I fear he may have never truly enjoyed his life for even a single day."

"That is something very sad. My da taught me early on that life should be enjoyed, as well as worked."

"I agree with him. If there is nothing but strict adherence to work, we suffer in other areas. In our spiritual well-being, for instance. I think we should devote time to spiritual renewal. My father thinks that kind of thought is a waste of time. He believes God will show us what He will and draw from us the things He wants. Otherwise, prayers and spiritual meditations should be left to Sunday services."

"I know a great many people who are like that. They put God in a trunk until they need Him. That would never work for me. If I didn't have my quiet time with God, I doubt I could face tomorrow or even the rest of the day."

"I agree. There is just something special about sitting with God in the still of the morning. Then taking time to reflect on His mercy and goodness through the day. I recall to mind some Scripture or promise He's given, and it bolsters my spirit." Charlie closed the ledger book. "Some folks would call me overly religious, I suppose."

"I wouldn't. In fact, your words could well be my own." Melody hoped he didn't think her forward. "I would go so far as to say our hearts are one on that matter."

Charlie smiled. "It does me good to hear you say as much. It's a comfort knowing someone understands, especially when living so far away from friends and family."

"Well, you have a friend in me, Charlie Decker. You needn't fear being alone. You should stop by and see Da sometime. He loves a rousing game of checkers and to tell tales of Ireland. You might find yourself completely entertained."

"I might at that. I'll try to take you up on the offer as soon as possible."

Melody bid him good day and headed back to the Coopers' house. She checked in with Mrs. Cooper, then went immediately to work in the garden. Mr. Cooper had ordered a load of manure, and she had promised to help spread it around the garden.

Working in the garden was another moment when Melody found time to meditate upon God and pray. She hadn't done much gardening here in Cheyenne, but elsewhere she had learned quite a bit about growing fruits and vegetables. Potatoes had always been a mainstay to her Irish ancestors, and now in America was no exception. Da loved potatoes in almost any form. A good boiled potato with a few pinches of salt was an entire meal to him. Melody had already made sure to plant several hills of potatoes in the community garden near their tent, knowing they would benefit the others if she and Da moved on. Mrs. Cooper was anxious to get her potatoes planted as well.

Melody and Mr. Cooper had managed to thoroughly mix the manure into the plowed soil when Marybeth Vogel and her daughter, Carrie, arrived.

"I brought those potato eyes," Marybeth announced, holding up a bulging flour sack. Carrie had a smaller sack and held hers up as well.

"Perfect timing. I was just getting ready to make rows. I should be able to have all of those planted in no time at all." Melody went to where Carrie stood. "Thank you for bringing me potatoes, Miss Carrie."

"You welcome." Carrie grinned and handed her sack over to Melody.

"I'm glad you found the Hendersons' already had these drying. That saves a lot of time," Melody said, coming to take the sack from Marybeth as well.

"Edward and I planted quite a few hills. Should have a large crop just for ourselves. I told Mrs. Cooper that we would definitely have plenty left over if she wanted them."

"With the boarders, they use a lot of potatoes. We have them most every evening and sometimes with breakfast."

Melody took the bags to a wooden table and deposited them. "What else are you and Miss Carrie doing today?"

"We've been quite busy," Marybeth replied. "Sorry we missed your birthday last Monday. Carrie and I have been making you a present."

"Oh, you didn't need to do that. Da and I celebrated by eating out, and it was quite good. Then Da surprised me with my gift. He always comes up with unusual ones. This year he gave me stock in the UP. He said it wasn't worth a lot just yet, but it would be, and I should hold on to it and even add to it if I have the chance."

"And how goes the search for a husband?" Marybeth asked, her expression showing doubt.

"I have no idea. Da told me he had been approached by quite a number of gentlemen. He's still making his choices."

"Oh my. Doesn't that make you nervous?"

Melody shrugged. "It did at first, but then I remembered that I don't have to pursue any of the men. If none of the men Da deems acceptable strikes me as a match, then I'll just move on with Da."

"But I want very much for you to stay here."

"I want that too." Melody had never wanted anything more.

"I wanna dig," Carrie announced.

Melody went to the gardening table and took up a small gardening shovel. She brought it to Carrie. "Here you go. Dig all you want." She glanced over Carrie at Marybeth. "Oh dear, I forgot to ask if that was all right with you."

"It's fine," Marybeth laughed. "She's quite good at digging."

As if to prove it, Carrie immediately went to work. Melody watched for a moment, then clapped her hands. "Very good, Miss Carrie. You dig very well."

"I dig and dig," Carrie replied, never stopping in her work.

Melody couldn't help but chuckle. "She's very helpful. May you have a dozen more just like her."

"Not a dozen, hopefully, but I'd settle for a few more. What about you?"

"I've always wanted to be a mother," Melody admitted. "I figured by twenty-six I'd already have three or four, but it hasn't been what God had planned. I'm trying my best to be content with how things are, but I have to admit there are times when I feel quite empty at the sight of others with babes in their arms."

"Me too." Marybeth met Melody's gaze. "I'm so hoping we'll have children."

"I know, and I'm praying that for you as well." Melody knew that Marybeth had raised her little sister since she was an infant. But it wasn't the same. Marybeth wanted to have Edward's children and to know what it was to carry that life inside of her own body. Carrie was special, and would always be so, but Melody understood how Marybeth felt.

For a long moment neither woman said anything, but the unspoken longing seemed to wrap around them.

"I'm praying for just the right husband," Marybeth said. "Someone you can love and who will love you as you deserve. I know you want to stay behind when your father moves on—I want that too—but even more I want love for you. I want you to fall in love with the right man and for him to love you as you deserve. You've become like a sister to me, and I can confide in you that a marriage of convenience is not nearly as satisfying as one of true love."

"I'm sure you're right." Melody glanced away to where Carrie continued her labors. She had prayed for God to send just the right man and for his love to be sincere. She would continue to pray for God's grace to make her the right woman with the amount of love that her husband would need. The proposition Da had recommended wasn't a simple one, to be sure, but Melody trusted both her earthly father and her heavenly one. Neither had ever let her down.

⌒〜

"And why would ya be wantin' to marry me daughter," Clancy Doyle asked Jefferson Lane.

Jefferson hadn't been sure he even wanted a wife, but with Melody's hand up for grabs, he thought it couldn't hurt to consider the matter. After all, the Doyles had a considerable amount of money in the bank that he hoped would be used for a dowry, and Jefferson needed a thousand dollars to prove to his father that he was successful so that the man would match it. Just the thought of having that kind of money at his disposal was enough to make Jefferson consider marriage to Melody Doyle.

"I find Melody a very amiable person. She's kind to everyone she meets, and my mother taught me that such a quality was important. God calls us to love one another, and you certainly cannot do that without kindness. Not only that, sir, but she's beautiful, and when I see her, my heart beats a bit quicker." He smiled. "I've long been moved by her grace and beauty."

"And for sure I'd be wantin' me son-in-law to find his wife appealin'," Mr. Doyle said, his expression quite stern.

Jefferson sat only inches from the tent flap opening, but every muscle in his body felt ready to spring if the older man so much as made a threatening move. He supposed Mr. Doyle sensed his uneasiness and probably used it to his advantage. Folks all around town knew Mr. Doyle was quite capable in a fight. He had a reputation for putting men much bigger than himself on the ground. But only with cause. It was often conceded that Mr. Doyle was never one to be fighting just for the sake of fighting. With that in mind, Jefferson didn't intend to give the man any reason to want to fight him.

"And are ya a God-fearin' man, Mr. Lane?"

Jefferson had been expecting this question. He didn't attend church, and Mr. Doyle would no doubt know that for himself.

"I am God-fearing," Jefferson began. "However, I'm not religious. I haven't yet found a church that I felt at home in. My mother trained me in the ways of God and the Bible when I was young, and when I was older my father did as well. I put my trust in God long ago and know that the Bible says salvation comes alone through Jesus. I'm certainly not opposed to attending church, but not having been here even a year, I find it easier to study the Bible at home on Sunday." The mix of truth and lies was easy enough for Jefferson to share.

"A man is a fool who stands as his own counsel." Mr. Doyle's eyes narrowed slightly. "However, I do understand yar thinkin'. I've been there meself. I'd encourage ya to come join us at the Methodist services on Sunday night. We meet at the school."

"Yes, I know. Melody invited me to attend on Easter. I didn't make it because I was feeling under the weather. However, I hope to go this Sunday."

Jefferson could see that his answer helped Doyle to relax a bit. He knew from comments others had made that the older man was definitely firm on his beliefs about God. He had known from his first thoughts to seek Melody as a wife that he would have to convince both that he was a man of God. Given his background, Jefferson knew all the right things to say and do. It shouldn't be that hard to convince them of his sincerity.

"And ya have a good job, do ya, Mr. Lane?" the interview continued.

"I do. I work for Cheyenne Savings and Loan. I've been managing it since the owner's son fell ill and had to move back to Chicago. Now another son has come to take the helm, but he's very much dependent upon me."

"And do ya like what ya do there?" Clancy Doyle's gaze never left Jefferson's face. It seemed the man was looking straight into Jefferson's soul.

"I do, for the most part. I enjoy meeting the folks from town and helping them with their needs. I've studied money handling and bookkeeping and find it very satisfying when all those ledgers add up and match." Jefferson smiled. At least that much was true.

"And what about a home, Mr. Lane. Would ya be livin' in a place of yar own or a rented apartment?"

"I currently live in a small apartment, but my savings are growing every day, and I intend to purchase a home of my own in the near future." Another lie, but hopefully the older man wouldn't realize it. Besides, what should it matter if Jefferson wanted to remain in the rented place? It was his decision as the head of the house, not Clancy Doyle's as father to the bride.

Clancy took out his pocket watch and checked it. "I'll have to be askin' ya to go now. Me daughter will be comin' home most any time. It's best that she not be here for the interviews until I figure out which men are worthy of her courtship."

Jefferson jumped up, quite anxious to leave. "I appreciate that you would consider me, sir."

Melody's father looked him over one more time, leaving Jefferson with the distinct feeling of being livestock at auction. It really was ridiculous that in this day and age a woman would be managed in such a way. Worse still, that he should have to endure it for the sake of marrying someone with money.

8

I've selected five different fellas to pay court to ya," Da told Melody as she served their supper. "Ya can be considerin' each choice."

"Five? Well, I suppose that will be more than enough." She put a bowl of her father's favorite corned beef and cabbage on the table and took her seat. She began dishing up the food as her father sliced into the fresh loaf of soda bread.

"It's a variety, to be sure. Their ages range from yar own to about fourteen years older. All have good jobs, seem to have good reputations in the community, and find ya attractive."

Melody laughed. "Well, I suppose that's a good thing." She placed a bowl of food in front of her father, then dished up her own. Once that was done, she took a piece of bread offered by her father and set it beside her bowl to wait for him to pray.

"Oh, gracious Father in heaven, we thank Ya for all that Ya've given. Bless the food and the day that we might serve Ya faithfully. Amen."

"Amen," Melody replied. She took up the bread and began to butter it. "So when will we start to see these fellas paying court?"

"Yar first outin' is Friday the twenty-fourth. And the second is on Saturday the twenty-fifth."

That was barely a week. Melody cut her bread into four equal pieces and took a bite. She trusted that her father had found good men to consider, but the entire matter still made her uneasy. After all, this was a lifelong mate she was searching for. Could she really figure out who to marry in a little more than a month?

"I want to be warnin' ya about that Jefferson Lane, the fella at the bank. He's not to be trusted."

Melody pushed aside her concerns and looked at her father. "He wants to court me?"

"Aye. He came to see me." Her father sampled the corned beef and smiled. "Yar a good cook, daughter."

"I'm glad you like it." She waited a moment, then posed another question. "So what about Jefferson made you uneasy?"

"He's a liar. I could tell he was lyin' the minute he opened his mouth. He couldn't look me in the eye for long at all. I'm not sure what he's up to, but I'll not have him courtin' ya."

"That's just as well. He doesn't appeal to me at all. Whenever I go to the bank, he's all sweet talk and attention, but there's something quite unappealing about him."

"That's the devil in him. Ya cannot be courtin' Jefferson Lane without keepin' company with his master as well."

Da dug into the food with more gusto than Melody had seen in a while. She knew he'd lost quite a bit of weight since she was the one to take up his clothes. It did her heart good to see that he'd gotten his appetite back.

"Well, you needn't fear, Da. I will steer clear of Mr. Lane."

"I'm glad to hear it." He took a bit of coffee.

"I'm enjoying my new job," Melody said. "I've been able

to help Mrs. Cooper with their garden. Of course, it's just getting started."

"Potatoes should have been in by St. Patrick's Day," Da commented.

Melody nodded. "I told her as much, but she wasn't too worried. She felt certain we'd have more than enough time for them to grow. Said some old-timer told her we'd be having a long summer."

Da seemed to consider this a moment. "That would please the railroad owners. They want very much for this railroad to be completed by next year or sooner."

"I read in the newspaper that the stretch that's coming up after the mountains is mostly desert-type land. Hot and dry. Full of snakes and other wild things."

"I heard it as well." Da dipped a piece of bread in the broth. "Such places are not a favorite of mine. I prefer the green."

"I do too. This area is as dry as I care for."

"The boys will have plenty to contend with as they build. I've heard there may be Indian troubles as well."

Melody shivered at the thought of her father and the others being under attack. So far the native peoples they'd encountered had been a mix of friend and foe. Sometimes the Indians would sneak into the camp areas to steal cattle. Just last year Cheyennes had placed a branch across the tracks, thinking to derail a locomotive engine. They had instead derailed a handcar and killed most of the repair workers who were heading out to tend to the tracks. Those were exactly the kinds of incidents that caused the railroad to bring in the army to keep the peace.

There had been more warnings as the railroad moved west. Melody had been concerned about attacks on the town of Cheyenne, but with Ft. Russell close by, most of the citizens felt that the Indians wouldn't chance an all-out attack.

Desiring not to dwell on the topic, Melody quickly spoke up. "I saw you had a letter from Ireland. Was the news good?"

"To me way of thinkin' it was. Me brother, yar uncle David, wrote with news."

"I'd love to hear about it." She hadn't been sure why Da had said nothing about the letter, but hopefully now she'd find out what it was all about.

"The family is good. They've been thriving. David's girls are all married now and have wee ones of their own. Liam and Seamus, me younger brothers, are doin' well with their families."

Melody had never met her uncles. She had, however, heard stories of Da's youth and the trouble he and his three brothers got themselves into. Usually, it ended in a huge brawl and even some nights spent in jail. She was glad her father had settled down to being a godly man who only fought when absolutely necessary.

"I'm glad they're all doing so well. Was there anything else?"

"There was, and I've been meanin' to tell ya about it," her father said, putting down his spoon. "Ya won't have known this, but me brothers and me shared in our da's business."

"A business? What kind?"

"A whiskey distillery. Ya know I had a problem with the stuff and me life was ruined at one time because of drink. When our da died and left us the business, I wasn't involved much. When I got right with the good Lord, I knew I didn't want any part of running it. I just felt it could lead me back to trouble. I picked up and moved to America instead. Last year, I finally wrote to me brothers and told them I'd like them to buy me out. The letter from David was an agreement to do so and told me they'd be arrangin' a transfer of money to America. I don't know all the particulars just yet."

"I had no idea." Melody wondered if her father's share would make him wealthy enough to stop working. With his back not yet improving, she worried he would just further irritate it if he hurried back to work. She thought of how she might pose the idea that he remain home for a longer recuperation.

"I never spoke of the business because it wasn't important to me. I never intended to be a part of it and didn't figure it mattered to us. However, the extra money will be somethin' I can leave to ya. It'll help ya after ya marry."

"I was just thinking it might help you, Da. Your back is still not healed, and who can say if it will be in another month. The money might allow you to rest and fully heal. I know you love what you do and the men you supervise, but you aren't a young man anymore."

"Aye, and that's for sure." He looked momentarily saddened by the conversation. "Those days are gone forever."

Melody didn't care for his melancholy tone. "Still, after a long rest, you might be just as capable as you've always been. I think the worst thing you can do is rush your healing."

"I'll give it a thought. In the meanwhile, this is one of the best suppers I've had in a while. It's been ages since we had corned beef."

She smiled at how quickly he changed the subject. "Yes, it's definitely been a long time."

Jefferson was more than a little excited when Melody Doyle made her weekly bank visit. He poured on the charm, hoping she would find him appealing and encourage her father to let him court her.

"You're looking quite lovely today, Miss Doyle," he said, greeting her at the door. "I must say that shade of blue does wonders for your eyes."

She offered him a smile. "Thank you, Jefferson. You're looking quite dapper yourself."

He grinned. This was a new suit, and he'd hoped she might notice it. "It's the finest cloth to be had. I arranged for it to be custom-made."

"Well, it certainly looks to fit you." She drew out cash from her handbag. "I've come to make a deposit in our account. Now that I'm working, I'm hoping to build up our savings again."

Jefferson took the money and moved to stand behind the teller's cage. He proceeded with the transaction, hoping to engage her in talk of a night out soon.

"I spoke to your father. You know, about the arrangement to court you."

"Yes, I'm fully aware of the arrangement." She offered nothing more.

"Well, I was just thinking we could perhaps take dinner together one night next week."

"Not unless my father has approved it. He's already arranged for me to go out on Friday and Saturday. You would have to speak to him."

Jefferson frowned. "I did speak to him. I thought once we had discussed my intentions, I would be free to pay you court."

"No, Da doesn't do things the conventional way. Goodness, if he did, he wouldn't have advertised for a husband." She toyed with her purse. "Da has his own ways and reasons."

"Did he say anything about me?"

"He said you came to see him. Otherwise, Da hasn't told me much about any of the would-be suitors. That's also his way."

Jefferson counted out the money she'd given him and had her sign a receipt. After giving her a copy, he quickly went back to the topic at hand. "I don't understand. Will he contact me, or will I need to see him again?"

"I would imagine you'd need to speak to him directly. I cannot speak for him, Jefferson."

Just then the office door opened, and Melody turned. Charles Decker came from his office, and he smiled when he caught sight of Melody.

"How do you do this fine day, Miss Doyle?"

"I insist you call me Melody. Otherwise, I won't answer to you."

He laughed and gave a little bow. "I yield to your request, Melody. How are you?"

"I'm good. I was just telling Jefferson that Da has started choosing suitors for me to meet. I have a Friday night supper and a Saturday outing on my schedule already."

Decker frowned. "I still think it's a bad way to find a husband."

"It's not the old-fashioned way of meeting someone by chance or even through mutual friends or family," Melody agreed, "but Da is determined."

"But why this way?"

Jefferson was surprised that his boss cared so much about the matter. It wasn't like he was on the roster to date Miss Doyle.

"I don't know," Melody confessed. She looked quite thoughtful for a long moment. "I think Da blames himself that I didn't marry young. I stayed with him and took care of his needs, and I think now it's all catching up with him. Since he hurt his back, he's had time to dwell on far too much."

Charles nodded and ran his hand back through his hair. "I suppose it just seems . . . well, unsafe."

Melody laughed. "Out of all the men in the world, I trust Da the most to know the truth of a man's character. He has a gift of discernment that is unlike any I've ever seen. He always knows when a man is playing him false."

Jefferson felt a momentary tightness in his chest. Was that possible? Could a man ever be able to know the heart of another man? The deep, secret parts of that heart? He frowned and felt the tightness move to his forehead as his eyes narrowed. Surely that wasn't true. If it was, Jefferson was in trouble.

Much of what he'd said had been insincere or outright lies, but he had felt confident that he'd played the role well. Now he had his doubts. If what Melody said was true, then Mr. Doyle would not be allowing him to court his daughter.

"Will I see you both at church on Sunday?" Melody asked, looking first at Jefferson and then settling her gaze on Charles.

"I'll be there," Decker replied with a huge smile.

Curse the man, he was always so happy. Jefferson wasn't sure what Charles Decker had to be so joyful about. From what little he'd heard the man say, he knew Charles didn't even like banking.

Jefferson knew very little else about Decker, except that he had two older brothers. Jefferson had no desire to work with Jacob again, but at least he had been more settled about the process. Charles seemed to need to prove he was on top of each and every matter, whereas Jacob had been relaxed about the business.

It had been Jacob's idea to set up a bank in Cheyenne, and he had bored Jefferson with lengthy stories about how he'd put together reports and charts to prove to his father what a wise investment a savings and loan operation could be in Cheyenne. Jacob had been certain Cheyenne was to be the next Denver or Kansas City, with the railroad leading the way for settlement. Jefferson thought he was probably right enough about how the town would grow. The Union Pacific had great plans. If they carried through, the entire area would be a crossroads for travel, ranching, and all sorts of industries.

"You are apparently miles away in your thoughts, Jefferson."

He looked up at the sound of his name. Melody stood watching him, almost studiously. "I am sorry. I have so much on my mind today. Did you ask me something?"

She shook her head. "It wasn't important. I'll be on my way. My lunchtime is nearly over." She moved toward the door, and Jefferson started to come around the cage area to help her, but Charles was there first. He opened the door.

"I shall see you at the Coopers' later this afternoon. If you need help with planting, I can assist."

"Thanks, Charlie. I'll keep that in mind."

Once she was gone, Charles closed the door and headed back for his office. "You should probably go to lunch soon," he told Jefferson.

Jefferson waited until Charles had closed his office door to sneer. He was coming to hate the man. Jefferson wasn't exactly certain it was anything personal. He hated all men who had a position of authority over him. He always had.

Jefferson knocked on Charlie's door a few minutes later. He didn't wait for Charlie's call to enter but opened the door. "I'm leaving for lunch," he announced.

Charlie was going to reprimand him for not waiting until his knock was acknowledged, but he said nothing about it. "Enjoy your meal, and please leave my door open so that I can keep an eye out for customers."

Jefferson didn't reply and turned to go. Charlie watched as he headed out the front door. He was a strange man, to be sure. His attitude was almost childish at times. He seemed snobbish with certain people but fawned over others. He definitely took an interest in Melody Doyle.

A few moments later, the front door to the bank opened, and Charlie got to his feet and went in greeting. He found Melody's father and extended his hand.

"How good to see you up and around, Mr. Doyle. Is the back doing better?"

"A wee bit," the man admitted. "Have ya a moment of time? I'd like to ask ya some questions regardin' international bankin' matters."

This took Charlie by surprise. "Of course. Come into my office. I've been wanting to talk to you as well. I'll need to leave the door open in case other customers come by. My assistant, Jefferson Lane, is at lunch, so I'm afraid I must keep watch over all."

"That's no trouble to me," Mr. Doyle replied. "Before we talk business, maybe ya could tell me how yar enjoyin' Cheyenne."

Charlie chuckled. "It's quite a change from Chicago, but, you know, I am enjoying it very much. I think I've a mind to call it home."

"And why would that be?"

Leading the way to his office, Charlie gave a shrug. "It just feels right. I prayed about it after my father asked me to take the position. It felt right then as well. God wants me here for His purposes. That's all I know." He motioned to the leather chair situated in front of his desk. "Please have a seat."

"Are ya enjoyin' workin' for the bank?"

Charlie took his seat as Mr. Doyle did the same. "I find it acceptable work, but truth be told, I'd rather be teaching."

"Teachin'?"

"You seem surprised." Charlie shrugged. "I was born into a family of bankers. I've done my best to honor my father's wishes, which were to continue the family tradition in banking. My two older brothers had no difficulty with the expectation, and I'm doing my best to follow in their footsteps."

"But yar heart isn't in it?"

Charlie lost his smile. "No. It never has been. I love teaching and have long wanted to start a school for boys. I remember a wonderful man who taught at my private school. He made stories come alive, and even mathematics held wonder and fascination. He was also a master of music, and I took a year of piano studies with him. I was never all that good, but he taught me about music and the composers, as well as a variety of instruments. It was all so fascinating. I knew that I wanted to be like him and share knowledge with others— help draw out their talents. That's what he did for me."

Mr. Doyle eased back in the chair. "But ya cannot go against yar da."

"No." Charlie shook his head. "I've never even really explained my heart to him. Oh, he knows that I fancied the idea of teaching, but that's all. I didn't want to disappoint him."

"Is yar father a difficult man?"

"He is a stern and serious-natured person," Charlie replied. "He is very business minded. That's something he got from his father. At times, rare though they are, Father allows himself to relax. But he is devoted to hard work and serving his community. I greatly respect him."

"Aye, but do ya love him?"

It was such an odd question to be asked by a man who was nearly a stranger. Yet Charlie didn't find it at all offensive. Clancy Doyle had a way about him that put men at ease. Charlie thought for a moment of what Melody had said about her father's discernment.

"I do love him. He's never been a man to show great affection, but I feel confident he loves his family. And I find myself wanting to please him more than any earthly thing."

"And why would that be?" the older man asked.

"I want his approval, of course." Charlie shrugged. "Doesn't every man want his father's approval? The same is true of my walk with the Lord. I want His approval, and so I do my best to live the life He calls me to live. I look to follow His Word and ways."

Mr. Doyle nodded. "A good answer, to be sure. Now, I have somethin' else to discuss."

"Ah yes, international banking. Please tell me what you wish to know." Charlie tried not to show any disappointment. The fact was, he was quite enjoying sharing his heart with Clancy Doyle. But work came first.

"Actually, I've another topic of discussion."

Charlie eyed the man for a long moment. "And what would that be?"

"Me daughter, Melody." The older man grinned. "I'm wonderin' what yar feelin's for her might be."

9

Friday evening, Melody and her father greeted Jackson Malbry. The forty-year-old was of medium build and height. He extended his hand to Melody's father, and the two spoke briefly.

"I was afraid it would be raining this evening. Saw that cloudbank come up in the west," Jackson said, giving Melody a slight smile. "Didn't want it to spoil our dinner."

Melody shrugged and took up her shawl. "A little rain couldn't hurt us. In fact, the garden would greatly appreciate the watering."

He nodded while Da asked him something about his workday. Melody studied the man carefully. He had a reddish glint to his brown hair, and his eyes were a sort of hazel color. He seemed nervous, but who could blame him? This wasn't exactly a typical course of events.

"And we've definitely had an increased number of orders," Jackson was telling Da.

As Melody understood it, the man was a wainwright. He owned a shop where he built and repaired wagons and carriages.

"'Tis always good to see business doin' so well." Da turned to Melody and gave a wink before fixing Jackson with a stern look. "I'll be expectin' nothin' less than gentlemanly conduct from ya, Mr. Malbry. Have me daughter home by eight, or I'll come lookin' for ya, and the outcome won't be pleasant."

"I'll have her home by eight," the man said, nodding. "And of course I will treat her with the utmost respect."

"Good. Then off with ya both, and have a lovely time."

Jackson nodded, and Melody hurried through the tent flap. She wasn't sure what kind of evening she was headed for, but Jackson seemed companionable. She whispered a prayer hoping the evening would go well, even if he wasn't the man God had in mind for her husband.

"Your father can certainly be intimidating," Jackson said after they'd walked a few minutes.

Melody couldn't help laughing. "That was Da's good side. You don't want to get on his bad side, that's for sure. But you can relax now. I don't want to have any pretense between us. My father wants me to marry quickly, before he leaves with the railroad. I desire to remain in Cheyenne, and marriage was his idea so that I would have someone to watch over me."

"Yes, he told me. I'm not opposed to an arranged marriage," Jackson replied. "My mother and father were arranged and did quite well."

"I did wonder what kind of man would show up when Da put out the call for someone to be my husband."

"I am surprised you weren't already spoken for." He looked at her, and Melody couldn't help but smile again.

"I was busy taking care of Da. And Da can be quite intimidating too. A great many men weigh the odds and walk away rather than deal with my father. That's why I'm still single, Mr. Malbry."

"Call me Jackson. May I call you Melody?"

"Of course. I see no reason to stand on formalities, especially given the circumstances."

"I hope you don't mind walking to the supper club. I'm a little embarrassed to admit I don't own a carriage. Seems each time I start to build myself a wagon or carriage, someone in dire need talks me into selling it."

"You're kind to let them buy something you intended for yourself. But no, I don't mind walking at all. I walk everywhere, every day. I'm used to it. And you'll find that I'm no grand lady requiring finery. I'm pretty capable and work hard. I have a job at the Coopers' boardinghouse, and I intend to keep it for a time because Mrs. Cooper is rather desperate for the help. Would you have problems with that?"

He considered that for a moment. "I never thought of having a wife working a job since I can easily provide for my family. It doesn't seem fitting for a married woman to hold a job."

Melody was disappointed by his reply. She didn't want to let Mrs. Cooper down, and if she married Jackson Malbry, it was clear that she would most likely have to quit.

"However," Jackson continued, "what with Mrs. Cooper being in great need, that changes things. I've always been one to help my neighbors out. You could continue working for her, and . . . well, it might sound strange, but . . . take no pay."

Melody was surprised by his answer. So many men were money hungry, yet here was a man who would allow his wife to work for no pay in order to help a friend.

"You have a kind heart, Jackson. I like that idea very much."

He smiled. "I'm glad you think so. I know I'm considerably older than you. Fact is, I was married once before. We were childhood sweethearts. My wife died from pleurisy twenty years ago, only a year after we married. We had no children. I wasn't of a mind to marry again, but the idea of growing older without someone . . . well, it makes for a lonely life."

Melody felt great sympathy for the man. He had faced the loss of a loved one. A childhood sweetheart. The very thought touched Melody deeply. Perhaps she could be the one to mend Jackson Malbry's broken heart.

On Saturday, Bruce Cadot showed up to take Melody out for a day of fun at the McDaniel Museum. It was more than a simple museum and, in fact, had a variety hall and saloons. The performances ran the gamut from lectures to ballets and everything in between. Melody had heard that it was most entertaining.

After a brief introduction, the couple headed to the museum, with Bruce offering nonstop talk all the way.

"I got out of the army last year, and then my father died. He was the last of my kin. He left me a little money, so I came here to get homestead land. I have cattle and am about to take on even more."

"So your desire is to have a large ranch here in Cheyenne?" Melody asked him.

"Yes, ma'am. I grew up with cattle, and it's in my blood. I know I can make a go of it as long as I can find me some good hands."

"And a wife would be one of those . . . hands?"

"No, not at all. I need a wife to run the house and give me . . . well, I want a family. A big one."

Melody could see he was rather embarrassed by his declaration. "I want children too. I appreciate that you would bring up the matter. I think it's important to discuss all the details. After all, it wouldn't serve either of us well to court and marry only to find we didn't want the same things."

"No, ma'am. That would be a disaster."

As they reached the museum, the McDaniel's famed hurdy-gurdy played loudly and constantly. Folks in the area were used to the noise, while newcomers were often seen with their hands over their ears. Sunday was the only day of the week that Professor McDaniel, as he was known to call himself, silenced the beast.

Melody thought it a pleasant sound and didn't mind the music it made. Bruce laughed and led her toward the free museum. "My beeves wouldn't care for the caterwauling of that thing at all." She laughed.

The museum advertised itself as having 1,001 marvels, with free admission to any man who drank at the saloon. Melody didn't have to wait long to see how Bruce might handle the situation.

"We'll pay," he told the admission clerk.

After Bruce paid for their tickets, she questioned him. "You don't drink?"

"No, ma'am. My mother and father were completely against it. They said it was a sin, and I believe if it's not, then it can definitely lead to that."

She found his comment rather reassuring. So many of the men in town lost themselves in liquor. Her own father had suffered greatly from drink. He would appreciate Bruce's teetotaling ways. No doubt he had questioned the young man all about it.

"I appreciate your thoughts on the matter." Melody allowed him to lead her into the museum. "My father gave up drinking when he got right with God."

"Your father is . . . well, he's rather intimidating. I'm glad he's a Christian."

Melody laughed. "It doesn't stop Da from fighting when the moment requires it. I know he can be a bit frightening. But have no fear, Bruce. You've passed Da's first inspection and made it this far. Tell me about your parents. Were they people of God?"

"My folks were very religious," Bruce continued. "I was brought up to fear God and to honor Him. That was always important in my family."

"Mine too." Melody considered the man as he paused to look at a display of what was labeled *Rare Egyptian Artifacts.*

Bruce Cadot was her own age. Da had told her that she was, in fact, a few months his senior. With blond hair that held a slight wave to it and brown eyes, Melody was certain he was one of the handsomest men she'd ever met. But even being as good-looking as he was, Bruce didn't seem to think much on that matter. He was nothing like Jefferson Lane, who knew he was handsome and expected compliments from everyone around him.

"It says that plate there is over four thousand years old. I can't even fathom that much time. It would have been long before Jesus walked the earth."

Melody nodded and studied the dish. "It is hard to imagine anything that old that a person could actually touch and hold."

"When I think of how often I broke one of my ma's dishes, it's a real wonder to me that these things are still around." He grinned at Melody. "Guess it's a good thing they aren't wantin' to show off my ma's dishes."

They both laughed at that.

They progressed to the next marvel, but Melody's thoughts

weren't on the exhibits. Bruce seemed far more lighthearted and fun to be with than Jackson had been. He was her own age, and no doubt they would have a lot in common. Maybe he was the one.

Charlie was hopeful Melody would join them at the table for breakfast on Monday morning. Mrs. Cooper had insisted Melody eat with them, even if she was the hired help. The Coopers saw their boarders and staff as family. Charlie thought it a wonderful way of looking at things.

Unfortunately, after pouring coffee for each person, Melody disappeared. After grace was offered, Otis asked about her absence.

"Melody is in the garden," Mr. Cooper replied. "I was able to lay my hands on ten dozen onion bulbs and a variety of seeds and vegetable plants. She's working to get it all put into the ground."

The conversation continued regarding gardens and weather. Charlie downed his bacon and scrambled eggs, then grabbed up a piece of toast and stood. "Excellent breakfast, Mrs. Cooper." He hurried from the room before anyone could question his rapid exit.

He went upstairs and changed into more informal attire, then slipped down the back stairs and made his way outside. Usually, he spent the early hours before heading to the bank reading his Bible and writing letters. This morning he had other ideas.

Clancy Doyle had taken him off guard. Instead of wanting to focus on his banking situation, the older man had told Charlie flat out that he felt, after prayer and contemplation, Charlie was the man God had sent to marry his daughter.

The news had come as a surprise to Charlie, but not nearly the shock he might have expected.

The more the older man talked about his thoughts on the matter, the more Charlie felt it was the truth that had been staring him in the face the entire time. Melody was, by his own admission, most everything he'd ever wanted in a wife. And the more he considered her being by his side for the rest of their lives, the more it seemed a perfect fit.

But, as he'd told her father, he felt it was important that the two be friends first. Charlie had seen far more success in romances when that element was in play. Clancy had agreed to say nothing but planned to allow Melody to go on her outings with the would-be suitors. He knew already that none of them would be her choice. Charlie wished he could be as confident.

Melody was on her knees in the rich garden dirt planting onion bulbs. She had her long brown hair braided down her back. It stuck out from under her sunbonnet, which she'd casually tied around her neck.

"Good morning," he said, kneeling to join her. "Looks like rain, so I thought you might like some help."

"The threat of rain is why I didn't stay for breakfast. I told Mrs. Cooper I could have a good part of the garden planted in the time it would take to eat. A fresh rain will do wonders for the new plants."

"I agree." He grabbed up a handful of onion bulbs from the little basket beside Melody. "How are you planning this out?"

She motioned to the narrow line. "This is the second row, and I figure there's enough for a third row as well. I've already staked it out."

Charlie noted the string she had tied from one stake to

the other to mark where the long row would be. "I can get that planted. You go ahead with the second one."

"Put the bulbs close, just a few inches apart. That way I can pull green onions when they're ready, and that will give the others room to grow."

Charlie got to his feet and took up the hoe at the end of the garden. He carefully followed the string to dig a shallow row. Next, he plopped in the bulbs just a few inches apart, as Melody had instructed.

Melody finished her row before he did and was taking up the string and walking the line to stomp down the dirt by the time he grabbed the last of the bulbs and finished his row. Dark clouds were moving in ever closer.

"I knew we could have that done in quick order." Charlie grinned as she untied the string from the third-row stake.

"There's still plenty to plant, but don't you need to get to the bank?"

"It's my bank, so I can go in when I want." He chuckled and shrugged. "I don't suppose I sound very much like a bank president, do I? My father would question my sense and loyalty."

"Well, I wouldn't want to get you in trouble over radishes and squash."

"Well, the truth is, I was wondering how your dates went with the would-be suitors?"

Melody straightened and stopped midstep. "Well enough, I suppose. Jackson Malbry was the first. He was very kind-hearted. The man deserves to find himself love, but I don't think that it will come from me. We had a nice enough supper, but frankly, I didn't feel we had much in common. He has his wagonmaking and is God-fearing, but I think his heart will forever belong to his first wife. He spent most of our time together talking about her and the dreams they had together. Made me sad."

"I'm sure losing someone you love is tough to get over. I'm surprised he responded to your father's announcement."

"It was probably the easiest way to find a companion. He's lonely. That much is clear. Still, I think I'd forever live in the shadow of a woman he's loved since childhood."

"And the second beau?"

"He had potential but wasn't quite right. Bruce Cadot is his name."

"I know Mr. Cadot. He borrowed money from the bank. He seems very industrious and driven to succeed."

"Yes. His ground is about twelve miles outside of town proper. I don't know if I could be happy as a rancher's wife. I like living in town. I've never seen myself as a farm or ranch wife. The isolation would be too much. I've always had people around me. We've been like one big traveling family since starting up with the UP, and before that we lived in a dozen other towns while Da worked for a variety of railroads. City life is what I know and appreciate."

Charlie could understand that. He didn't figure he'd be very good at living on a farm or ranch himself. Cheyenne was isolated enough, but it was clearly growing, and there were new people coming in daily. With that came a sense of anticipation that excited him. Each day the town was changing, and who could say where it would all end up?

"Bruce needs a wife who understands working with animals. I told him I probably wouldn't be of any use to him. I'm rather afraid of roosters. Had one attack me right after we moved to Omaha. I don't know how to ride horses or hitch a wagon. If I can't walk to where I'm going, I just don't go."

She continued walking down the line of planted bulbs.

"So my conclusion is that neither Bruce nor Jackson would make a good husband for me. Well, perhaps I should reword that. I wouldn't make a good wife for them."

Charlie breathed a sigh of relief. "There's nothing wrong with that. Just keep praying about it. God will show you the right person."

"I agree." She reached the end of the row and bent down to take up the stake and remaining string. "Want to help me mark out the next row?"

"Sure." He went to her and took the stake and string. "Just show me where you want it."

"About twelve inches from the last row." She drove her stake into the soft ground at one end. "Just take it down there and line it up."

Charlie did as she asked, and when the row was straight, Melody gave him the okay to put his stake into the ground. Then she went to the back of the house and took up a box. When she returned, she placed it on the ground near the new row.

"I have seeds, so we'll need to trench it out under the line and then plant them." A rumble of thunder sounded from afar. "Guess we'll need to get it done quickly."

"You plant, and I'll come behind and cover them up," Charlie offered.

Melody nodded and went to work. They had the row taken care of in no time at all and moved on to the next and a new package of seeds. By the time it started to sprinkle, they had planted most of the seeds and a few of the plants.

"I could never have managed without you, Charlie. Where did you learn so much about gardening? I figured you probably grew up in luxury and gardening was something done by servants."

"Well, you're right about my life being one of ease and wealth, but my mother loved to garden, especially herbs and flowers. We had a head gardener named Ezra. I liked talking to the man and hearing his stories. He came from free black folks, and yet they suffered much the same as people in slavery. My folks were good to him and treated him as a valued member of the family and cherished employee. My father, although not as strong in his faith as my mother is, always referenced the Bible saying, 'The worker is worth his wage.' He paid his staff better than most, and our help always stayed on rather than leaving in search of greener pastures."

"And Ezra taught you to garden?"

"He did. I learned a great deal from him." Charlie grinned. "So if I ever do have a home of my own, I'll be able to fix up a suitable garden and raise my own crops."

She laughed. "You do surprise, Charlie Decker."

"In a good way, I hope."

Melody nodded. "In a very good way."

10

Friday evening, the first of May, Melody found herself sitting across the table from Dr. Leonard Smith. The man talked incessantly about his service during the War between the States and his practice after the war. She knew from what he had said that he was thirty-eight years old, hailed from Pennsylvania originally, and he'd come west after hearing doctors were scarce in the area.

When the waiter came, Melody was more than ready to order, but to her surprise the doctor insisted on ordering for them both.

"We'll have the lamb, cooked well, and the mixed vegetables. Also bring us bread but no butter." Dr. Smith handed the man the chalked menu board they'd been given to consider. "And we will both have hot tea." He glanced at Melody. "Stimulates digestion."

She nodded, not knowing what else to do. She hadn't planned on having any of the things he had ordered but, thankfully, knew she could live with his choices. At least it wasn't liver.

"Now, where was I?" he asked.

Melody opened her mouth to speak, but Dr. Smith quickly continued. He repeated something he'd said earlier about amputations being the bigger part of his surgeries during the war and continued by explaining that, here in the West, there was a pleasant enough absence of them.

"I've not had to remove an arm or leg—not even a foot—in some time. Although I do not have any difficulty with amputations. In fact, they can be quite fascinating. You have to make certain to tie off all of the blood vessels, and the arterial flow is of the utmost importance. If you damage the artery and veins that return the blood to the heart, the patient will not live. He will most likely see the death of tissue, which will spread up the remaining limb.

"However, as I mentioned, there aren't a lot of amputation cases here." He fixed Melody with a smile. "Which allows me time to seek out a mate. Something I've long needed. After all, I intend to have at least four children. Do you have regular cycles?"

Melody was stunned by this very personal question. "I beg your pardon?"

He gave her a brief wave of his hand. "I am rather forward, I'll admit. But as a physician I am used to seeing the body and its functions as less than a private or even intimate matter. It's important to your fertility that you have regular monthly cycles. Do you?"

Melody nodded, still unable to say what she was really thinking.

"That's good to know. I would imagine that you are quite fertile, then. I have no reason to believe that I'm less than capable of producing heirs, and so that much is established. Is your general health good? No night sweats or fainting spells?"

"Fainting at night?" Melody clarified.

He frowned. "Or during the day."

She had never received such an interrogation. "No. No fainting or sweating."

"No sweating at all?"

She couldn't help but giggle. "When I work hard, I sweat. Goodness, Dr. Smith, I feel like I'm enduring a physical examination."

"Not yet, but that would be wise before marrying."

She rolled her gaze heavenward. The beautiful copperplated ceiling tiles caused her to point upward. "Lovely ceiling, isn't it?"

The doctor glanced upward for a moment and then back to the table. For once, he said nothing, and Melody breathed a sigh of relief. She wouldn't be marrying Dr. Leonard Smith. Although if she needed something amputated, he would be the first one she'd call on.

On Saturday evening, Melody was introduced by her father to Samuel Sullivan, a twenty-eight-year-old Irishman with gray-blue eyes that seemed to take in everything at once.

"Samuel works for me," Da explained. "I've known him since Omaha, and he's a good man."

Melody extended her hand, and Samuel bowed over it. "Pleased to meet you, Miss Melody."

"And I'm pleased to meet you, Samuel."

"Just Sam." His eyes seemed to twinkle. "Or folks close to me call me Sammy."

"I like that."

He smiled at this, then turned to her father. "And how is it going with you, sir?"

"Well enough, Sam, well enough. I hope to be back with ya, once I have me daughter settled." Da turned to her. "Sam was workin' as one of my section hands, but he's accepted a position with the railroad that will keep him right here in Cheyenne."

"How nice. What will you be working at, Sam?"

"I'll be working in the shop. I'm learning to make repairs and replace parts when they wear out. I've been saving my money and intend to build a house. I've already bought the lot. Got it at a discount from the UP."

"How nice." Melody liked the man well enough for a first-time encounter.

"Well, go on with ya now. Sam wants to be takin' ya to one of Professor McDaniel's shows. *Hamlet*, didn't ya say?"

Melody had heard of the Shakespeare play but had never seen it. "How very unexpected. I will look forward to that."

It was the first time Sam looked a little uncomfortable. "I hope you like it. I've never been to a play, but one of the boys said women like that sort of thing."

"We shall explore the matter together, then," Melody replied. "Shakespeare is quite popular, but I have never attended such a performance, although I did hear a couple of his plays read to us in school."

With that, they made their way to McDaniel's and, after purchasing their tickets, entered the variety hall and took their seats. The entire room was soon filled, with every seat taken and a couple dozen people standing around the back of the room.

Once the play began, Melody found herself caught up in the story. The actors were quite good at their roles, and the costumes captivated her. The performance was like nothing she'd ever seen.

She glanced over at Sam, who seemed only slightly interested in the tale of murder and revenge. By the end of the
first act, Sam was soundly asleep, and while Melody found
herself wanting to see the play, she gave Sam's arm a pat.

He stirred and opened his eyes. "Oh, sorry. I worked hard
today."

"Why don't we just leave. We can go ahead to supper as
you planned and then head home."

He nodded without even a pretense of argument. He
helped her from her seat, then led the way out. Melody gave
one backward glance toward the stage. Maybe someday she'd
have a chance to see *Hamlet* through to the end. She very
much hoped the young man was able to find justice.

Outside, the skies were still light and people plentiful.
Sam gave her an apologetic look. "I didn't mean to fall asleep
like that."

"It's not a problem. I know railroad work takes a lot out
of a man. Da always came home on Saturday ready for rest."

"I sure hope he'll start feeling better, but . . ."

His words stopped, and Melody gave him a quizzical look.
"But what?"

Sam pushed his hands deep into his pockets. "Well, some
of the boys are worried that he's worse off than he lets on.
Maybe really sick."

"Why would you say that?"

He shrugged and kept walking. "Just the way he's been. A
couple of the fellas talked to him when he came to see the
railroad doc. They said he didn't look good at all, and they
wondered if maybe . . . well, they wondered if he hurt himself
worse than they thought when he fell."

Melody couldn't imagine that was the case. "Da is doing
good. He's still enduring some pain, but he's much better.

I'm sure he'll be rejoining his team soon. June first is what he's told me."

Sam seemed relieved. "I hope you're right. We'd hate to lose him. He's a good one. I wish he'd settle down here in Cheyenne so I could still be around him. He's taught me a lot."

"Has he now?" Melody laughed. "He's taught me a great deal too. I suppose we have that in common."

"I reckon we have a lot in common, Miss Melody, but maybe just as important is how I've admired you for a long time. I think you're one of the most beautiful women I've ever seen, and your reputation for kindness is well-known. Everybody who works with your da knows you're a good cook. We've always enjoyed it when your da brings in your cookies or handpies. You're really quite the gal."

She sobered for a moment. "If that's how you feel, why didn't you seek to court me prior to Da's announcement?"

He chuckled. "Your da told us back in Omaha that you were off-limits."

Melody shook her head. "That sounds like him. But that was then, and this is now."

"Look, I didn't speak about his health to worry you. I hope you won't say anything to him about it."

"Of course not."

Melody could see the concern in his expression. Maybe the poor man feared losing his position, but Da wasn't that petty regarding a man speaking his opinion. On the other hand, there was the tiniest nagging doubt in the back of her mind. What if Sam was right, and Da was worse than he let on?

Monday was as fair a day as Melody had seen that year. She arrived at the Coopers' with sunlight dawning on the horizon. Da had only come halfway with her because they met up with Edward Vogel on his deputy marshal rounds. Edward had offered to walk her the rest of the way, and Da hadn't even offered a reason why he shouldn't. It wasn't like Da to hand over his responsibilities to someone else, even in something as simple as escorting Melody to her job. Still, she tried not to let it worry her. Maybe Da had plans and needed to get back to the tent.

After tying on her apron, she went to work in the kitchen scrambling eggs and making coffee. Mrs. Cooper was busy frying up bacon and chatting about the church bake sale they were soon to have. They had definitely fallen into an easy partnership.

"If we keep having the sales, we'll have money for a church before we know it."

"It'd be lovely to have our own place of worship," Melody agreed. "And to have services during the day instead of at night."

"So many churches share the school. Did you hear that the men were joshing about having a prizefight to raise money? I guess so much money changed hands at the fights last week that it caught their attention. They said it in jest, but it is rather startling that good men would bet money on other men beating each other to a pulp."

"Yes. It's never been of interest to me, but Da seems to enjoy a good fight."

"How is your father? He looked quite pale on Sunday."

It was yet another reference to her father being ill rather than just injured. "I believe he's doing all right. The pain sometimes gets to be a bit much. I have encouraged him to go back to the doctor and see if something more needs to be done for his back."

Mrs. Cooper met Melody's gaze. "I hope—pray, really—that it's nothing serious."

"Of course not. I don't think there's anything to worry about."

But throughout the day, Melody couldn't let the matter go. She left on her noon break and headed home just to see how Da was faring. If he was ill, she would surely see signs of it. She was a block away from their little tent community when she spied her father on the street. He was walking quite slowly but with great determination. She decided to follow him and was surprised when he made his way to the bank.

She didn't follow him in but headed back to the Coopers', wondering what he'd been doing. Da hadn't said anything more about his brother sending money from Ireland, but she guessed that this was probably the reason he was at the bank. He had told her he was determined to get the transfer set up and money safely deposited before heading west with the railroad. It would make sense if that was what he was up to now. The fact that he was banking for himself convinced Melody that her worries were for naught. Da wouldn't have bothered if he'd been feeling poorly.

Later in the day, Melody went to the garden plot to check things out. There wouldn't be any signs of growth just yet, but she couldn't help reviewing the work that had been done and plan for the next tasks. Mr. Cooper had ordered more plants, as well as two apple trees from a nursery in North Platte. Seeing she could do nothing more, Melody figured it was time to head home.

"Melody, Melody, never contrary. How does your garden grow?" Charlie teased, his smile lighting up his entire face.

"It's too early to tell." She got up from where she'd been kneeling. "How are you doing today, Charlie?"

"Quite well. Tell me, have you had any more suitors?"

"I did. An obnoxious doctor and a sweet railroad worker." She began gathering her gardening tools.

"And?"

She glanced at Charlie, who seemed completely interested in what she might have to say. "And nothing. The doctor ordered my dinner for me because, as he told me later, he knew best what I needed to eat. He talked nonstop about his work during the war, and I'm not completely sure, but I believe he's dreadfully sorry that more amputations aren't needed here in Cheyenne."

Charlie's eyes widened. "Amputations?"

She nodded. "Apparently, there was a wealth of them to be done during the war, and now he finds the task missing in his daily duties." She couldn't refrain from laughing. "In the absence of amputations, he's looking for a wife."

"I can't believe the man would speak of such things while courting."

"That and even more. It's a good thing I'm not easily embarrassed or offended."

"Maybe that was part of his testing for a wife."

Melody hadn't considered that. "Maybe so. Anyway, after the good doctor, I went out with one of Da's railroad workers, Sammy Sullivan. An Irishman who has taken a job here in Cheyenne at the UP warehouse. He took me to see *Hamlet*."

"Oh, a wonderful play. What did you think?"

"We only made it through act one, but I would like to see it through to the end someday. Sam fell asleep, and I took pity on him. We left and went to dinner, then returned to the tent, where we found Da already asleep. We said goodnight, and Sam went home to bed while I tidied up and wondered how poor Hamlet was going to prove his father was murdered."

"I'll take you to the play one of these evenings when you aren't seeing anyone else. It's really a very good play. Lots of intrigue, and I think you'd like it very much."

"Thank you, Charlie. It'd be nice to just enjoy an outing without worrying about interviewing a husband."

He smiled and bent down to adjust the wooden stake Melody had used to mark the new row of squash she'd planted.

"Did Da come to the bank today?" She hoped Charlie might give her insight as to why her father had visited him.

"He did. Came in while Jefferson was gone to lunch. We had a nice discussion about the town and railroad. I enjoy talking with your father. He's quite knowledgeable."

"Yes, for an uneducated man, he can definitely hold his own."

"How much schooling has he had?" Charlie asked.

Melody carried her things to the gardening shed. "He quit after sixth grade. He was a troublemaker and not at all interested in what they had to teach. Da got himself into a world of trouble after leaving school. He took up smoking and drinking, but most of all he loved fighting. Only God was able to pull him back from the dark path he'd taken himself down."

"He plays a good game of checkers, I must say."

This surprised her. "When did you play checkers with Da?" she asked over her shoulder before going back to securing her things in the shed.

Charlie leaned against the door frame and laughed. "A fella should have some secrets, shouldn't he?"

"Sorry, I didn't mean to pry." She laughed. "But I did suggest it. Remember?"

"I do, and he was quite receptive. And I lost graciously."

"You didn't lose on purpose, did you? Da hates when people do things like that."

"No, he beat me fair and square, although it was close. He said I was a worthy challenger."

Melody turned to face him. "That's high praise coming from Da. Sometimes he finds it difficult to find someone willing to go up against him. I suppose they fear him more than desire a relaxing game. Da can be imposing, as you well know. I can play when Da is desperate for a game—and I'm pretty good—but it's not my favorite thing. I prefer reading a good book."

"I enjoy that myself. What do you like to read?"

"Almost anything. I've enjoyed fictionalized stories, as well as biographies of great men and women. I very much like to read about faraway places, and if there are illustrations, then all the better. I do hope we get a library in Cheyenne one day. I positively love libraries."

"I do as well. I could lose myself for hours in the library back home."

"What do you like to read, Charlie?"

"Geography has long been a favorite subject of mine. Geography stirs up images of places and that leads to events and history. It's all very captivating."

"Would you like to teach geography and history?"

Charlie sobered. "I'd like to teach most anything. I enjoy sharing knowledge, as well as gaining it. There is something quite satisfactory in teaching what I know."

"Some of my favorite people in the world were those who taught me in school," Melody said. "When I was in first grade, I attended a school with two teachers: a man and a woman. The woman was Miss Merriweather. She was always so happy and encouraging. She taught all of the regular subjects, but then went so far as to teach us about proper manners and etiquette. She was there the next year as well, and I learned so much about how to speak properly. It's always amazing to me how little things like that can make such a big difference."

"Indeed. Proper manners and social training are acquired skills that will take you far."

"If you had your own school, would you teach such subjects?"

"I would," he replied most enthusiastically. "I find it's often neglected in a boy's upbringing. And out here, it might be especially relevant. Maybe save someone from getting a punch in the nose." His grin was infectious.

Melody laughed. "I believe you would make an excellent teacher, Charlie. You have a sense of humanity and a lightness of spirit that naturally draws folks to you."

"You're kind to say so. Hopefully, one day I will find a way to make my dreams come true."

"God has a plan, Charlie. Da always says that those good things we long for are the desires that God has put in our hearts. Trust Him to know what to do with your dream. If God gave it life, He'll be good to grow it to fruition."

Charlie thought of her words that night as he readied for bed. He found her faith and wisdom to be exactly what he needed. Her encouragement was reassuring that he was finally on the right path. Including his growing desire to court and marry her.

It had all happened so fast, however. And he was still somewhat stunned by the fact that Melody's father had been the one to come to him. But Clancy had no doubts that God had chosen him for his daughter's husband, and he spoke with such conviction that Charlie had no doubts either.

He smiled at the thought of Melody's sweet expressions.

The way her eyes would widen just a bit when she found something to be a wonder. Of late, he'd even begun to imagine what it would be like to take her in his arms . . . to kiss her.

A sigh escaped his lips as he closed his eyes. He could see her smiling back at him. Reaching for him.

Friendship first, Charlie. Friendship first, then romance.

11

Throughout the next week, Melody focused on her work and tried not to worry about her father's health. Thankfully, no one else spoke of it, but she couldn't help bringing it to mind. When she sat down to tea with Marybeth and Granny Taylor, Melody wondered how she might share her concerns with them. They were always good to advise her.

"We were caught up on everything, and even supper was well on its way to being done, so Mrs. Cooper told me to take an hour or so and come back later when the laundry I hung out would be dry," Melody told Granny Taylor and Marybeth. She had gone to see Marybeth and found Granny just happened to be there as well.

"I'm so glad you came over," Marybeth declared, pouring the tea. "Carrie just went down for her nap, and it will be so nice just to visit. Granny stopped by to show me some of her new embroidered quilt squares."

Granny picked up her bag and opened the top. "I've been busy with this all winter, as well as other projects." She pulled out a big stack of squares. "The flower drawings were all done by my daughter-in-law and sent to me in the mail. She's quite the artist."

Melody took one of the squares and studied it for a moment. It was a rose, and Granny had used various shades of pink to embroider it. "This is beautiful." She gently touched the embroidery before handing it back.

"And just look at this iris," Granny said, holding it up. "It almost looks real."

Melody nodded as Marybeth handed her a cup of tea. "You look upset about something," Marybeth said to her with a look of concern.

Granny lowered the square. "I thought as much myself but hated to say anything just yet. I thought perhaps you'd come around to telling us what's on your mind."

They both knew her so well. "I suppose my biggest worry is Da."

"I thought him rather pale on Sunday," Granny said. "Jed's been worried about him too. Wondered if he'd taken ill."

Melody shook her head. "I suppose I've been so busy I hadn't really noticed, but you aren't the first person to comment on Da's health. I honestly don't know if there is something wrong."

"Is he eating all right?" Granny asked.

"Well, he eats supper with me, but not that much," Melody admitted. "Not like he used to eat, but since he's not working, it seemed natural that he wouldn't eat as much. He never eats breakfast with me now since I have to leave so early. He says he'll eat when he gets back. As for lunch, I have no way of knowing. But now that I think about it, there's never much missing. And he has lost weight. I've taken his pants in twice."

"That does sound concerning," Granny replied. "An idle

man who isn't eating much shouldn't be losing that much weight."

"Has he complained of more pain than usual?" Marybeth asked. She handed Granny her tea, then took a seat. "It could be his back isn't healing as fast as he'd like."

"I've wondered the same. He does move slower than before. I just figured it was due to the injury, but what if it is something more?"

"Has he gone back to the doctor since the accident?" Granny asked.

"Yes, he's gone a couple of times and reported it all to me. At least, I thought he had. I don't know what to think. You don't suppose he's hiding something from me? He's never been that way before."

"Hopefully it's nothing." Granny sipped her tea and nodded toward Marybeth. "This is quite delicious."

"It's a special tea that Mrs. Henderson used. She left it here when she moved away, and I thought you might like it."

Melody listened to the women discuss the tea, but her mind was fixed on Da and his condition. Was he lying to her? Was something more wrong with him, and he didn't want to worry her with the details?

"So tell us about the courting. Has your father picked out a lot of suitors for you?"

Granny's question broke through Melody's thoughts. She smiled and shrugged. "I've seen four different men so far. None of them are a good fit for me, however. Like I told Charlie the other day, maybe I'm just too picky."

"A girl should be picky about her husband," Marybeth said, passing a plate of refreshments.

Melody took one of the pieces of shortbread. "That's how I see it. None of them are the type of man I would choose.

And all for different reasons. And now, worrying about Da and what's really going on with him, I don't feel like going out with anyone else. How can I think about getting married when Da might need me?"

"You can't let your heart be troubled over this, Melody," Granny assured. "God knows what's going on even if you don't. He has it all under control. Just focus on praying for your father."

"I know you're right, Granny. I've told myself to pray on it more than once. I know that prayer is the answer. I suppose just coming out and asking Da about it is also in order. Still, I hate to impose on him. He's very private, and when he wants to tell me something, he does. He's never been one to keep things from me."

But Da was also the type of person that didn't share things with anyone if he was deeply troubled by it. If Da was sick and hadn't yet managed to think through the matter, he wouldn't be open to talking to anyone else about it either.

"How's your job coming along?" Marybeth asked.

Melody was glad for the change of topic. "I love it. I've enjoyed helping Mrs. Cooper. She's well-organized and keeps things running with little chaos. We have our wash days, our cleaning days, and, of course, every day we cook, and I tend to the garden. The men are all quite gentlemanly and interesting.

"I arrive every morning at five thirty. Da walks me over since it's still so early. Mrs. Cooper insists I join them for breakfast, and so I do. At the table, the men talk about their plans for the day and what their jobs will entail. It's like having a family of brothers. Charlie even helps me in the garden from time to time. We talk about church and things going on in Cheyenne. He's even taken to playing checkers with Da."

"I like Charlie. He reminds me of my son Elmer," Granny said. "We had him to dinner last Sunday before church. He told us of his love of teaching, as well as learning. He's a naturally gentle soul."

"I like him too. Maybe too much." Melody found it easy to talk about Charlie.

"Can you like someone too much?" Marybeth asked.

"You can if you're supposed to be looking for a husband, and he's not one of the ones you're looking at."

"And why aren't you looking at him? He's a fine young man," Granny interjected. "I think Charlie would make a fine husband."

"I do too," Marybeth agreed. "But Charlie isn't on Da's list. They've played checkers, but Charlie didn't ask to court me. If he had, I'm sure Da would have approved him." Melody tried not to let the matter ruin her day.

The women fell momentarily silent. Melody had no desire to continue focusing on Charlie. It was embarrassing to be developing feelings for someone who obviously had no feelings for her.

"There have been quite a number of families moving into the area," Granny said. "The railroad is hiring new workers to remain here in Cheyenne. Jed tells me the Union Pacific has advertised in papers back east and in the South for workers interested in relocating to Cheyenne. And word has also gotten out that the land is good for raising cattle and sheep."

Marybeth nodded. "Horses too. Edward is trying to convince his family to move out here. His father has a horse farm that Edward's sister helps with. Her husband is a lawyer, so there would certainly be work for him as well."

"I told my son Robert about the potential for ranches. He and his wife, Susanna, are less than content with Texas.

Susanna has trouble with the heat and the dampness. I told them they might consider moving up here where it's dryer. I would love to have my grandchildren around me."

"How did you end up here in the first place, Granny?" Melody asked.

The old woman smiled. "The good Lord told Jed and me to come, so we did. Believe me when I tell you, I had no thought of moving away from Texas in my old age. Jed was a cattleman, but out of the blue, he tells me that God wants him to take up working for the railroad. He signed over the ranch to Elmer and Robert with their promise to share some of the land with their married sister, and Jed up and went to work for the railroad. Of course, railroads in Texas were a mess after the war. The South had most of their lines torn up, and the locomotives themselves needed work. Jed found mechanical work on the engines and cars to be something he enjoyed. He took to it like a fish to water. So when there were advertisements about the Union Pacific needing men, Jed felt God was calling us north. I have to say, God has used my dear husband in great ways. Jed easily shares God's Word with his fellow workers. Some of the men are now going to church."

"I'm so glad you came north, Granny. I don't know what I would have done without you." Melody had long found the woman to be the best of confidants.

"Well, you must remember that even when it seems strange, if the Lord pushes you in a particular direction, pay attention and go. Remember Abram being called to leave his country and people? That was us, and we don't regret it. God has blessed us in many ways."

Charlie stacked up the books that held all of the bank's transactions for the last year. He felt it was his responsibility to know everything he could about the bank and its customers, and studying the transactions was one way he could know both.

Jefferson was working to enter some figures in the daily ledger when Charlie came into the front room with the other books in hand.

"I'll be leaving early and taking the books home with me this weekend. With exception to the daily ledger you're working on."

Jefferson looked up and narrowed his eyes. "Why would you need to do that?"

Charlie laughed. "Because it's a good way to understand what's going on in the life of the bank." He shifted the books. "I haven't been here long enough to know the customers or their transaction routines. Jacob informed me of things, but I want to read for myself and watch the story unfold."

The younger man looked like he might protest or, at a minimum, comment on the matter, but he turned instead to continue writing in the ledger he had.

Charlie gave it no more thought. "Be sure to leave the receipts for the day on my desk and lock up when you're done." He glanced at the grandfather clock in the corner. It was just seconds away from chiming four o'clock. "Will we see you at church, Sunday night?"

Jefferson didn't bother to look up. "If I can make it, I will."

"Well, it would be good to have you there. If not, I'll see you Monday."

With that, Charlie headed out onto the streets of Cheyenne. He couldn't say that Jefferson had grown on him with time. If anything, the man was even more pretentious and full of himself, and Charlie found such people intolerable. Still, he had to work with Jefferson Lane, and treating him with respect was something he could and would continue to do.

As he headed home, Charlie found himself thinking no longer of Jefferson or the bank, but rather of Melody Doyle. He wondered if he'd find her out in the garden. It hadn't rained for a while, so she would need to water. She might even be planting additional vegetables. There had been some talk of tomato plants.

Mrs. Cooper was in the front sitting room when Charlie came through the door. She was straightening up several newspapers on a side table and glanced his way.

"Hello, Charlie. You're early tonight."

"Yes, ma'am. Thought I'd bring some work home to do. How are you, Mrs. Cooper?"

She shrugged. "As well as can be expected. We're having baked chicken tonight, and Melody made us two apple pies."

"That certainly will hit the spot. Is Miss Melody in the garden?"

"She is. I would expect she's finishing up with the watering."

Charlie nodded. "Well, I'd best take these ledgers upstairs and get changed. She might need help."

Mrs. Cooper smiled. "She might at that."

Charlie was headed back down the stairs ten minutes later. He didn't bother to see where Mrs. Cooper might be, just headed out the front door and around the house, where he found Melody pumping water at the well.

"Afternoon," Charlie said, coming up to where she was working. He took over pumping the water, and when the pail was full, he picked it up. "Where to?"

Melody smiled. "I'm nearly done. I'm on the last row." She followed him across the yard to the garden.

Charlie held the pail while she used the large ladle to scoop out water to sprinkle over the row of dirt.

"How are you this fine day?"

"Doing well. And how about you, Charlie?"

"I've had a productive week. Signed up six new depositors and had three loans paid back in full."

"Sounds very productive. I baked pies today, so you'll get a chance to sample my work."

"I heard about that from Mrs. Cooper and must admit my mouth is watering at the thought. I've heard from several people about your great cookies and pies. By the way, how's your father?"

Melody glanced at him for a moment. "I'm not sure I know. Several people have suggested he might be ill and not simply recovering from his fall."

Charlie frowned. "I'm sorry to hear that."

"Da never makes his feelings known unless he has to." She continued serving up water down the line, where Charlie knew they had planted seeds.

They reached the end, and Melody straightened, took the pail from Charlie, and emptied out the last little bit of water. She plopped the ladle into the bucket with a thud.

"I suppose I'll be heading home now. Da has someone lined up to see me tomorrow, and I need to talk to him in order to know what to expect."

"Your heart isn't in this, is it?" Charlie asked.

She didn't even try to hide her feelings. "No. Not anymore. I'm too worried about my father to think about securing a husband. I'm sorry I ever brought any of this up, in fact."

"Why don't I walk you home and say hello to your father?

I haven't seen him since he was in the bank. Maybe he'll perk up with a game of checkers."

"Oh, Charlie, I know he'd enjoy that, and maybe you can watch him and see what you think about his health. I just want to make sure he's getting all the care he needs."

"Of course." He gave her a smile, knowing that her heart was heavy.

"But you'll miss supper."

"I'll eat something when I get back. Mrs. Cooper will put something aside for me. I'm sure of it."

Melody turned to head back toward the house but managed to lose her footing. She dropped the bucket as she reached for Charlie. He grabbed hold of her and steadied her. For a moment, he held her close and gazed into her eyes. He didn't want to let her go.

"Oh, thank you, Charlie. I stepped on the hem of my skirt."

He said nothing. He wasn't sure he could even speak. The moment was strangely magical to him. Melody Doyle was in his arms, and it felt very right.

Realizing the moment was lasting longer than it needed to, Charlie let her go. "Are you steady now?"

"Yes, thanks to you." Her expression suggested that she, too, had been moved by the experience. That surprised Charlie in a way that blurred reasonable thinking. Was she starting to develop feelings for him?

"I, uh, well, I'll go ask Mrs. Cooper to save me some supper," he stammered, not knowing what else to say.

"Actually, if Da doesn't mind, you can eat with us. I'll let Mrs. Cooper know that you're coming home with me. I'll ask her to save you a piece of pie."

"I'd like that." He felt his heart race. *Be calm, Charlie. Don't make a mess of things.* He drew in a deep breath and let it out slowly. "I like your father a lot. He's a good man with great insight. He values work, but also play. I wish my own father would have paused for a game or two, but business is all he thinks about."

"It doesn't sound like you two are very close."

"Sadly, we're not. At least not as close as I wish." Charlie followed her to the pump, where she hung the bucket for the next person to use. "Father has always focused on the family by way of the business. If the business is doing well, he presumes the family is too."

"What a strange way of things."

"I've often thought that myself. My father is a wonderful man. A well-respected man. But he's never offered an abundance of affection or encouragement. And he has so seldom ever smiled that I can't help but wonder if he even knows how these days." Charlie could see his father's stern, almost severe expression. It saddened him to think his father had never known true happiness. Charlie pushed the thought aside. "But that's not important right now. We have checkers to play."

She looked at him oddly, and Charlie thought she might question him about what he'd said. Instead, she nodded and turned away. "I'll let Mrs. Cooper know we're leaving."

Melody disappeared into the house and was only gone for a few minutes. When she returned, she had rolled her sleeves back down and carried her shawl.

"I'm ready."

They headed around the house and down the street. Charlie couldn't help but enjoy her company. In fact, the more time he spent with her, the more he was assured that they were the perfect match. He was already losing his heart to her.

He hadn't given a lot of thought to securing himself a

wife when he came west. He knew he was more than old enough and had established himself in his profession. And while he hadn't purchased a home of his own, it was just a matter of time. Up until now, he'd not had any need for a place of his own. In Chicago, he had remained in his father's house, and here it seemed reasonable to board where someone could take care of his needs. But after speaking to Melody's father and examining his heart, Charlie knew a wife was exactly what he wanted and needed—no, Melody was what he wanted and needed.

"I just never thought of Da being sick, as well as injured," Melody began as they walked. "Da's always been so healthy and vital. Never a moment of illness. His fall was the first bad injury he's had in years. And that's saying something for a section hand supervisor. Accidents are commonplace in his line of work, but Da always seems to have God's hand on him."

"Yes, your father seems to put his trust in God completely. Still, pain can alter the way a man thinks or acts."

"You sound like someone who knows."

"Not firsthand, but there were a great many men I saw in the war who were injured . . . some badly enough to die. It wasn't an easy thing to see."

"I'm sure it wasn't. I doubt I'd be any good at nursing men through those kinds of injuries. I'd probably break down and cry alongside them."

"That's because you have a tender heart." Charlie glanced over at her. She looked so worried, and he found himself wishing he could ease her of that burden.

They reached her tent a few minutes later. The flap was open to let in the fresh air, but Mr. Doyle sat on a chair outside. He got to his feet and extended his hand.

"Charlie Decker, how nice to be seein' ya again."

"Charlie walked me home, and I'm thinking you two could have a game of checkers while I finish getting supper on. Da, don't you think we should ask Charlie to stay for supper?"

"I wouldn't want to be any bother or extra work." Charlie glanced from Melody to Clancy Doyle.

"Nonsense," her father replied. "It's our pleasure to have ya. Melody, bring the checkers and a chair. I'll pull up the barrel."

Melody glanced at Charlie, then nodded. Smiling at her father, she leaned over and kissed him atop the head. "This will be a grand evening."

12

Melody woke up in the middle of the night to hear her father making his way outside once again. His nighttime visits to the privy were coming more and more often. Granny had said that older people were that way sometimes, but she couldn't help but worry, what with so many people suggesting Da was ill.

She heard him return and asked, "Are you all right, Da?"

"I'm fine, darlin'. Just go back to sleep."

He settled into bed, and it wasn't long before Melody heard him snoring. She supposed she was worrying for nothing. Charlie had been with them all evening, and he didn't seem to notice anything amiss, at least he'd said nothing about it. Of course, they hadn't been alone long enough for him to say anything even if he had.

Thoughts of Charlie sent Melody to thinking back on her near fall. Being in Charlie's arms had caused her to see him in a new light. She really liked Charlie. They had a lot in common and talked so easily about all sorts of things. Charlie was kind and gentle in his nature, and he loved God. Those were such important things to her.

But things were also just different with Charlie. There was

no pretense to their relationship. She openly told him about her outings with other men, men she was considering for a husband. Charlie always asked how things had gone and never seemed upset to hear what she had to say.

He wasn't looking for a wife, and even if he were, he hadn't applied to court Melody. He knew all he had to do was talk to Da. And Da already liked him, so there wouldn't be a problem with getting Charlie approved.

She frowned. He obviously enjoyed her company, so the situation had to be that Charlie simply had no interest in getting married. Perhaps he couldn't see past her being anything more than a friend.

Well, good. She needed a friend. Given that something was obviously going on with Da, Melody had already decided to put an end to the scheme of finding a husband. She wasn't going to leave Da until she knew he was well and able to take care of himself. She knew there was another outing with a new prospective husband slated for today around noon. Jason Oberling wanted to take her for a picnic near Crow Creek. She would have to endure it, but then she'd let Da know that she didn't wish to have any more outings arranged.

But what reason will I give him? It wouldn't be easy to convince him, but she supposed she might as well tell him that she just wasn't ready to leave him. Not because of his needs but because of her own. That wasn't a lie. She felt the need to see him through whatever physical problem he was dealing with, and if it turned out that she would have to move down the line with him . . . well, so be it.

Charlie came to mind again. She wouldn't like leaving him any more than she would Marybeth or Granny. He'd become such a good friend. She sighed and closed her eyes. Maybe once morning came, she'd feel better about all of it.

But morning shed no more light on the matter. Because of the night's interruptions and the fact that it was Melody's day off, she didn't wake up until nearly six. Da hadn't even gotten up yet. However, he wasn't long to follow her. But he seemed tired and looked pale.

"Are you feeling all right, Da?"

"Me back is always sore after a night on that cot. But don't ya be worryin' about it, darlin' girl."

But she did worry, and her concerns were growing every day. "Coffee's on, and I'm getting ready to make breakfast. Are you hungry for anything in particular?"

"No, can't say I am." He sat down at the table. "Coffee will suffice for me."

"You haven't been eating much lately, Da. I'm worried about you. You've lost a lot of weight. I'll fix something you'll enjoy."

Her father chuckled. "Ya worry too much."

She honestly didn't know what to say to that. Maybe she did worry too much. After all, Da had never been sick a day in his life. Or maybe she should say, a day in her life. Seeing him dealing with the effects of the accident was also different. The other accidents he'd had with the railroad work had been different. Most didn't even require a doctor's long-term care. So maybe she was just giving in to her fears.

When Melody put breakfast on the table with Da's favorite flapjacks and ham, she whispered a prayer that he would eat. Instead, he only picked at it while telling her about the man she'd see later.

"Jason is a good fella. He's partners with his cousin and co-owns Oberlings' Mercantile. Ya know the place."

"Yes, I do. It's a very nice store." Melody poured her father more coffee, as it seemed to be the only thing he was interested in.

"Jason plans to be stayin' in Cheyenne, and even now he's buildin' a house."

"That's good news." Melody sliced into her flapjack. "You should eat your breakfast before it gets cold, Da."

"I'll be gettin' to it. Don't fuss."

She nodded and focused on her plate. Whatever was going on with him, he wasn't going to say a word. She knew it. It sent a sense of sadness washing over her. If Da wasn't speaking about the matter, it must be bad.

Melody could almost hear Granny Taylor admonishing her not to borrow trouble. The Bible would tell her the same. So why was it so hard not to worry?

Da cut up the flapjack and ham and took a bite of each. He pushed the food around as he talked to Melody about the day and what he planned to do while she was away on the picnic. He didn't take another bite of food.

Melody cleaned up after breakfast, mended some clothes, and then went out to check the community garden. There wasn't much to be done, however. Waiting for things to grow was hard. At least it was right now. Melody desperately wanted something to focus on besides her father's health.

She returned to the tent and readied herself for the outing she would have with Jason. Since it was a picnic, she dressed in a simple brown serge skirt and calico-print blouse. The calico had blues and browns as well as bits of rose and gold. It seemed to draw out the blue in Melody's eyes, and she'd always liked the blouse for that reason. But she didn't want to attract Jason and gave some consideration to choosing a different top. Finally, frustrated by her own jumble of thoughts, Melody kept the calico.

Jason was prompt and showed up right at noon. He and Da talked outside the tent for a few minutes, discussing the weather and railroad. Melody found herself wishing she could just cancel the entire affair but knew that was hardly the polite thing to do. Jason had already gone to the trouble of packing a picnic. The least she could do was go along and eat it.

"Well, here ya are," Da said when Melody stepped from the tent. "Melody, this is Jason Oberling."

She squared her shoulders. "Mr. Oberling, I'm pleased to meet you."

"Pleased to meet you, Miss Doyle."

She didn't suggest he call her Melody. There didn't seem any sense to it. No use getting the man's hopes up.

"Well, ya best be off, then," Da said, seeming almost anxious to get rid of them.

Jason helped her up onto his buckboard, then sat beside her, taking up the reins for the dappled gray horse.

"That's a lovely horse you have," she offered.

"He's rented. The wagon too. Never had much need for one of my own but figured we had a little way to go to get to Crow Creek."

Melody nodded. "I suppose that makes sense. I walk everywhere myself."

He glanced over at her, seeming to size her up. "You're a fine figure of a woman, if I can say as much."

"Well, you just did, so I suppose I'll have to be amenable to it." She worried her words were too harsh. "Thank you for the compliment."

He gave a slight smile. "I have to say that your pa's way of hooking you up with a husband is rather strange. I never figured to find a bride this way, but now that I've joined in, it seems just as conventional as any other plan."

He sounded so happy about the prospect that Melody couldn't bring herself to tell him she'd changed her mind. They rode out from town and headed for a popular gathering spot along Crow Creek. Mr. Oberling rambled about the weather and the town, but Melody paid little attention. From time to time, she nodded or said just enough to let him know she was sort of listening.

"I like that you're a quiet woman. Most women seem to think they've got to be sayin' something all the time. Like they can't stand to just enjoy the peace and quiet."

Melody started to respond but instead just nodded. If he liked quiet, she was more than happy to give it to him.

When they finally reached the place, Melody didn't wait for Mr. Oberling to help her down. She went to the back of the wagon as he came around. He gave her an approving nod, as if pleased she was capable of taking care of herself.

"I'd be happy to carry something."

He handed her the blanket. "Appreciate that. I can manage the rest."

She saw other people enjoying the day but knew she wouldn't be among their number. She couldn't enjoy the day, not when there were so many unanswered questions about Da.

He took up a large basket from the back of the wagon and motioned to a place. "That looks like a nice spot."

She looked to where he was glancing. It was situated near a stand of pines, and not far away were several families. It offered privacy, but not too much.

"It looks quite nice."

They made their way to the spot, and Melody spread the blanket. Once that was done, Mr. Oberling put the basket down and then offered Melody his hand to help her sit. Once they were both comfortable, Mr. Oberling started bringing the food out of the basket. He offered Melody a plate, then took up a towel-wrapped bundle.

"I hope you like ham-and-cheese sandwiches."

"I do." She accepted one from him and put it on her plate.

A carriage arrived with two sets of couples. It kicked up a bit of dust, causing Melody to shield her sandwich. Mr. Oberling gave it little attention and instead reached into the basket. He took out a covered bowl. When he removed the cloth, Melody was surprised to find what looked to be very thinly sliced fried potatoes.

"My cousin's wife made these. She worked back east in Saratoga Springs for a man named Crum. He made these chips as a snack for people to eat while they waited for their meal. But I like them just as much as part of my meal. Try one." He extended the bowl toward her.

Melody picked one out and tasted it. It was crunchy and salty. She liked it very much. "It's like when I accidentally fry the potatoes too long."

"We've grown to eat them all the time. Can't get enough of them myself." He took up several and popped them into his mouth and began crunching away.

He put other things out on the blanket, then drew out a couple of jars of liquid. "This is lemonade. I got a taste for it during the war, and now we make it and sell it at the store. Sells well. Just citric acid, sugar, and a little lemon oil. Not too much of the oil, though. It can be too strong otherwise. I'm hoping maybe once the railroad goes all the way through that we'll be able to get real lemons in."

"I remember having fresh lemonade when we lived back east," Melody said, looking rather apprehensively at the jar being offered her. "Only had it a couple of times. Lemons were scarce and expensive."

"To be sure. We drank this on the battlefield when we could get the ingredients. Chemists keep the oil and citric acid. Give it a try."

Melody opened the jar and tasted it. It wasn't half bad. She smiled and gave Mr. Oberling a nod. "It's tart. I like it."

"For some reason, it's good to quench the thirst for a long time." He opened his own jar and had a long drink.

He looked at Melody. "I suppose you'd like to know more about me. I hail from Albany, New York. Lived there until after the war. I was a sergeant with the Third New York Infantry. Got injured too. Not bad, took some shrapnel to my side and back. Lost my brother Hal."

Just then, a small dog came up to their blanket. He was pale brown with short hair. It was obvious he hadn't been eating a lot, as his ribs were clearly visible. Melody thought to offer him a piece of her sandwich, but Mr. Oberling would have none of that.

"Get out of here, cur. Go on now." He waved his arms, and the dog scurried away. He looked back at Melody and shook his head. "Someone ought to shoot that mangy beast."

She thought he was probably just exaggerating his thoughts, but when the dog returned, he threw a rock at it. When that failed to get results, the man went to the wagon and took up a shotgun from behind the seat. He aimed it at the dog, and Melody couldn't help but scream.

"No! Don't shoot!"

The dog ran from the picnic and hurried down the creek toward one of the families, who by now was watching to see who had cried out.

"How could you threaten a hungry animal like that?" she asked, getting to her feet.

Mr. Oberling looked at her like she had suddenly lost her senses. "What's got you riled up?"

Melody planted her hands on her hips. "How could you threaten to shoot a helpless animal? He was hungry. Didn't you see how skinny he was?"

The man shrugged and lowered his shotgun. "Not my problem. He isn't my dog."

"And you most assuredly won't be my husband!"

She stormed off toward the road and marched all the way back to town without so much as a glance over her shoulder to see Mr. Oberling's response. The man was absolutely heartless. How had Da not discerned the man's temper? Was his physical condition starting to interfere with his ability to hear God's voice? Fears for her father grew. Something wasn't right, and for too long now, she'd ignored the truth. She put aside her anger at Mr. Oberling and picked up her pace. She was glad to no longer be looking for a husband, as she had a feeling Da was going to need all of her attention.

Charlie added one of the columns on the page of the bank ledger for the third time. It didn't match up with one of the corresponding columns. It should have, but something was obviously written down wrong. He would have to go number by number. For all the erasure marks and questionable writing, it was a wonder that anything added up correctly. Some of the handwriting was so illegible, Charlie was guessing at the entries.

He frowned and set the book aside. Was Jefferson purposefully making a mess of the ledgers in order to steal from the bank? It could have been Jacob who made the mistakes, but it continued after Jacob had left Cheyenne. That most likely made it Jefferson's responsibility. Charlie didn't like to think ill of the young man, but there was no denying it had happened on his watch.

Charlie eased back on his bed and closed his eyes. He'd been poring over the books most of the morning, and now that it was a little past one, food was uppermost on his mind. He'd missed any chance at the boardinghouse lunch. It was served promptly at noon on the weekends and would mostly likely already be over with and cleaned up.

He thought of Melody and her father. Melody was on a date. Hopefully it would be her last. Maybe Charlie would grab something to eat and take it by the tent to see how Clancy was doing. Melody had said he wasn't eating well. Perhaps if Charlie brought him something, he'd feel obliged to eat.

Clancy Doyle was good company, and Charlie had enjoyed their time together the night before. Their supper had been simple but good, and Clancy told several stories about Ireland and his youth. Unfortunately, there hadn't been an opportunity for Charlie to speak to Clancy alone, and he hoped he might rectify that while Melody was busy elsewhere.

He closed the bankbook and took up his coat. The heaviness of what he planned to discuss with Clancy slowed his steps. When he reached the bottom step, Mrs. Cooper just happened to be there.

"Charlie, you missed lunch."

"I know. I just realized that."

"Well, don't tell the others, but I made you a couple of roast beef sandwiches. They're in the kitchen. Come along."

"I was just going out to check on Melody's father. Do you suppose I could impose on you to wrap them up so I can take them with me?"

She gave a nod. "Of course, Charlie. That's kind of you to visit Mr. Doyle. I hear he's not doing as well as he could be."

"Yes. Things do seem to be difficult for him. I'm hoping maybe a visit this morning and a game of checkers will help."

"You're a good man, Charlie Decker."

The older man was sitting outside the tent, just as Charlie and Melody had found him the evening before. He was reading a newspaper when Charlie happened along.

"Afternoon, Clancy."

"Good to be seein' ya again, son. Kind of thought ya might be back." Clancy lowered the paper.

"You did, huh?" Charlie gave a knowing nod. Since their first discussion at the bank, he'd felt as if the man knew what Charlie was thinking. "I brought a couple of roast beef sandwiches. Would you care for one?"

"No, but thank ya, Charlie. Go grab a chair from the tent, and ya can be speakin' yar mind."

Charlie did as Clancy instructed. He placed his sandwiches on the little table and took the chair outside. He was hungry and thought about retrieving his food, but instead, he sat beside the older man, a sadness coming over him. "You have to tell her the truth."

"I know. I've been wantin' to do just that since our first talk, Charlie."

"It's not right that I know and others suspect, and yet you've said nothing to her."

"I'm dyin'." The words were offered simply and without emotion. "What else can I be sayin' to her?"

Charlie nodded. "But she doesn't know. She thinks you've nothing more than a back injury to overcome. Although, by now, she's starting to figure out something's not quite right."

"Me kidneys are failin'. Doc says the time's not long."

Clancy gave him a tired smile. "For sure that will be hard news to take in."

"You have to tell her just the same. She can't just go on thinking you're going to recover."

"I know that, and I've been plannin' to tell her. I wanted to see if she took to any of the young men I picked out. But there's only one that I feel confident of, and that's yarself. It's always just been you, Charlie."

Charlie nodded. "I've lost my heart to her. I think she's starting to feel something for me as well. I want her for my wife. I love her."

"We did it yar way, Charlie. I said nothin' about yar interest. Let ya be friends, just as ya wanted. I like what I see. Ya have me blessin' to marry her."

"So the time has come to be honest with her. She deserves to know the truth, Clancy."

"Aye, Charlie. And for sure, I'll be tellin' her. I'll do it today after she comes back."

Charlie started to say something, but the sight of Melody marching down the street toward the tent community, a look of pure anger on her face, stopped him. He looked to Clancy and nodded his head in her direction. "It would seem that she's back."

Clancy gave a nod. "Aye, and she's ragin', to be sure. I know that look."

Charlie couldn't help grinning. "Good. That means she didn't much care for Mr. Oberling."

"It would seem that way," Clancy said, chuckling. "So much the better for ya, Charlie."

13

Melody was surprised to see Charlie sitting with her father outside the tent. She was still seething over Jason Oberling's reaction to an innocent dog invading their picnic. A part of her knew she'd overreacted. It was a good excuse to make it clear to him that she wasn't interested in furthering their relationship, but she felt guilty for treating him poorly. Her guilt only served to make her all the angrier. And then there was Da and whatever was going on with him. That was starting to make her just as angry. How dare he not be honest with her?

"Well, yar back early and without the fella who took ya," Da observed. "What seems to be the trouble? Did he harm ya?" Da's expression turned from curious to concerned.

"No, Da. He didn't harm me, but he tried to shoot a stray dog, and it made me mad. I can't believe a starving pup deserves to be shot. He was just trying to get a free meal." She shook her head. "People can be so disappointing, and I'm tired of their nonsense. I don't intend to go out with any more of these men. If they come calling, you'll just have to let them know I've changed my mind and will remain with you. When the railroad sends you west, then I'll be at your side."

Da shook his head. "Ya shouldn't be lettin' one bad-tempered fella spoil ya on all of them. Why, Charlie here is a good man and doesn't deserve yar rage."

She gave Charlie a slight smile. "Sorry. I feel no malice toward you. You've been a dear friend."

"I'm glad to hear that," Charlie said, grinning. "And just for the record, I'd never shoot a stray dog. I would have invited him to the picnic."

Melody glanced into his eyes, and for a moment, she forgot about her anger and worries. He really was the best of friends. No doubt he was here to try to help Melody figure out Da's situation.

"Did ya have lunch yet, Charlie?"

"No. I did bring a couple of roast beef sandwiches, though. You'll find them on the table inside. But how about I take you and your father out to eat at one of the cafés? You can save the sandwiches for later."

Melody looked at her father. Maybe with Charlie's invitation to lunch, Da would eat a decent amount of food. "What do you say, Da?"

"Maybe Charlie could be eatin' his sandwiches and take ya to supper this evenin'. I'm wantin' to spend some time talkin' to ya first."

Melody nodded. Maybe she would finally get some answers about what was going on with her father. She looked to Charlie. "Would supper work?"

"I'd be happy to take you to supper. Your father too, if he wants to come along."

"We can be seein' about that later," Da replied.

Charlie got to his feet. "Then I'll get my sandwiches and

take my leave. I'll return around five thirty, if that suits you, Melody." He disappeared into the tent and quickly returned with a dish towel–wrapped bundle. Unfortunately, it reminded her of the picnic.

She pushed the thought aside. Da wanted to talk to her. Hopefully he'd tell her what was going on with his health. Of course, she couldn't be sure that's what he intended to talk to her about, but she prayed it would be in regard to his condition.

"Until this evening," Charlie said and took his leave.

Melody watched him go, then turned back to her father. "What do you want to talk to me about?"

Da smiled. "What would ya be wantin' me to tell ya?"

She took the seat Charlie had vacated. "I want to know how you're feeling and if something more is wrong than what you're telling me. People keep saying you don't look well or that they're concerned about your health. I know you aren't eating or sleeping well, so I figure something must be wrong."

Her father nodded. "I've been meanin' to find a good time for this discussion. I didn't want to worry ya none nor give ya cause to be grievin'."

Melody laced her fingers together and lowered her gaze. She already knew the news wasn't going to be to her liking. She could sense it and had been afraid of knowing since people had first started mentioning her father's condition.

"Go ahead then, Da. I want to know it all."

"Me kidneys are not farin' well. Doc says they haven't been for some time. It's the reason I've lost me appetite and make the frequent trips out in the night. It's also causin' me some pain."

"Along with the back injury from when you fell?" she asked, not wanting him to continue but certain he must.

"There wasn't any real injury from the fall. Nothing more than some pulled muscles, anyway. The fall wasn't that far. No, most of it has been me kidneys."

"Why didn't you just tell me that? What can we do about it?"

"Well now, that's the point to all of this. I know ya won't want to be hearin' this, but there's nothin' that can be done. Me kidneys aren't good."

"But surely there's something someone can do. We don't have much in the way of doctors here, but we could go to Denver. Or better yet take the train east to Chicago. There are some very good doctors there, I'm sure. Charlie could probably recommend someone who would know. A big-city doctor might know how to help you." Melody was already thinking of how the railroad would give them free passage at least as far as Omaha. Maybe Charlie's family could offer them guidance once they got to Chicago.

"No, the doc already checked into such things. I'm afraid there's naught to be done."

Melody wasn't ready to accept that thought. "I'm sure someone, somewhere has better information regarding your problem, Da. We can't just give up and not try. We just need to get to a bigger city."

"Melody, me darlin', no one wishes more than me that I could be givin' ya more time. But the truth must be faced."

She met his gaze. "The truth?"

He smiled wistfully. "None of us lives forever. I won't be here much longer."

"No!" She shook her head. "It can't be that bad."

"Aye, but it is." He reached out and took hold of her arm. "Ya need to be strong, me darlin' girl."

Tears came against her will. Melody wiped them away with

the back of her sleeve, then took hold of Da's hand. "This can't be. I won't let it be." She drew his hand to her cheek. "You can't leave me, Da."

"Oh, me darlin', I wish I didn't have to. Ya know that to be the truth. Ya've been me pride and joy." He paused, causing Melody to look at him once again.

"Yar mam used to ask me if I regretted not havin' a son, and I told her I had no need of a son. I had yarself, and that was more than enough. Ya've always been a hundred times better than a son."

"Da, you can't leave me. Not yet."

"I still want to see ya married. That desire hasn't changed. Ya need someone to take care of ya."

"No. I won't be husband hunting while you're so sick. Let's work to get you well, and then we can worry about my need of a husband. I'm not convinced that there isn't someone who can help us."

"Melody."

Her name was almost spoken like a command. She didn't want to accept that there was no hope. She couldn't. She prayed silently for God to intervene and give them answers. There had to be hope.

"Melody, look at me."

She did as he bid. "I've had a good life, and ya've made me happy every day ya've been here. Don't make this harder than it needs be."

"But it is hard, Da. It's the hardest thing I've had to face since losing Mother. You tell me there's nothing to help with this problem, but I can't let that be the end of it. I'm certain there must be something we can do."

"I wish there were, but Doc has already tried to find other answers, and there aren't any to be had. Now, what I need from ya is to be strong. We can't be stoppin' what's going to happen, but we can walk this journey together . . . or I can walk it alone."

"No! I won't let you walk it alone. You know I won't."

"Then be me strength. Be strong in the Lord."

A thought came to her just then. "Does Charlie know?"

"Aye. I told him. We've been talkin' about all sorts of things since I first met him. I like Charlie a great deal. I think he's a good man. Honorable and godly. He's helpin' me with the money that's comin' from Ireland. There will be an account set up to take care of yar needs."

She didn't care about the money. It wouldn't keep Da alive. Hearing that Charlie knew about her father but said nothing bothered her. How long had he known? The thought of him lying to her was more than Melody wanted to consider. She hated to think Charlie would keep something that important from her.

She got to her feet and swallowed down the lump in her throat. After dealing with Mr. Oberling and the dog and now this, she felt the need for a long cry. Of course, she couldn't have it. Not in front of Da.

"I'm going to go see Marybeth. She said she'd have some eggs for us today. Do you think you might be able to eat some?"

"I'm not hungry, darlin'. But ya should go ahead and see yar friend. Maybe she can bring ya some comfort."

Melody looked at him for a long moment. "I can . . . stay if you need me to."

"Gracious no. Go on with ya. And go to supper with Charlie tonight. Ya'll be needin' him now more than ever."

She almost wished she'd never asked for the truth. If she hadn't asked she could pretend nothing was wrong. Never in all of her thoughts had she figured anything could be this bad.

She made her way to Marybeth's, where she found her outside with Carrie. They were hanging up clothes. Carrie, only two years old, was handing Marybeth clothespins and laughing. She was such a happy child.

Melody joined them and immediately went to work helping Marybeth with the laundry. Her friend gave a nod, but Melody said nothing. She was almost afraid to open her mouth. What if she started to cry in front of Carrie?

Marybeth picked up the last of the things, a large sheet. "Glad to have your help." She glanced at Melody and frowned. Melody looked away and pinned the sheet in place.

"Carrie, it's time to go inside for your nap. You bring the clothespins, and I'll get the basket."

"Don't wanna nap." Carrie pointed to Melody. "Wanna play wit Melody."

"Not today. You take a good nap, and I'll let you help me make cookies when you wake up."

"Cookies!" Carrie clapped her hands. "I get cookies."

"Yes, but first bring the clothespins and take a nap." They headed to the house with Carrie nearly running. The bag of clothespins thankfully had a drawstring that kept them from spilling out as she ran.

Once Marybeth had Carrie put to bed, she motioned Melody to sit in the front room and joined her. "What's wrong? I can see in your eyes that something isn't right."

"Oh, it's all more than I can bear." The tears came again. "Marybeth, my father is dying."

"What?"

"You know I've been worried about him being sick. Today he was finally honest with me about it. Apparently, his kidneys are failing. The doctor says there is nothing to be done. Da said he doesn't have much time."

"How can this be?"

"I don't know." Melody shook her head and let the tears fall. "What will I do without him?"

"You have us. We won't let you be alone. In fact, I bet if I ask Edward, he'd go and talk to your father about moving in here with us. That way you could take care of him in his . . . his . . . final days. And I could help as well."

"Da would never come here. He wouldn't allow himself to be that kind of burden." Melody sniffed back tears. "I just can't believe this is happening. Why would God take him from me? Where is the good in that?"

"I've often asked myself that question about losing my mother, stepmother, and father," Marybeth replied. "It hasn't even been a year since my father died, and I miss him very much. Seems you and I have a lot in common."

Melody nodded. "That's why I came here. I knew you'd understand. I don't even know how much time we still have. And worse yet, he told Charlie about it, and Charlie said nothing to me. Charlie even knew I was worried about Da."

"When did he tell Charlie?"

"I don't know. I just know that he did. Da admitted that much. I just feel it's a betrayal of our friendship that Charlie said nothing. I know we haven't been friends that long, but it seems like I've known him forever. We were able to talk about everything. Goodness, I even tell him about my outings with the men who want to marry me. Of course, there will be no more of that. I told Da that I have no desire to marry now."

"What did he say?"

Melody leaned back on the sofa. "That he still wants me to marry. He wants to have me taken care of so he can die in peace." She sighed and shook her head again. "I can't be courting someone with this weighing on my heart."

"You know what? We need to pray." Marybeth reached out to take hold of her hand. "We need to do it right now. God always has answers, and He won't fail to show you the right direction this time, just as He always has."

Melody knew she was right. "I agree. We need to pray He heals Da." She thought of Charlie. "And we need to pray that Charlie will be honest with me about why he said nothing."

Charlie was actually glad that Clancy Doyle wanted to stay home that evening. He wouldn't have been able to have an outing like this with Melody otherwise, and he was very much looking forward to it.

They walked to the restaurant, and Charlie told Melody about his day of going over bank ledgers. He said nothing about his fears that Jefferson was doing something underhanded and instead shared some of the things he'd learned about banking over the years.

"Of course, you already know that banking isn't where my heart lies."

"Does your heart lie, Charlie?" she asked him most unexpectedly.

"What?" He frowned, completely uncertain what it was she wanted to know.

"How long have you known about Da?"

"What exactly are you asking me?" He stopped on the boardwalk and faced her.

"How long have you known that Da is dying?"

He frowned. "He confided in me a week ago."

Melody studied him for a moment, then her shoulders sagged a bit. "Why would he do that? Tell you and not me?"

"I don't pretend to entirely understand, but I think it was

a man-to-man kind of thing. He came to talk to me about the money coming from Ireland."

"You lied to me."

"I would never lie to you, Melody. And I told your father that when he asked me to keep his secret until he could talk to you about it."

"You knew I was worried about Da's health, and yet you said nothing." She glanced down the street. "I thought you were my friend."

"I am your friend and Clancy's too. I didn't want to betray his trust, but had you asked me directly if I knew what was wrong with him, I would have told you. I swear I would have. But you never asked. You talked about him and what might be going on, but you didn't ask me if I knew."

"That's just a game, Charlie. It's still not right."

"I am not playing games with you, Melody. My intention has only ever been to keep your father's trust until he was ready to tell you the truth."

"He's known since he fell. Why didn't he just tell me the truth then?"

"You'd have to ask him that question. My guess is that he didn't want to spend his final days dying."

She frowned, drawing her brows together. "What do you mean?"

Charlie wanted so much to comfort her. "If I were him, I'd want to spend my last days living to the fullest, rather than spend them dying a little at a time with people crying over me or being sad." Tears were in her eyes, and despite it being in the middle of the boardwalk, Charlie put his arm around her shoulders. "I'm here for you, Melody."

She pushed him away. "I don't want you to be. I can't trust you to tell me the truth."

She stormed away, leaving Charlie to watch her go. He longed to run after her but knew it wouldn't do any good. She needed time to think through all that had happened and calm her anguished heart.

"God, please go with her. She's in such despair," Charlie whispered.

14

"Jefferson, we need to talk." Charlie had been dreading the confrontation all day, but it was apparent to him after studying the books that Jefferson had been taking money from the bank for quite some time. Somehow the young man had managed to do it right under Jacob's nose, and knowing his brother's eye for details, Charlie was quite impressed.

"All right, but it's nearly closing time, and I have plans tonight."

Charlie nodded. "I understand, but this won't wait. Please take a seat." He motioned for Jefferson to take the chair in front of Charlie's desk.

Sitting behind his desk, Charlie straightened and put his hands on the stack of ledgers. "I went through these. I'm sure you're aware of what I found."

"No. I haven't a clue," Jefferson said, looking bored with the entire matter.

"Jefferson, it's clear you've been changing entries and skimming money from accounts. There's no one else who could have done it. Not only that, but your initials are beside each entry."

"Anyone can put down initials. I have done nothing wrong."

"There are erasures and hard-to-read markings," Charlie continued, "and it started shortly after the bank opened and has continued throughout the year."

"I sometimes transpose numbers and have to fix them. I'm sorry. It's always been a problem of mine, but I always make the corrections."

"Jefferson, this isn't just a matter of transposing numbers and correcting them. You know as well as I do that money is missing from the bank. I came in at five this morning and did a physical count. You're the only one who could have taken it."

"What about your brother? Mr. Decker could just as easily be to blame. He was always very secretive about what went on with the books."

Charlie sat back and shook his head. "I'm afraid I need to let you go. I would appreciate it if you would return the money to the bank so that I don't have to file charges against you."

Jefferson jumped up and pointed a finger at Charlie. "I'm not taking the blame for your brother."

"This has gone on even after my brother left. How do you account for that?"

The younger man shook his head. "I have no idea. You're the banking genius. I've done my job and done it well. I remained faithful to see the bank open and running each and every day, even after your brother left. But did I get any thank-you for my efforts? A bonus?" He shook his head again. "No! Nothing. And now you're firing me for something I didn't do. I see no justice in this."

Jefferson left without another word. Charlie remained at his desk as he listened to Jefferson storm around the front room, gathering his things. When the front door slammed shut, Charlie knew he had gone.

He didn't know what to say about Jefferson's charges toward Jacob. Charlie supposed anything was possible, but Jacob seemed the least likely to do anything underhanded. He loved banking and wouldn't jeopardize anything related to his job.

No, it was clearly Jefferson who had done the deed. The missing funds totaled some six hundred dollars. That was far too much money to be a mere mistake in the books. The carbon copies of the receipts showed the discrepancies clearly.

Charlie closed his eyes. Now Jefferson was his enemy as well as Melody. He'd certainly made a mess of things in such a short period of time. He let out a long sigh.

Lord, what am I supposed to do now? What is it You've planned for me? You know my heart isn't in this job, but I have to earn a living, and I want to honor my father that my days may be long. I don't want to disappoint him.

He sighed again. *I didn't want to disappoint Melody either. I know once she thinks things over, she'll understand. She's a good woman, and she puts her trust in You, but right now she's dealing with so much. The news of her father dying is overwhelming, and I'm asking You to help her. Please, Lord.*

The front door opened, and Charlie wondered if Jefferson had returned. He got up and walked out to find Dr. Scott smiling in greeting.

"Charlie, my boy. I hope you don't mind this intrusion."

"Not at all. The bank day is pretty much done. I was just getting ready to lock up."

"Wonderful. Then you can walk with me as I make my way back to my office on Fifteenth."

It wasn't in the direction Charlie had planned to go, but he nodded anyway. "Just let me get my keys and lock up." Charlie secured the bank and turned to Dr. Scott. "I'm ready."

"Wonderful. I know it might seem odd for me to show up here unannounced, but I wanted to talk to you about church."

"I've very much enjoyed your sermons. I like straightforward messages, the kind without pretense or show."

"Good thing, because I have neither pretense nor show to offer. For me the Word of God is strong enough to stand all on its own."

"I agree. I've attended church since I was born. My mother said even as a baby I was most attentive." Charlie chuckled. "I love hearing the Bible recited and preached. The lessons it has for us there are so vital."

"I completely agree with you and have been thinking of what you said about loving to teach. I'm wondering if you would consider teaching a Sunday school class of six- to fourteen-year-old boys every Sunday afternoon at two. You can speak on anything in the Bible that you like, but I can also let you know what the Sunday sermon will be, and you can teach on that to give the boys insight into what I'll be talking about that evening."

Charlie didn't even have to think about it. "I would love to. I'm honored that you would trust me with such a position."

"People speak highly of you, Charlie. Even in the short time you've been here, you have made impressions."

"Thank you. I pray I won't disappoint you or God."

"Do you really suppose you can disappoint God, Charlie? Disappointment suggests an unfulfilled anticipation. A hope that things will go one way only to find they've gone another. Since God is all knowing, how can He be disappointed?"

"I've never really considered that point, but it makes

sense. I suppose instead of disappointment when we choose something other than Him, God is . . . saddened."

"I agree. God must surely face sorrow knowing the choices we make that will lead us to pain and injury. Imagine Him at the beginning of creating the heavens and earth. He knew it wouldn't go well for man, and yet He continued to create. He had a plan beyond what He knew would be man's choices. The plan was always to bring Jesus to a dying world.

"Some people think that Jesus coming to earth to die for our sins was an afterthought, but God knew the choices man would make before He ever put them in the garden. Jesus was always a part of the picture. Disappointment didn't figure into it."

Charlie nodded as the entire explanation came together in his mind. "I can see that now. I will endeavor not to lead God to sorrow over me and my choices." He looked at Dr. Scott and smiled. "And I will endeavor to serve our little church faithfully."

By Friday, Melody could hardly look at Da without feeling her tears come up anew. She couldn't bear the idea of losing him. It terrified her and left her feeling like a small child, stranded and alone.

She argued with herself constantly about the situation. She was certain there had to be someone who could offer help. She knew there was money in the bank and more to come when the Ireland money was delivered. There was surely enough to travel to wherever they needed to go.

She hung up her kitchen apron and glanced over at Mrs. Cooper. "I need to check the garden before I go."

"You tend that plot like a mother with a new babe," Mrs. Cooper declared. "I'm impressed with all of your work, Melody. You've been the perfect employee."

Melody forced a smile. "Thank you for saying so."

"Are you all right? You've seemed preoccupied all week."

"I have a lot on my mind, but, yes, I'm fine." It wasn't really a lie, Melody told herself. Da was the one who wasn't fine, but she wasn't yet ready to share that information with Mrs. Cooper.

Making her way outside, Melody grabbed her gardening gloves at the back door. She pulled them on as she approached the large garden plot. She spied a few weeds starting to grow. Also, there was a faint line of green down some of the rows she'd planted. The soil was good, and the rain they'd had, though minimal, had helped to grow the seeds into tiny plants.

As she weeded, Melody couldn't help but wonder what she should do next. She needed to better understand her father's situation and had already figured to check in with the railroad doctor sometime soon. Since the garden was in good order, why not leave early and go see him now?

She straightened and looked around. Everything was taken care of, and she'd even helped Mrs. Cooper by making a cake for supper. There wasn't anything left, and if she went now, she might avoid seeing Charlie.

Charlie.

Now, there was a big disappointment. She had loved being his friend and enjoyed the things they talked about. Charlie had been a good friend. At least she'd thought he was a good friend. But good friends didn't lie to each other.

But Charlie hadn't really lied, a voice seemed to whisper. He'd not volunteered to share information with her that he knew she'd want to know, but that had been done because of a promise he'd given to Da. He hadn't lied.

He really was an admirable man. She had to admit that much. The next time she met with Marybeth and Granny Taylor she would ask their opinion of the matter. It just wasn't easy to understand the situation on her own. Her thoughts were far too jumbled, and underlying everything was fear.

Melody had never been one to be afraid. She'd always been ready and willing to rise to the occasion and face whatever there was to face, but not this time. She supposed it was because she'd always known she had her father to help her. Da would never allow her to face anything alone. She had felt safe and secure, even when their finances had been bad, because she knew Da would have an answer.

It came to mind that maybe she put more trust in her earthly father than she did her heavenly one. She frowned and pulled off her gloves. Surely that wasn't the truth of it. She knew that God was in charge of all. That He knew all. She trusted Him.

Didn't she?

She went back into the house and deposited her gloves. She found Mrs. Cooper in the kitchen spreading melted butter on top of the dinner rolls she'd just pulled from the oven.

"I'm taking off a little early," she told the woman. "Everything is done, however, and I'll stay a little longer tomorrow if need be."

"You've done a great job. I'm sure you probably have your own housekeeping and shopping to tend to. Thank the Lord it's safer now for a woman to walk alone in Cheyenne. There are still some unsavory characters out there, but it's so much nicer."

"Yes," Melody said, again forcing a smile. "Thank you for understanding. I'll see you in the morning."

She hurried out of the house, hoping to avoid any further discussion. She didn't want to explain matters to her employer. At least not now. Faith Cooper was a good woman and would be sympathetic and understanding, but Melody had no desire to share her sorrows just yet.

The day was warmer than usual. Melody worried they'd have an unbearably hot summer and further Da's misery. Would he even be around for the summer months? How much time did he have left? She bit her lower lip. No matter how much time, it wouldn't be enough.

Melody headed to the railroad's hospital. Dr. Latham had been with the railroad for some time and knew the physical conditions of most of the UP employees. She knew her father respected the man.

When she arrived at the hospital, Melody learned that Dr. Latham was busy with a patient. She told the nurse she would wait—that it was important she speak with him. She sat and thought of exactly what kinds of questions she might ask. Her list was quite long by the time the doctor agreed to see her.

"Miss Doyle, it's a pleasure to see you." He ushered her into a tiny office and motioned to an empty chair. "Please have a seat."

"Thank you."

"What can I do for you?" he asked, taking a seat at his cluttered desk.

"Da told me about his kidneys. He said there's nothing that can be done, but I find that hard to believe."

Dr. Latham frowned. "It's sadly the truth. Your father's kidneys haven't been functioning well for some time. We just didn't realize it."

"Could something have been done if you had known sooner?"

"It's doubtful," the man replied. "There are so many things we just don't know about the body. We might have been able to stave it off for a time, but even that is uncertain."

"I can't believe there isn't a doctor somewhere who specializes in this kind of thing. We could travel to him, if I knew where he was."

The doctor nodded. "Your father and I discussed that very possibility, and I put out word to several colleagues back east and in California. No one could offer me much in the way of help. So, you see, we aren't just relying on my limited knowledge."

"But there has to be something we can do," Melody insisted.

"I'm afraid there isn't. His body isn't functioning well. His appetite is very low, and you know for yourself he's lost a lot of weight. I've given him medicine to help with the pain, but it doesn't help much."

She had no idea of Da having medication for the pain. He had said nothing about it. But then, he'd said nothing about being ill.

"I'm truly sorry, Miss Doyle. But even if there were a doctor elsewhere who had advanced treatments, I'm afraid your father is too sick to even make the trip."

Melody shook her head. "He doesn't seem that bad. He seems tired and isn't eating a lot, but . . ." She fell silent, seeing the look on the doctor's face. The truth of the matter was fixed. There was no hope of Da getting better.

"So there's not much time left?" she asked, already knowing the answer.

"No. Like I told your father last week, it could be just

about any time. The kidneys are an important organ in our body, and when they fail, the body cannot survive. I'm so sorry."

Melody drew a breath, but it was more of a sob. She barely managed to make it outside before she burst into tears. Her mind refused to accept the truth, but her heart knew there was nothing more to be done.

She did what she could to control herself and headed home. What else could she do? She had to be there for Da. Had to make his final days as comfortable as possible. A cloud seemed to come over her mind, and she found reasoning and planning impossible. In something of a daze, she continued walking.

"Melody?"

She heard her name called after a time. She stopped and looked around, uncertain of where it had come from. Then she spied him. Charlie. Where had he come from? How did he know she needed him more than ever?

But he hurt me. He lied to me.

No. He hadn't lied.

He drew near, and Melody felt her knees buckle. Thankfully, Charlie was close enough to catch her.

"What is it? What's happened?" he asked, helping her to stand.

She felt his arms strong and capable around her body. How she wished she could trust him.

"Melody, what's going on? Are you ill?"

"I . . . I talked to Da's doctor." Her vision blurred from the tears.

"I'm so sorry."

He hugged her close, his strong arms encircling her in a protective fashion. In that moment, Melody wanted nothing more than to remain where she was. Charlie might have kept information from her, but Da had made him give his word. Charlie had honored his promise. He wasn't a bad man. . . . He was her friend, and she could trust him.

She wrapped her arms around him, not caring what anyone thought. "He's going to die, Charlie. Da is going to die, and I'm going to be alone."

"Never alone, Melody. You have Jesus, and you have me. I'm not going to leave you, and neither will He."

For a time, all she did was cry. She let out all the pent-up misery and sorrow as if she could hand them over to Charlie and be done with them. Her entire world was falling apart, and she didn't know what she would do.

Charlie just let her cry, and when she began to calm, Melody straightened. "I'm sorry for being angry with you." She pulled away and drew out a handkerchief from her pocket. Dabbing her eyes, she shook her head. "It wasn't right. Da told you in confidence, and you kept his secret. That doesn't mean you lied to me. I understand that now."

"I'm glad. I never wanted to hurt you."

She regained control of herself and squared her shoulders. "I know you didn't do it to hurt me. Just please don't keep things from me in the future."

Charlie frowned. "I don't want to keep anything from you, so I need to let you know—"

"Melody! Melody!"

A young boy who lived in the tent community came running and waving his arms. "Come quick. Your pa is sick. He fell down on the ground."

15

Melody and Charlie ran all the way back to the Doyle tent. By now Da was sitting in his chair again and waving people away.

"He was out cold on the ground," one of the women told Melody.

"I'm fine. Just a wee bit light-headed."

"Thank you for sending for me." Melody knelt beside him. "What happened, Da?"

"Just as I said. I got a wee bit light-headed, and next thing I know folks are fussin' over me." He smiled. "But I'm fine now. Everyone can go home." The few remaining people gave Melody a nod and started back for their tents.

Melody studied her father, looking for any sign of injury. "Have you had anything to drink? Some water, perhaps? The doctor said you should keep drinking plenty of water."

"The neighbors plied me with offers of all sorts of drink." He chuckled. "I've had me fill of water."

"Then maybe we should get you inside, and I'll fix supper. Charlie, would you help Da?"

"Of course." Charlie reached down to help the older man to his feet.

"Thank ya, Charlie."

Melody brought the chair inside with her. There were only two inside, and they'd need three if Charlie stayed for supper.

She checked the stove and added wood to make sure it heated up quickly. Next, she went to the tiny icebox they kept and pulled out leftover baked chicken. "Charlie, would you care to stay for supper?"

"I'd like that very much."

"If the two of ya wouldn't be mindin', I'd like to go to me bed and rest. I'm not really hungry."

Melody swallowed the lump in her throat. Normally, Da would never have considered lying down while there was company. She wondered how bad his pain level was.

"Go ahead and help him to bed, Charlie. Da, where's the medicine the doctor gave you? I think you should have a dose of it."

"Could be," he replied. Another sure sign that he wasn't at all himself. "I keep it in the wooden box at the foot of my cot."

Melody let Charlie help him to bed first, then she opened the box and found the large bottle of liquid. It didn't look as though much of it had been used. She got a spoon and went to her father's side as Charlie returned to their eating area.

"How much are you supposed to have?"

"Doc said two tablespoons or so. More if I need it."

Melody nodded and measured out the medication. She helped him to take the first spoonful and then poured another. Da didn't protest but took the medicine quickly.

"I'll just be restin' now. Maybe even sleep for the night. Don't fret about feedin' me. Ya can eat with Charlie." He closed his eyes.

Melody fought back tears. How could she have not seen

how bad off he really was? His face was so thin it was nearly skeletal. A thick growth of whiskers helped to fill it out a little, but that was only another sign that Da was ill. He had always been faithful to shave every day.

She returned the medicine to the box and left the spoon in case he needed more in the night. Seeing Charlie sitting there, just waiting for her to return, Melody nearly broke down again. Instead, she went to work fixing food for their meal. At least it helped her to focus on something other than Da.

When the food was ready, Charlie offered grace. Melody was grateful for his silence and the kindness he'd shown her father. She wished so much that things might have been different. After they'd eaten, Melody gathered the dishes and checked on her father.

Da slept soundly. His breath was even, and he bore no signs of discomfort. She whispered a prayer for him and pulled up his cover. The evening was already much cooler.

"I could help with the dishes," Charlie offered.

She shook her head. "I think it'd be best for you to go and for me to get ready for bed. Da might need something in the night, and I'll need to be well rested."

Charlie hesitated. "I still need to talk to you about something."

"That's fine. I'll see you at church or maybe even tomorrow. We can talk then."

But she hadn't seen Charlie on Saturday or Sunday. Da had been feeling much worse and had agreed to take the medicine very nearly around the clock. This had left Melody no choice but to miss church.

Now, as Melody stood with Mrs. Cooper at the edge of the garden on Monday morning, she knew she would have to resign her job. It wasn't easy to let Mrs. Cooper down.

"As you know," Melody began, "we weren't in church last night."

"I did notice your absence. I hope everything is all right." The older woman looked out over the garden.

"The fact is, things aren't good. I hate to do this, but I'm going to have to stop working for a time. I'd like to come back to it, but for now I'm needed at home. You see, my father is dying."

"Oh no." Mrs. Cooper turned to her and took hold of Melody's arm. "Are you certain?"

"I'm afraid so. I had a talk with Da, as well as Dr. Latham. They have been dealing with Da's kidneys not working right for a long time. Dr. Latham has tried to find solutions, but there seems to be nothing we can do."

Mrs. Cooper gave her a hug. "I know how attentive you are. It's surprising you didn't notice it sooner."

"I know. It seems a lot of folks could see the problem before I could. I guess I was just too close to the situation and focused on other things. Da has always seemed like a pillar of strength, and I suppose I refused to allow myself to see his failings."

"Poor girl. Of course you can take as much time as you need. The job will be here for you."

"Thank you. I'm sorry if this puts you in a bind. I would certainly understand if you needed to hire someone else to help you."

"Nonsense. We'll get by. I can pay the neighbor boys a nickel to come pull weeds and water. There won't be any crops to harvest for a good while yet, so no need to worry about that. The rest of the work . . . well, it will get done when it gets done." She patted Melody's hand. "You go on now. Get back home to your father."

"Thank you."

She headed home still feeling bad for leaving Mrs. Cooper without notice. But in the back of her thoughts, Melody knew it wouldn't be a long absence. Da was so much worse that now he wanted only to lie in bed. He'd even taken to using the chamber pot.

She glanced heavenward, noting white fluffy clouds overhead. *How long, Lord? How long will I still have him with me?*

"Melody Doyle."

She turned at the sound of her name. It was Jefferson Lane. He walked up to her like a man with a purpose.

"I'm so happy to have run into you."

"Good morning, Jefferson. I'm afraid I haven't much time to waste. My da is ill."

He sobered and nodded. "I know. He's dying."

She was surprised by this. "How did you hear about it?"

"Your father was at the bank not long ago. He told Mr. Decker, and I couldn't help but overhear. I'm sure sorry to hear about it. I know that can't be easy on you, even if you are rich now."

"What are you talking about?"

Jefferson smiled. "The money coming from Ireland. It, along with the money your father already saved, will see you through for life. If you're careful. You certainly would need to be wise about investments, and I could help you with that."

"Why would I ask you to help me with that?" She hadn't meant to ask the question aloud, but since she had, she fixed him with a hard look.

"Well, it's just that you are looking for a husband, and I

have shown my interest to be considered. As your husband, I would have control over such matters. However, being the kind of man I am, I would seek your opinion and discuss the matter thoroughly with you. I believe that's what women are asking for now."

"I suppose women would like for men to be considerate of their interests and thoughts on matters of importance," Melody countered. "But the fact is, I'm no longer looking for a husband. I need to take care of my father, so I'm no longer accepting suitors."

"That's foolish, Miss Doyle. Your father will die soon, and you'll be without protection."

"Hardly that. I have the good Lord, first and foremost, and dear friends who will watch over me otherwise. Also, I'm quite capable. I'm a very good shot, and if need be, I'm not afraid to prove it."

Jefferson chuckled. "Now, Miss Doyle, you can hardly walk around with a gun strapped on like a gunfighter. And while friends are good to have, they can't be there in the middle of the night should someone attempt to rob your home. Not only that, but you live in a tent provided by the railroad. When your father passes, you will have to move."

"I have considered that, Mr. Lane. I have friends who have invited me to move in with them if need be. However, since, as you say, I am rich, I might just buy myself a house to live in."

"Yes, but the sorrows of losing your father will be great, and wouldn't it be better to have another with you who can share the load? I'm a good man, Miss Doyle. I would see your every need met."

"Well, perhaps in time I might feel differently, but for now my answer is the same. I am no longer in search of a husband."

"Perhaps you might hire me to help with the things that your father can no longer do. I could even help to care for him. I believe once you spend more time with me, you'll see how well suited we are."

"Hire you? What about your job at the bank?"

Jefferson shifted his weight and looked heavenward. "Well, that's an entirely different matter. You see, Mr. Decker fired me." He looked back at her, his expression downcast. "I still don't even understand why, but the truth doesn't seem to matter to him. I suppose when you own the bank you can do as you please."

"But Charlie doesn't own the bank. His father does. In fact, as I understand it, there is an entire board that has a share of the ownership. Charlie's father just happens to be the majority owner."

"Yes, well, it doesn't matter. I couldn't work for someone as heartless and mean-spirited as Charles Decker."

Melody almost laughed out loud. Charlie? Mean? Heartless?

"I have no idea of what transpired to cause Charlie to fire you, Mr. Lane, but I'm sure there was a very good reason. Now, if you'll excuse me, I need to make my way home. I've already been gone longer than I intended."

She swept past him and continued down the street. Melody was almost certain he would come after her or at least call out, but he did neither. She shook her head at the thought of Charlie being ill-tempered with Jefferson. It was ridiculous. She imagined even in firing Jefferson, Charlie had been nothing but kind and gentle.

Of course, just a short time ago, she had thought ill of Charlie too. How sorry she was to have held that attitude.

Charlie arrived at the breakfast table wondering if he'd see Melody as usual. Instead, Mrs. Cooper made an announcement just before her husband offered grace.

"Miss Doyle will be absent from us for a while. Her father has taken ill, and the doctors believe it to be such that he will die in a very short time. I beg your indulgence and ask that you arrange for your laundry elsewhere. I won't have nearly enough time to manage it all without Melody here to help." She turned to her husband. "You may now offer the blessing."

Charlie bowed his head for the morning prayer. He had been praying constantly for Melody and her father. He still hadn't had a chance to tell Melody that he'd fallen in love with her.

Given that she wanted no more secrets between them, Charlie wanted to make this clearly understood. He didn't want her accusing him of false pretenses. Charlie had only ever asked her father to let things unfold this way because he believed all marriages were better when the couple started with friendship. He'd seen it proven with family members. His eldest brother, Jacob, had known his wife for many years before they wed. They were good friends who had met through gatherings that included both families. She'd even lived just two houses down on the same street. Whereas Charlie's other brother, Warren, had married a woman he hardly knew at all. The marriage had been all but arranged by the fathers of the couple. They never seemed truly happy and fought all the time. At least anytime Charlie was in their presence there appeared to be some sort of fight ensuing.

There were, of course, close friends whom Charlie had watched court and marry. The ones who had a history of being friends first always seemed to have a much better foundation than the ones who were arranged or claimed love at first sight. He had wanted very much to be friends with Melody Doyle before anyone spoke of love and marriage. However, Charlie could now say without any doubt at all that he did love her.

That made him even more determined that she should know the truth of his arrangement with her father. No more secrets. He would tell her everything, perhaps even the fact that he'd lost his heart to her.

"Charlie, how did it go teaching Sunday school yesterday?" Mrs. Cooper asked.

He looked up and smiled. "Fairly well. The boys were quite energetic, so I had them marching in place for a time."

"Marching?" She looked quite puzzled.

"The Bible story I chose to teach on was Joshua and the Battle of Jericho. The Israelites had to march around the walls of the city, as you might recall. So I had the boys stand and march in place. That seemed to amuse them but also kept them busy. When the walls came tumbling down, so did they."

The men who were paying attention chuckled at this, causing the others to look up from their food. It was Otis who spoke, however, and it had nothing to do with what Charlie had just said.

"They are breaking ground today for the railroad line from Denver to Cheyenne. Just imagine how convenient that will be in the future," he announced. "We shall soon move about as easily as they do back east. Once the east and west lines close the gap on the transcontinental railroad, we will be able to travel without resistance from one end of the country to the other and all points in between."

"These truly are remarkable times," Mrs. Cooper agreed.

Incredible times, to be sure, but not enough so that the

doctors had a means to save Clancy Doyle. Nevertheless, Charlie said nothing and refocused on his breakfast.

Today wasn't going to be at all easy for him. The bank was his sole responsibility since he had fired Jefferson. And, quite frankly, the bank was of absolutely no interest to him, given Melody's situation. Sometimes it was very hard to meet his obligations when the heart beckoned him elsewhere.

16

I'm glad you felt you could stop by," Marybeth said as Melody headed for the front door. "I'm just as sorry as I can be about your father. Please let us know if there's anything we can do to help."

"I will, but I doubt there will be anything. Da is spending more and more time in bed. He just doesn't have the strength to do otherwise. While he sleeps, I cook or bake and clean. Sometimes I just sit by his side and watch him breathe. I know he wouldn't want me to do that, but I can't help it. When things were good, Da would almost always go out on Friday nights, to a fight or just to see the fellas, and he always invited me to come." She paused and tried her best to contain her emotions. "Now I wish I'd gone more often."

"Bye-bye," Carrie interrupted, wrapping her arms around Melody's legs. "I wuv you, Melwedy."

"I love you too, Miss Carrie." Melody hugged her back.

"Are you sure you won't stay and have supper with Carrie and me? Edward's gone off on his shift, so it'll just be the two of us. I'll be glad when he switches to daytime hours. It's coming soon, but not soon enough to please me." She paused to look at the clock on the mantel. "Look, it's already five forty. You don't want to have to be cooking something now."

"I'll be fine. I made some soup, and I want to try and get Da to eat something."

Marybeth pulled Carrie away. "You go play for a little bit in your room, and then we'll eat." Carrie skipped off across the room without another word. Marybeth touched Melody's arm. "Just know that no matter what happens, you have a home with us anytime you need it."

"The Taylors stopped by and told me the same thing. I'm relieved not to have to worry about that much. Charlie has been so good to help too. He's really been the best of friends to me and Da. Da likes him a lot, and they play checkers when Da is up to it."

"Charlie seems like a very good man."

Melody nodded. "I think so. I like him very much."

"Perhaps if things were different . . ." Marybeth left the rest unsaid, but Melody completely understood.

"Yes."

She headed for home, thinking about asking Dr. Scott to come by and see Da. She knew her father's time was passing far too quickly. It might comfort him to speak with the pastor. Knowing Da, however, he'd probably already discussed everything with the man in order to plan out the funeral arrangements. That would be like her father.

Remembering that she still needed to pick up a few things from the store, Melody hurried to cross House Street and make her way up Sixteenth to Armstrongs' Mercantile. They closed at six, so she needed to hurry. She'd nearly reached her destination when she saw Jefferson Lane with a large suitcase in hand.

"Jefferson, are you heading somewhere?" she asked as she came up behind him.

He turned, looking surprised. "Uh . . . well . . . uh, yes. I'm leaving for good. This town just doesn't agree with me."

"I'm sorry to hear that." She almost chuckled but refrained. "I thought you wanted to marry me."

He laughed. "I was just teasing you. I'm not looking for a wife right now, but when I do, she'll give me far more advantages than you could."

Melody refused to be wounded by his words. "I hope you find someone worthy of you, Jefferson." Perhaps that was unkind to say.

"I will," Jefferson replied, not seeming to realize he'd been insulted. "I've no doubt. Now, if you'll excuse me, I need to make some arrangements before I head out."

"Where are you headed?"

He smiled and shook his head. "It doesn't need to trouble you." With that, he tipped his hat and left her standing there, rather surprised by his abrupt, dismissive words. Da was so right about him. He was full of secrets and deception.

Melody went on her way. She reached Armstrongs' and found Cynthia Armstrong just preparing to lock the door. "I only need a few things," Melody told the older woman.

"Sure, come on in. The afternoon has been slow, so I figured I'd go ahead and close, but you're always welcome. What can I get you?"

Melody told her what she needed, and Cynthia gathered the few things together. "I heard your father has taken a bad turn."

"Yes. He isn't . . . well, he's not at all well."

"I'm sorry to hear that. I know we've enjoyed his company

the times he's come in for one thing or another. I hope he feels better soon."

Melody didn't feel like explaining and simply thanked Cynthia for her thoughts. She paid for her things, then gathered them and headed back to the tent. She'd already been gone for over an hour, and while she knew Da had probably slept through the absence, Melody was more than a little anxious to get back to him. Soon enough he'd be gone, and she wanted to spend as much time with him as she could.

Charlie had ended the workweek with nothing in mind but going to see Clancy and Melody Doyle. He hurried to the boardinghouse and changed his clothes, then made his way to where he knew he could buy some hothouse flowers. With a bouquet and the peppermints he'd purchased the day before in hand, he made his way to the tent community, hoping he could finally explain to Melody his interest in her and the arrangement he'd had with her father.

When he reached the Doyle tent, Charlie called out through the opening. "Is anybody home?" He hid the flowers behind his back.

Melody appeared almost immediately. "Hello, Charlie."

He smiled. "Evening. I hope you don't mind my stopping by. I thought I'd play checkers with your father if he is up to it."

"He's still asleep. Been sleeping all afternoon, in fact. I thought I'd wake him and see if I couldn't get him to eat a little soup. You're welcome to stay and have some as well. I didn't make a lot, but I doubt Da will eat that much."

"Maybe I could go over to one of the restaurants and bring something here for us. You need to eat more than soup. You're losing almost as much weight as your father."

She glanced down at herself. "I guess I've just been too busy thinking about Da."

"That's understandable." He looked over his shoulder, and seeing no one else was around, Charlie turned back to Melody. "Look, before we do anything else, I need to talk to you. I have something to say, and I don't want to put it off anymore lest you think later that I lied to you."

She frowned. "All right."

He presented her with the flowers. "These are for you."

Melody gasped and took the bouquet from Charlie. "They're beautiful, but I don't understand."

"That's part of what I've come to say. I have feelings for you, Melody. Very deep feelings."

Her brows knit together as her expression changed to confusion. "But you didn't ask Da to court me."

"Oh, but I did. Well, I should back up. Your father came to me and . . . Oh, I'm making a mess of this. When he came to the bank, we discussed the entire matter. However, I didn't want him to say anything to you. I didn't want to do as the others were doing with their obvious desires and intentions of a quick wedding."

"Again, I don't understand."

He smiled and shrugged. "All of my life, it seems, I've watched people court. My brothers were much older than me, and I watched how they did things and learned from it. I believe, with great conviction, that it's better to become friends first. In all the relationships I've watched, the ones who were friends first seemed to be the closest and sweetest couples. I wanted us to be friends first, Melody."

"I see." She smelled the flowers and seemed to consider his words.

"I asked your father to say nothing and to let us get to

know each other first, and he agreed. However, as upset as you got regarding him telling me about his medical situation before telling you, I wanted to let you know about our agreement. As I said, I care for you, and I don't want anything to cause problems between us. I especially don't want you thinking I lied to you."

"Thank you. I appreciate that you care about my feelings." She smiled. "I appreciate our friendship as well. I agree that friendship is an important foundation for romance. My da and mother were good friends before taking up romantic interests."

"Mine were as well. They still are, and I believe it has made all the difference in seeing them through bad times, especially given my father's serious nature."

She stepped back. "You might as well come on inside. I'll wake Da and see if he's of a mind to eat a little, and then maybe you two can talk or play checkers."

"I brought him some peppermints. He mentioned sometimes being nauseous, and I know peppermint can soothe the stomach."

"That is very kind of you, Charlie. I'm sure he'll be happy to have it."

She led the way inside and placed the flowers on the table. "I'll see to these in a moment." She turned up the lantern and made her way to where her father slept.

"Da? It's time for supper."

He stirred and opened his eyes. Seeing her, his eyes lit up. Clancy's love for Melody was evident in his expression.

"Da, Charlie's come to see you. He's brought you peppermint to calm your stomach."

"Charlie. Good to see you," Clancy managed to say.

"Good to see you. I thought if you were up to it, we might play a game of checkers."

"We might at that."

But Charlie could see the man had very little energy. His color was even more gray than it had been the day before.

"I have some soup for supper, Da. Won't you let me help you to eat a little?" Melody asked.

Her father closed his eyes. "In a moment. I think I'd just like to rest a bit more."

She looked at Charlie and nodded. "That's all right, Da. You rest. Charlie and I will have a good long talk." It appeared the man had already fallen back asleep.

Charlie followed Melody back to the table, where she was already taking up a large glass jar. She dipped out water from a bucket and poured it into the jar. Charlie watched as she arranged the flowers. He felt a great desire to take her away from all of this. She lived like a pauper, even though there was now plenty of money for her to draw on. This was the only life she had ever known—one of sacrifice and few extras. She didn't even have a decent vase in which to place her flowers.

He wanted to change all of that for her. He wanted to give her a better life. A real home and furnishings. He wanted to dress her in beautiful things that would complement her delicate features. That thought made him smile. She couldn't possibly be more beautiful than she was right now in her simple white blouse and navy skirt. She could have all the finery in the world, and it would pale compared to her natural beauty.

"You have such an odd look on your face, Charlie. Are you all right?"

He forced himself to focus on her words. "I'm just fine.

Would you like me to go get us some dinner? I could take a couple of plates and have one of the restaurants fill them."

She shook her head. "Soup is fine by me, Charlie. I don't have much of an appetite. Seeing Da waste away, knowing he won't be with me much longer . . . well, food doesn't seem so important."

"But you can't allow yourself to get sick. If you don't take care of yourself, you'll be no use to your father."

"I know you're right." She gave a sigh. "I just don't know how to put it all aside and carry on as if nothing's wrong. He's always been there for me." Tears came to her eyes. "Oh, Charlie, I don't know how to be me without him."

"You were all prepared to live in Cheyenne alone."

She nodded. "I know. I was thinking about that. However, I always knew that Da would be just down the line. I knew he'd visit me, or I could go to him. I just figured he'd always be around. Now when I think of living in Cheyenne alone . . . it terrifies me."

He came closer and took Melody into his arms. "I know it's not the same as having your father nearby, but you have good friends. Be assured of that, Melody." He pulled her closer. "And you have me. I love you." He lowered his lips to hers and kissed her for a very long moment. She wrapped her arms around his neck and held on to him as though she might fall away if she let go. Charlie trailed kisses on her cheek and whispered against her ear, "You'll never be alone."

Jefferson paced the hotel room floor. He had to wait until morning—until the stage was ready to pull out of Cheyenne for Denver. He should have timed things better, but he had been in a hurry. Since it was Friday, he knew Decker would be away from the bank for two days. That would give Jefferson time to get away, taking with him a little more than a thousand dollars. He'd hoped to get more, but the larger safe was inaccessible. Still, one thousand dollars was a lot of money, and it would see him well on his way to a better future.

He forced himself to sit and stretched his arms over his head. Decker had fired him but neglected to take his keys. Jefferson had thought immediately of returning to give them back, but then the idea of robbing the bank had been too much of a temptation. The small safe was the one Jefferson used daily while employed. He'd known there would be no chance of getting to the large safe in Decker's office. So once Decker had left for the day, Jefferson made his way to the bank and simply took what he could.

He smiled to himself at the thought of Decker showing up Monday morning to find he'd been robbed. Jefferson wondered if he'd immediately think his former employee was the culprit, especially since the front door would be locked and secured. Perhaps Charlie would forget about Jefferson having a set of keys. Maybe he'd presume someone had picked the lock to gain entry. That's what Jefferson hoped. He'd been very careful to leave everything seemingly untouched. That way when the town deputies made their rounds, they would see nothing amiss, even if they checked the lock. There would be nothing and no one to suggest a problem until Monday.

By Monday, Jefferson would be long gone. Gone with a thousand dollars. And given the plans he had for hiding away, no one would ever find him. He would be just fine for as long as it took.

The pure pleasure of imagining Charles Decker's face

was enough to keep Jefferson entertained throughout the evening. It would only be better if he could have remained in town to see the man's reaction in person. Jefferson had thought of hiding the money and then returning to Cheyenne, but he was sick of the town and the people. No, the sooner he was out of here, the better. He would eventually head back east to bigger opportunities, and one day he'd be as rich—maybe richer—than his father. Then he wouldn't need anyone. He'd be the one in charge. He'd be the one ordering people around.

Melody was awake long into the night. The feel of Charlie's arms around her, his lips on hers, was still firmly etched in her memory. His whispered words of love echoed in her ears. She could still see the intense look of love in his eyes as he pulled away. She wrapped her arms around her body and sighed.

He was there all along. Being her friend—showing her kindness and understanding. Listening to her talk of her outings with other men, and all the while wanting to court her. He was an amazing man, and she'd nearly pushed him out of her life altogether. A part of her had wanted to wake Da up and ask for his opinion of Charlie, while another part of her already knew that he approved. Da would never have allowed Charlie so much inclusion in their lives otherwise. She thought of all that was yet to come. Charlie. Her father. Her life in Cheyenne. Already it seemed that things were happening faster than she could keep up with. Before summer was out, she might very well become an orphan and a wife.

17

E veryone settle down," Charlie said, getting the dozen
or so boys ready for Sunday school. "Remember when
we talked about the Battle of Jericho? What did God
call Joshua and the Israelites to do?"

The boys finished taking their places, and one boy raised
his hand.

Charlie smiled. "Yes, Bobby?"

"They marched around the walls, and the walls fell down."

"Exactly right. God brought the walls down, and His
people were able to lay claim to the city. This wasn't the
way that the Israelites thought God would give them Jericho.
Marching around the walls didn't seem at all a likely way
for the obstacle to be removed. Yet sometimes that's how
it goes with God. He does things in His own way, and while
it doesn't always make sense to us, we need to do what God
calls us to do."

The boys were listening much better than they had the
week before, and Charlie was pleased to see they seemed
genuinely interested.

"Have you ever been told to do something a certain way and it didn't make sense to you, so you didn't do it that way?"

Most of the boys nodded. Charlie smiled. "And what happened?"

One of the boys blurted out, "I got a whuppin'."

The other boys laughed, and Charlie nodded. "Remember to raise your hand if you want to speak. Anybody else?"

One of the older boys named Mark raised his hand, and Charlie called on him. Mark came to stand beside the desk. "Once, when we lived in Missouri, my ma sent me out to pick berries. She always told me to beat around the bushes to make sure there weren't any rattlers or other snakes. I thought it was silly and decided not to do it. Then I got bit by a rattler and almost died."

The other boys looked at Mark in surprise. Perhaps a little admiration too. Not many of them could boast of living through a rattlesnake bite.

"That's a very good example, Mark. Thank you for sharing it." Mark sat back down, and Charlie continued. "Sometimes the instructions or rules we're given to follow make no sense to us. God calls us to trust Him no matter what. It doesn't mean we'll have an easy time of it, but obedience to God is always best. Yielding to Him will always bless us in the long run, so do what God tells you to do, even if it doesn't seem right by the world's way of doing things."

"And we won't get bitten by a snake," another of the boys replied.

Charlie didn't reprimand him. Instead, he smiled. "Obedience often keeps us from bad situations. Today we're going to talk about a man who didn't want to obey God's calling, and he met up with some very bad times. His name is Jonah."

Charlie was still feeling exhilarated on Monday morning. He had declared his love to Melody, although she'd said very little in return. He knew her feelings were overwhelmed—a mixture of grief and surprise. He hoped he'd made things better for her . . . more reassuring rather than confusing.

She hadn't been at church, so he'd had no chance to speak to her, and he felt that rather than go and impose himself on her at such a difficult time, he'd give her a day or so to think about all that had happened. It would also give him time to consider his next move.

He unlocked the bank door and let himself in. It was bittersweet to find the place empty. Jefferson used to beat him in and got things set up and ready to go for the first customers of the day. Now that fell to Charlie to do. Only his heart was not in it. Especially after his successful time teaching.

Last night he had written his father a long letter explaining his desire to teach. For the first time, he wrote in detail what teaching meant to him and why he no longer wanted to work in the bank. He promised his father he would stay with it until another man could be hired to take over the savings and loan, but he also asked that his father make it soon. Charlie intended to take money left to him by his grandfather and invest in building a small school. He wanted it ready for the fall so he could start advertising for students right away.

He knew it would take a lot of work to get teaching materials and books ordered for September, as well as desks and chairs. After writing his father the letter, he had started making a list of what he needed to purchase. First atop the list was a house and property where a school could be built. He saw no need for anything fancy regarding the school. A simple building, say, twenty by twenty, would be plenty big enough. He figured he could take on twenty boys at most. In his mind, he saw it set up with simple wooden tables and chairs, a large chalkboard, and maybe a big table where they could conduct science experiments. The very idea excited him so much that he could hardly focus on the day ahead when there was so much to plan.

For instance, where in town should the land for the house and school be? Charlie felt certain he needed to have Melody's thoughts on the matter. He was even more confident after their time together that she was the one for him. They might not marry for a while. He knew her focus right now would be her father, and there was no way of knowing how much longer he had on earth. Then there would be her time of mourning. She might be someone who didn't feel comfortable marrying before a substantial amount of time passed after her father's death. Still, he thought it only right that she know his intentions toward her and that he get her opinions on a place to live.

There was already a property Charlie had in mind. A house was being built next to an empty lot where Charlie could easily put in a school. He liked the idea of keeping the school and house close together. That way he would never be all that far from home. The property was situated on the northeast side of town in an area that was just starting to see settlement.

He smiled at the thought of making his dreams a reality. As he went about his bank duties, he couldn't help but make mental lists of all he would need to do for the school. Maybe later in the day he could close the bank for a time and go visit the land agent.

Humming to himself, Charlie went to the small safe and unlocked it in order to put money in the teller's cage. The empty interior stopped his humming immediately. He went to the cash drawer in the teller's cage. Had he forgotten to put the money away on Friday?

He turned the key in the lock and gained access to the drawer but found that it, too, was empty. He hurried to his office. The door was still secure. He let himself in and looked around. Nothing appeared disturbed, but neither had the front office. He went to the larger safe and opened it. The money was there, much to his relief.

He pulled out the ledger and the notes he'd left himself last Friday. He counted the money in the safe and noted that it was all there. The only money missing was a little over one thousand dollars from the smaller safe.

There was only one other person who had access to the bank and to the small safe and cash drawer: Jefferson. Charlie hit his forehead with the palm of his hand. He'd forgotten to demand Jefferson leave his keys when Charlie fired him. He didn't want to jump to conclusions, but that seemed the only logical answer. Everything had been locked up tight. There was no sign of damage, and nothing but the money Jefferson could access was missing.

With a heavy sigh, Charlie grabbed his hat and headed out of the bank after relocking everything. He thought of going to see Jefferson first but instead made his way to the police station. It was probably best to let them confront Jefferson. Charlie might very well punch the man in the nose if left to his own doings.

After seeing the police and giving them his thoughts on all that had happened, as well as Jefferson Lane's address, Charlie went to the telegraph office and sent his father a telegram. The letter he'd written the night before would have to wait. Now was hardly the time to walk away from his responsibilities. Charlie might hate banking, but he didn't want to let his father down, especially given that he'd been the one who neglected to get the keys back from Jefferson.

He returned to the bank and shortly after found Judge Kuykendall at his door. The man was a part of the local vigilante committee, and he assured Charlie that a posse had been formed to go after Jefferson Lane.

"He's gone?" Charlie asked, not completely surprised by this news.

"Yes. The marshal went to question him and learned from his landlord that he'd departed on Friday. The marshal then checked with the railroad ticket master and with the stage company. It seems Jefferson was on the Saturday morning stage for Denver. Hopefully the posse will bring him back with the money still on him."

"I suppose there's a possibility that Jefferson didn't take the money, but I don't know how anyone else would have gotten in here and taken it without some sign of forced entry. Jefferson had keys."

Judge Kuykendall nodded. "It seems to point to him, but he will have a chance to defend himself. We don't want to jump to hasty conclusions, even when all the evidence points to him."

Charlie nodded. He felt the same way. If he was wrong, and Jefferson hadn't taken the money, Charlie didn't want the man to be unjustly punished. Still, there was the matter that Jefferson had already taken about six hundred dollars by adjusting the books. He felt compelled to tell the judge.

"There's something else about Mr. Lane that I didn't mention to the police."

By late morning, almost everyone in town had heard that the Cheyenne Savings and Loan had been robbed. Charlie wasn't surprised when people started coming in to demand their money, fearful that the robbery would keep them from being able to withdraw their savings.

"Rest assured, folks, the bulk of the money wasn't taken. You can withdraw your funds if you truly feel the need, but I can assure you that your money is safe, even if I must put my own money in to see you paid out. I would like to encourage you, however, to leave the money here with the bank." He knew a great number of people heard nothing he said. They were afraid, and the thought of losing their money was uppermost in their minds.

"Banking procedures will continue as before. You can make your loan payments and make deposits to your savings accounts. It's banking as usual," Charlie assured.

Little by little the people headed home, some taking their money and others feeling confident enough of Charlie's words that they left their money in the bank. When noon rolled around, Charlie was once again alone. He couldn't help but fear this might well be the end of things for the little bank.

Melody arrived around one o'clock to brighten his day. She was dressed in a lightweight gown of blue and white. He'd never seen her wear it before and thought how pretty she was.

"Hello, Charlie." Her voice was just a whisper. "I hope you don't mind my interruption." She held a basket in front of her and shifted it to her left arm. "I heard about the trouble."

"It's good to see a friendly face." His smile almost immediately faded, however. "Unless, of course, you're as worried as everyone else and have come to withdraw your money. I assure you your money is safe."

"I wasn't worried about the money," Melody said, holding up a basket. "I guessed you probably wouldn't be able to get away for lunch. I know it's a little late, but I have fried chicken and fresh soda bread."

He hadn't gone to lunch for fear that if he closed the bank, even for half an hour, people might think the worst and start a riot. "Bless you. I'm starving. Bless you, too, for not being afraid that the bank doesn't have your money."

Melody shrugged. "We've never had much money and have always lived frugally. If the money is gone, I really don't know what I'm missing."

Charlie chuckled. "You are something special, you know that?" He wanted so much to take her in his arms, but he held back.

"I'm just me. Plain and simple." She nodded toward his office. "Would you like to eat in there?"

"Yes. Let me take that for you." He took the basket from her and led the way to his office. He was at odds as to how to broach the subject of all that had transpired between them but felt he should at least acknowledge what had happened.

He placed the basket on his desk and turned to face her. "I, uh, well, there's a lot I'd like to say, but given the circumstances, I don't want to rush you."

"Oh, Charlie." She smiled and pushed back her sunbonnet. "What else needs to be said?"

He chuckled. "Well, you never did say what you thought of the matter."

"I thought I did." Her brows raised as she stepped closer. "I specifically remember putting my arms around you like this." She stretched up and clasped her hands behind his neck. "Then I raised my face to you . . . like this."

Charlie did what came naturally. What he'd wanted to

do since she came into the room. He lowered his mouth to hers and kissed her.

Melody was the one to pull away this time. "Do you remember now?"

"I do. I guess you were plenty vocal on the matter."

She laughed. "Charlie, you are something else. Something so unexpected."

He wanted to kiss her again but held off. "You are as well." He crossed his arms to keep from taking her in them. "I never expected to find love in Cheyenne, but I've been thanking God all weekend that I did. That He sent you my way."

"I've been thanking Him as well, Charlie. For you. I wasn't at all sure how I could possibly get through this situation with Da, but knowing you're there for me helps a great deal."

"How's your father?" The intensity of the moment fell away as they focused on Clancy.

"About the same. He sleeps most of the time, but the doctor said that's to be expected. The medicine makes him sleepy."

Melody went to work pulling out a plate for Charlie. She had included some sugar cookies with the bread and chicken, and Charlie reached for one first thing.

"I'll start with dessert." He bit into the cookie with a wink.

"It would seem to meet with your approval. That is, if the look on your face is any indication." She put the food on his plate and handed it over. "I'm sure sorry Jefferson did this to you. Da told me he didn't think the man could be trusted. Jefferson had asked to court me, but Da refused him.

"Then Jefferson told me the other day that he wanted to spend time with me and help. What a laugh that is, considering what he did. I saw him on Friday night, and he had a large suitcase with him. Said he was leaving this town for good. I asked him about the fact that he supposedly wanted to marry me, and he said he had only been teasing. The man doesn't have any honor."

Charlie put the cookie aside and sat down to eat the fried chicken. "Of course, we don't know for sure that Jefferson Lane is responsible, but if not him, then I don't know who it could be. The place wasn't broken into. The person responsible appeared to have keys, and I'm afraid when I fired him, I failed to get those back."

"Don't be too hard on yourself, Charlie. It's not like you intentionally forgot. You had a lot on your mind."

"That's for sure. I've been going over the books with a fine-tooth comb and realized Jefferson had been stealing money from the bank. When I confronted him, of course he denied it. Even suggested my brother was responsible, but then I reminded him the losses continued after Jacob returned to Chicago. Jefferson never did admit responsibility."

Melody sat in the chair opposite Charlie's desk. "So now what?"

"Now people are terrified that their savings have been lost. I told them even if I had to use my own money, they wouldn't be out. The bulk of the bank's money was locked in the safe behind me. Jefferson didn't have the ability to open it, so the money is still there. Unfortunately, that didn't do much to assuage folks' fears."

"People are that way. When we arrived here last summer, there were rumors of Indians attacking folks in the area. Someone thought they'd seen a bunch of mounted warriors on a nearby ridge, and even though there was no evidence of anyone being there, people were unwilling to listen to reason and wouldn't calm down until the army posted men around the town. When the army got back from searching for the Indians, they announced that the attacking warriors that had been spotted were nothing more than a small herd of dairy cows." Melody smiled. "People had just let their imaginations go wild."

Charlie grinned. "Attacking dairy cows, eh?"

She nodded. "It's always something. Da taught me to refrain from getting too excited about things until I have all the facts. 'Be keepin' yar wits about ya, me girl.'" Melody did her best to imitate the older man.

Charlie laughed. "Sounds like him."

She sobered. "I'm going to miss him so much, Charlie. Dr. Latham came by and checked on him. He said Da will pass in the next few days. I don't want to leave him alone, so our neighbor is sitting with him now, even though he's just sleeping. I should get back."

Charlie hated to think of Clancy Doyle leaving them. He'd come to truly enjoy the older man's company, as well as his philosophies on life and spiritual insight.

"I won't let you go through this alone, Melody. I want you to know that."

She nodded. "I do. My friends are making known their desires to help me through, and I so appreciate their kindness. But there's an emptiness that Da's passing will leave that no one person can fill. A big emptiness that terrifies me."

"No person can fill that emptiness, but Jesus can. He'll be your comfort and assurance of better days to come. Your father wouldn't want to leave you with an empty spot in your heart. He'd tell you to let the Lord make things right."

Melody considered his words a moment. "I want to be strong like that, Charlie. I want to just give it to God and trust Him. I know He's good and able to ease my sorrow, but . . ."

"But what?"

She didn't answer for a long time and instead looked down at her hands. Charlie thought maybe she wouldn't answer.

"It's so much easier to speak the words than to walk the path." She raised her head and met his gaze. "I'm afraid, Charlie."

His heart nearly broke at the fear in her eyes.

"What if my faith isn't strong enough? What if I fail this test?"

"You won't. The devil wants you to think you will, but you won't. God has promised He'll never leave nor forsake you. You have Him at your side, and His strength will be enough. His grace will be sufficient, just as it was for Paul."

"When I was a little girl, I came to God out of fear. Fear of hellfire and eternal separation from Him. My mother told me that Jesus had died in my place to pay for my sins. That made me sad, but she said without that sacrifice I could never be right with our heavenly Father. I remember praying that Jesus would save me and that I would belong to Him. I've always found such comfort in that, and even in the pain of losing my mother, I found solace in knowing God was there for me.

"But Da was there for me too. I think I saw Da as God's representative on earth. Although I couldn't see God, I could see my earthly father and knew that I was safe and cared for. Now Da will be gone, and I don't know what will happen, Charlie. What if I walk away from God?"

"Do you really think that's possible? God has chosen you for His own. He knew that you would accept Him and choose Him in return. Do you suppose He'll let you just walk away now?"

"But people do. They leave the church and forget about God."

"Yes, but God doesn't forget about them. I've seen those people too. God doesn't just let them flounder out there alone. He's always speaking to them, wooing them to return home—to hear His voice and obey. They sometimes don't even know that it's God, but they know there's something familiar to it. They can't leave it or ignore it. You'll never forget God, Melody. You love Him too dearly. It wasn't your da who saved you. It was Jesus. And it was Jesus shining through your father that made him so loving and compelling to you. You might not see it right now, but you will in time. Trust God, Melody. He will never let you down. And He will never die."

18

Melody woke up to the sound of moaning. At first the gut-wrenching sounds seemed far off, beyond the tent, but then the sound came again. This time much louder. She jumped up off her cot, pulling on her robe as she made her way to the other side of the curtain.

She found her father writhing. "Da, let me give you some medicine," she said, grabbing the bottle.

Her father groaned and twisted, barely able to speak. "It's time I be . . . be goin' to . . . the hospital."

She was surprised by this. Da had said nothing about being taken to the hospital. He hated being fussed over. She gave him his medicine, then recorked the bottle before coming back to his side.

"Are you certain you want to go to the hospital, Da?"

"Aye. 'Tis what I want. I don't . . . don't wanna . . ." He stopped speaking and grabbed his midsection. The pain was so intense that Melody felt herself tense as her father cried out. She had no idea what she could do.

Da reached out to take her hand. "I don't wanna die here. Get me to the railroad hospital."

She nodded. "I'll get dressed and get help."

Without waiting for a response, she hurried to pull on her clothes and boots. Da continued to toss and turn. She prayed for God to ease his pain, knowing the only real healing would be in death. Once dressed, Melody was uncertain where to go. It wasn't that far to Marybeth and Edward's house. Of course, there were people in the tent community who would gladly help her. But it was Charlie she wanted. Charlie she needed.

"I'm going to get help, Da. Will you be all right?" she asked, knowing she was really asking if he'd still be alive when she returned.

He seemed to sense this and gave a weak smile. "For sure, I'll be here."

She nodded and ran from the tent, making her way to Mr. and Mrs. Cooper's boardinghouse. Faith Cooper was in the kitchen working on breakfast when Melody burst in through the back door, her sandy-brown hair flying out behind her.

"Da has . . . taken bad . . . needs to get to the hospital," she said, panting for breath. "I need Charlie."

"You wait here. I'll get Mr. Cooper to fetch him." The older woman left the kitchen and was only gone a few minutes. "Mr. Cooper can hitch the wagon and come along too. The men can carry your father to the wagon and drive him to the hospital."

"Thank you." Melody had regained her breath, but her heart continued to race. She knew the end was near, and it was hard to think of what would come next.

"Sit and have a cup of coffee." Mrs. Cooper poured a cup and put an ample amount of cream in as well. "This should help a bit."

Melody sipped the hot liquid, but it did nothing to ease

her fears. She tried to pray, but the words failed to come. Finally, all she could do was silently beg God to help.

Mrs. Cooper disappeared for a moment, and when she returned, she held a hairbrush and piece of ribbon. She didn't even ask Melody if she wanted help but went to her and began to brush her long hair.

"I'm sorry that you and your father must go through this," Mrs. Cooper said in a soothing manner as she continued to draw the brush through Melody's hair. "This is no doubt one of the hardest things you've had to face. Be assured, however, God is here with you. He will never leave you."

Melody found strange comfort in the rhythmic strokes of the brush, as well as Mrs. Cooper's encouraging words. After a moment, Mrs. Cooper began to braid Melody's hair into a single plait down the middle of her back, putting order to chaos. Oh, that she might be able to do the same thing with Melody's mind and spirit.

Charlie was there in no time at all. He went to her side as Mrs. Cooper finished tying off Melody's braid. "Mr. Cooper said he'd meet us outside just beyond the garden." He helped Melody to her feet.

"Thank you, Mrs. Cooper," Melody said, searching the older woman's face. "For everything."

Charlie led her outside, his arm around her shoulder. "What happened?" he asked.

"I woke up to Da crying out. The pain was so intense he could scarcely draw breath. I gave him medicine, but I doubt it's helping much. He asked to go to the hospital, so I know it's not good. He doesn't want to die in our home."

Charlie nodded. "I'm glad you came to get me."

"You were the only one I wanted." She met his gaze. "The only one who could help . . . me." She had known plenty who could help her with Da, but Charlie was her own selfish desire. Charlie would help her face the hours to come.

"I'm glad you felt that way."

Mr. Cooper arrived with the wagon and drove them back to the tent. Melody jumped from the wagon seat unaided and rushed into the tent, almost fearful Da hadn't kept his word to be there.

He was still alive, but the medicine was already starting to cloud his thinking. He opened his eyes, but Melody wasn't sure he even saw her.

"Da, Charlie and Mr. Cooper have come to take you to the hospital. We're going to move you now."

He nodded, then closed his eyes again. "Charlie's the one," he murmured.

Melody frowned as the two men entered the tent. The one for what? To take him to the hospital?

The men carefully wrapped the blanket around Da and lifted him. Charlie had Da's head and shoulders and Mr. Cooper his feet. Together they moved as one to place Melody's father in the back of the wagon.

"It won't be a very comfortable ride," Mr. Cooper said.

"Charlie, help me into the back, please. I'll cradle his head." Melody hiked her skirt as if to get up on the spoke of the wheel, but Charlie lifted her in his arms instead. She was surprised by his strength. He placed her in the wagon as if she weighed nothing at all. Then he climbed in after her.

By now a few of the tent-community neighbors had come outside to see what the commotion was. Men took off their hats and bowed their heads. The women nestled close to their men. Death was never easy to face.

Mr. Cooper headed the wagon in the direction of the railroad hospital while Melody held her father's upper torso in her arms like a baby. Charlie sat close to her side, support-ing her.

"We'll be there soon, Da."

They hit a rut, and Mr. Cooper called out an apology, but Melody simply held her father tighter as he groaned. She tried to forget about his pain and glanced heavenward to the clear blue of the open skies. It was a beautiful day to go home. She imagined her father meeting Jesus face to face. He would no doubt laugh and embrace his Savior with great joy. The kind of joy Melody had always known him for. She wondered if he'd see her mother right away. Perhaps his parents?

She brushed back graying hair from his face. The action caused him to open his eyes. He seemed to recognize her without any trouble and smiled.

"Me darlin' girl . . . love ya so." His voice was just a whis-per. "Don't . . . be . . . afraid."

She felt the tears form in her eyes. She wanted so much to be strong for Da, but she couldn't fight back her emotions.

"I love you, Da. I love you so much. I wish you didn't have to leave me."

His face tensed, and he closed his eyes again.

Melody felt his uneven breathing continue. The breaths came further and further apart. "We're almost to the hos-pital, Da."

He said nothing.

Mr. Cooper arrived at the wooden-framed hospital at the corner of Seventeenth and Hill. Melody allowed Charlie to help her disengage from her father. She scooted off the back of the wagon and waited while Charlie jumped down and took hold of her father. He carried him in his arms, not even waiting for Mr. Cooper's help.

Together they made their way inside. With it being so early, there was only one orderly and nurse in residence. The orderly quickly directed Charlie to a room. They worked together to situate Melody's father on the available bed.

"What seems to be the problem?" the orderly asked.

"My father is a patient of Dr. Latham's," Melody replied. She went to her father's side and took hold of his hand.

The nurse came in and began examining Da. "This is Mr. Doyle," she told the orderly. "He's suffering from severe nephritis. He's in the final stages." Melody wasn't sure how the nurse knew the details of her father's condition, but she was relieved. With her emotions on the edge of being out of control, Melody wasn't sure she could have answered many questions. The man gave a solemn nod. Everyone there now knew the situation.

The nurse finished her exam and looked to Melody. "When did you last give him his medicine?"

"Just before we came here. He was in horrible pain. The worst yet."

The nurse nodded. "There's nothing else to be done. I'm sure Dr. Latham already told you. We can give him more medication if the pain returns, but he seems at peace for the moment."

Melody nodded and squeezed her father's hand all the more. Charlie came to stand beside her and put his arm around her shoulder. He didn't say a word, but then, nothing needed to be said. Melody had anticipated this moment. She hadn't allowed herself to dwell on it for too long of a time, but she knew what was happening. Dr. Latham had explained the situation and what was to come. Her father would be in excruciating pain, and they would medicate him with the strongest remedies available. This, unfortunately, would cause him to sleep and probably never awaken again. All she could do was wait for Da to draw his last breath.

"We will see to it that no one disturbs you," the nurse said, motioning to the orderly. "I'll let Dr. Latham know when he gets in."

Melody said nothing. She kept her gaze fixed on Da and did her best to remember all the good times they'd had together.

"Clancy, if you can hear me," Charlie said, bending down to speak to the unconscious man, "I want you to know that I'll see to it that Melody is safe and cared for. You don't have to worry about leaving her alone. She will never be alone as long as I have breath in my body."

It touched Melody that Charlie would go out of his way to offer her father comfort in his final moments. She wanted nothing more than for Da to rest easy and know he was free to leave this world without worrying over her.

"You told me I was the one," Charlie continued. "Said you knew we were meant to be together. I see you were right, and I'll not let you nor Melody down."

Melody thought of her father's words back in the tent. *"Charlie's the one."* Now she understood what he meant. How precious it was to know she had her father's approval to spend the rest of her life with Charlie. Da had been determined she wouldn't remain in Cheyenne alone. Now she wouldn't.

The minutes turned into an hour, then two. Dr. Latham arrived at eight o'clock. He came into their room, listened to Da's heart and breathing, and turned to Melody. "It won't be long now."

"I know." She tried her best to sound brave. Thoughts of life without her father, however, were anything but comforting. She constantly reminded herself that she had people who cared about her, people who had offered her a refuge and their love. But it wasn't the same. It would never be the same.

She remembered their typical mornings when Da would ready himself for work on the railroad. They would share breakfast and laugh about something that had happened the day or week before. They would talk about things that they hoped to accomplish that day. And, always, they shared Scriptures and prayed. They would never do that again.

Melody stroked her father's cheek. His color had turned a pasty yellow-gray. There was more of death to him than life, and Melody felt the need to speak her final good-bye.

"I love you, Da. With all my heart. I will miss our long talks and your good advice. I'll miss your sense of humor and quick wit. Everything about you has been a blessing." Tears slipped down her cheeks.

"I wasn't ready for this . . . wasn't ready to say good-bye, but I know it must be done." She leaned down and kissed his forehead. "*Beidh tú i mo chroí i gcónaí*," she whispered. "You will always be in my heart."

Her tears dampened Da's cheeks, but Melody knew he wouldn't mind. There were two more shallow breaths and then nothing. She put her ear to his chest. The silence there left her no doubt that he was gone.

Melody stood and turned to Charlie, who already held his arms open to her. With no words spoken, she walked into his embrace and cried. He held her close . . . protected . . . loved. Melody had no idea what the future would hold for her now, but she knew it would be a little less lively and joyful without Da.

Charlie held Melody and let her weep. He thought of verses in the Bible that he might speak to offer comfort, but nothing seemed as right as just holding her tightly. After a few minutes, Dr. Latham rejoined them and pronounced Clancy Doyle dead.

"Your father has made all of his arrangements, so I'll contact the undertaker to come and get his body."

Melody pulled away from Charlie just enough to address the doctor. "Can they let Dr. Scott know too? He's our pastor."

"I'm sure they will. Your father was very explicit in his plans. He told me he didn't want you having to worry about a thing."

Melody watched as Dr. Latham pulled the sheet up over her father's head. Charlie felt her tense with the action and suggested they leave.

"Let me take you home."

She shook her head. "I need to tell Edward and Marybeth. They loved Da very much." She turned to Dr. Latham. "If anyone needs to reach me, I'll probably stay with them for a time."

"That's good. I wouldn't want you to face this alone, and I know your father wouldn't want that either."

"She won't be alone," Charlie said. He touched Melody's shoulder. "Come on. I'll take you there now."

Melody allowed him to lead her outside. Mr. Cooper had gone back to the boardinghouse shortly after dropping them off at the hospital. Melody started walking but seemed aimless in her direction.

"Why don't we go to the tent and get the things you'll need?" Charlie turned at the corner and headed her in the right direction.

They walked for several blocks before she spoke again. "I'm glad he's out of pain."

"Yes," Charlie agreed. "It's hard on you—us—to lose him, but none of us wanted him to suffer."

"I wish I'd known sooner that the end would come so fast."

"I don't suppose anyone can know for sure how much time they have left. The important thing is that you made that time special for him. You were there to care for him and to encourage him. No man could ask more of his daughter."

They reached the tent, and Melody just stood and looked at it for a moment. "The tent belongs to the railroad, but what's inside is ours. I suppose I shall have to find a place to store everything. Marybeth said I could stay with them, so I can probably move our belongings into their woodshop."

"I would imagine. Why don't you just pack the things that you'll be needing in the week to come? I can help if you need."

"If you just sit and keep me company," she replied, "I can pack it all myself. There's not that much to worry about." She frowned. "I don't have a black dress."

"That's easy enough to get. I'll help you figure it out after you settle in with Marybeth. I'm sure she'll have ideas as well. Probably better than anything I could come up with."

Melody hesitated as she glanced toward the tent. Charlie saw her bite her lower lip. This was her first time facing her home without her father. No doubt it was a daunting thought.

"Would you like me to go first?" he asked.

"Please."

The word was barely whispered, but it was enough for Charlie. He stepped around her and pushed back the flap. He tied the waxed canvas to the side to allow the light to filter in. Even at that, it wasn't very bright inside, so he lit the lantern as he'd seen Melody do on other occasions.

"There, now you can see better."

Melody walked inside and silently surveyed the room. "It won't be the same without him here."

"No. I don't suppose it will."

"I'm glad I don't have to stay here alone."

Charlie felt an overwhelming urge to take her in his arms. He went to where she stood and paused only a moment until he saw her reach for him. Pulling her close, Charlie's heart overflowed with love for her. He couldn't imagine his life without her.

19

T his room is yours for as long as you need it," Marybeth
Vogel told Melody. "If you need anything at all, you have
only to ask. Just consider our home yours."

Melody glanced around the room. "I'm so grateful to you
for taking me in. I couldn't bear the idea of staying at the
tent without Da. Just being there made me sadder than I can
even put into words."

"I know how that feels. Coming home after my father's
funeral was almost more than I could stand, and I had Carrie
to take my mind off things. Still, the house was so incredibly
empty without him, and I'm sure your tent felt the same way.
And even though Cheyenne is much safer than it was even a
few months ago, it still wouldn't be wise for you to stay there
alone. It's far too easy for someone to break in to a tent."

Melody nodded and plopped down on the edge of the
bed. She really wasn't worried about her own safety right
now—it was the dreaded void left by her father that seemed
more threatening.

"I don't know why, but I thought we'd have more time. I
mean, I knew he was failing quickly. He slept almost around

the clock and wasn't eating or drinking anything." She could remember times when Da had eaten huge meals and had greatly enjoyed himself. He always loved a good meal and appreciated her cooking. "I don't know how to go on without him in my life. I just didn't plan for this."

"I know. It's a hard thing to face."

"I wouldn't have wanted him to have to go on hurting. The look of pain on his face was more than I could bear. I guess I feel guilty and angry at myself for not having seen it sooner. For not having known how bad it was."

"He didn't want you to know," Marybeth said, coming to sit beside her. She took Melody's hand. "He wanted to spare you the pain and sorrow for as long as possible."

"I know, but I was so selfish. I took a job because I wanted to prove to him how I could remain behind in Cheyenne, even if we didn't find someone for me to marry. I wanted him to see that I could take care of myself."

"And you can. You're strong and capable. You can go back to work for Mrs. Cooper and live here with us, or, if you don't want to share the house, you could live in the little woodshop out back. We lived there quite snugly, and I know you could as well."

"Thank you. Thank you for everything. I feel so silly in some ways. I mean, I had planned to stay here without him. But I knew I could visit him if I needed to. I could talk to him about my troubles. This isn't the same at all." She paused and looked at Marybeth. "He has been my mainstay. My everything."

Melody shook her head. "I keep thinking that somehow I replaced God with Da. I never meant to, but I did. I would talk out a thing with Da until I felt I understood or had an answer. I shared all my joys and plans with Da. I asked Da for directions and advice. I'm ashamed to say it, but my prayers are hollow when compared."

"God gave you a good father for the very purposes you mentioned. Don't feel guilty for seeking his guidance. Maybe you did lose sight of God—I can't judge that. However, I know God is still there waiting for you." Marybeth smiled. "He'll be happy to guide and direct, cheer and encourage. God will show you where to go from here."

Melody knew she was right. "I guess I need to spend some time in prayer."

"Then I'll let you be alone to do so." Marybeth got up and headed for the bedroom door. "Just rest and pray. You'll find it helps more than anything else."

Knocking sounded from downstairs. Marybeth frowned. "I wonder who that might be." She left the room, and Melody could soon hear her talking to someone. In a few minutes, she returned.

"Sorry to bother you, but it's Dr. Scott. He wants to talk to you. He said it won't take long."

"It's not a problem. I wanted to speak to him as well."

Melody made her way downstairs and found the older man waiting for her in the front room. She could see the compassion in his expression.

"Dr. Scott."

"Melody, I'm so sorry to hear about your father."

"Thank you. Won't you sit down?" She hurried to take a chair as she felt her strength giving way. It was as if she'd run a long race and didn't have the ability to take even one more step.

"Would you care for some coffee or tea, Dr. Scott?" Marybeth asked.

"No. I have no need for either. I just came to let Melody

know that her father arranged everything. The service will be this Saturday on the thirtieth. Your father wanted a very simple service."

"That sounds like Da." Melody knew her father wouldn't want people dwelling on his death. He would prefer people focus on life, and not even his, but rather the life abundant they could have in Jesus.

"What time and where?" Melody asked.

"Ten o'clock. If it's not raining or stormy, we'll hold the services at the grave. Your father said he hated the thought of having to hold his funeral indoors."

Melody smiled. "He loved being outside. Even when the weather was questionable, he preferred to be in the open air."

"That's what he told me. The undertaker will wait for everyone to gather at the depot and then lead the processional down Fifteenth Street to the cemetery. If we have inclement weather, we'll simply meet at the school as we would for Sunday services. I'm getting the word out to all I know and asking them to do the same. I know the editor at the *Leader* plans to put in a small funeral notice."

"I have to admit, I'm glad to have the matter already arranged. Da was so good to have taken charge. I wish, however, that I would have known sooner just how bad things were."

"He waited until the last minute to tell most of us," Dr. Scott replied. His tone was full of sympathy. "He told me he didn't want people spending his final days mourning him before he was gone." The doctor smiled. "He said that he wanted to live his days to the fullest, right until he drew his last breath, and he couldn't do that if everyone had already buried him."

She understood exactly what her father had said. Understood and respected it, but that didn't stop the pain of loss from tearing at her heart.

Dr. Scott got to his feet. "There was just one more request your father had."

She looked up. "What was that?"

"He didn't want you wearing black. Said he'd prefer no one wore it, but he had no say over other folks. He did feel he had a say over his daughter, though, and he didn't want you to worry about the mourning rites or processes. He wanted you free to marry Charlie as soon as possible and to move forward with your life in happiness. He said to tell you this so you knew it came from him." Dr. Scott paused and looked as if he were thinking hard to recall something to mind.

"*Gan aon chiontacht i ngrá.*" The words came with difficulty from the older man.

Melody smiled at his Irish. Her father's last message for her. "'No guilt in love.'"

Later that day, Edward Vogel came to the bank to update Charlie on the posse hunting for Jefferson Lane. "About two dozen men have headed south to search for him. They'll follow the stage line and inquire at each stop as to whether Jefferson was seen. There are a couple of good trackers among the men, so we feel confident they'll find Lane."

"I appreciate knowing about that. I received a telegram from my father. He intends to be here on the second of June. It would be nice if we could have the matter wrapped up by then."

"Our men are determined to find him. The vigilante committee members are doing less and less and will soon be disbanded altogether now that we have a good police force in place, but they wanted to participate in this. Many of them had money in your bank. It's their way of making sure they get it back."

Charlie ran his hand through his hair. "I wish they wouldn't worry. I told them I'd back it with my own money if need be. I have an inheritance I can draw from."

Edward shook his head. "You're a good man to do such a thing, but isn't it really your pa's responsibility? After all, it's his bank."

"But it happened under my leadership, and I am, therefore, the one who must make it right. I failed to get the bank's keys back from Jefferson. Had I done that, he wouldn't have had a chance to take the contents of the smaller safe. I never even thought about it." Charlie shook his head. "I'm not cut out for this job."

"Don't be too hard on yourself, Charlie. Nobody blames you."

Charlie met Edward's gaze with a smile. "You haven't met my father."

Edward shrugged. "No, I guess I haven't. Sounds like he's pretty hard on you."

"He's just got his ideas of how things need to be, and when they aren't, he takes that as his cue to put everything in order. He'll blame me for this and rightly so. I just hope he'll forgive me and understand that the decision I've made was made before Jefferson took the money."

"What decision is that?" Edward narrowed his eyes. "You aren't pulling out, are you?"

Charlie laughed. "No, just the opposite. I've found a house I want to buy, along with the land beside it to build a school for boys. I want out of the banking business. This proved to me once and for all that this job isn't for me. I'm not a banker, and my father is just going to have to accept that."

"Sure glad you aren't planning to go. I was just starting to think of you as a friend."

"Of course I'm your friend, Edward. I figure God put us together for a reason. Maybe catching Jefferson is the purpose. Who can say?"

"Well, whatever the purpose, I'm glad you're sticking around. I'd best head out. I still have to make the rounds. Working during the day now has me kind of mixed up. I got so used to working at night that it still seems I ought to be sleeping."

"Thanks for coming by to tell me about the posse."

"No problem."

Edward was hardly gone two minutes when the front door opened again, and no fewer than a half dozen brawny men entered. Charlie recognized most as railroad workers and freighters. Men with the muscle to impose their will. He made his way to the front of the bank to greet them.

"Afternoon, gentlemen. How may I help you?"

"You can give us our money," one of the men asserted. The others nodded their heads in agreement. "And don't be tellin' us we shouldn't worry about whether it's safe," the man continued. "We know it ain't."

"We've been workin' and just got back to town to hear there was a robbery and our money might be gone. I worked hard for that money," a tall, well-muscled man declared. He probably had forty pounds on Charlie.

"Don't try to change our minds neither," a shorter but equally robust man with a beard and mustache said. "We want our money *now*."

Charlie knew that it would be easy enough to make a

scene about the money and how they didn't need to worry, but he also knew it wouldn't change their minds. He called each man to the teller's cage one by one. He prayed, asking God's guidance in his words and manner. The last thing he wanted to do was further upset these men. He looked up their accounts and counted out their money and had them sign the receipt.

"I appreciate that you trusted us with your business. I'm sorry you feel you can no longer work with us. Given the circumstances, however, I understand. I accept responsibility for this."

This seemed to surprise the men, who in the beginning looked as if they were just itching for a fight.

"Well, it . . . it ain't you personally," one of the men said, stuffing his money in his trouser pockets.

"No. It's not you, Mr. Decker." This came from a man Charlie had seen at church.

He smiled. "I know it's not me. It's the situation that has angered you. You're worried that if you don't take your money now, someone else might. I completely understand. You have to look out for yourselves. There are a lot of bad people in this world. I hope you have a good day, gentlemen."

He left them standing there in the lobby and went back to his desk. Charlie had hoped after the initial run on the bank that people would settle down and not worry if the bank could keep their money safe. Now, with these fellas taking out their cash, Charlie worried word would get around, and people would once again get stirred up and come to demand their money. If they did, Charlie wasn't sure if there would be enough cash to cover all the withdrawals.

The men left without another word, and Charlie was relieved to see that it would soon be closing time. A wave of discouragement washed over him. All of his life, he had tried so hard to please his father and do as he asked. If it hadn't been for his father telling him how much he needed him, how now more than any other time it was imperative that Charlie do as he requested . . . Charlie wouldn't even be here.

But if he hadn't come to Cheyenne, he never would have met Melody or Clancy. He never would have met the woman he intended to marry. Never dared to dream of a boys' school to the point where he was ready to purchase the land and see the place built.

He supposed the good was bound to be mingled with the bad, and yet it seemed almost too much to think about. In some ways, he wondered if he would lose his father just as Melody had lost hers. Would this be the final thing that caused his father to turn away from him once and for all?

It wasn't that his father was unreasonable. Not really. He was assertive and focused on the vision he had for his family and business. He had his plans and didn't brook interference. Father was a man of strength and character whose impeccable reputation for getting things done had made him a man of high regard in the Chicago area and elsewhere.

Charlie buried his face in his hands. "God, I don't know what I'm supposed to do now. I don't want Father to think I'm walking away because of what Jefferson did, but it sure didn't help things at all.

"I also feel Clancy's death deeply. Even though I didn't even know him that long, I feel as if I lost a dear friend. And, of course, there's Melody and my feelings for her."

He raised his head and looked for a long while at the ceiling. Was God even listening? Charlie had never felt so alone.

20

Jefferson stretched and got up from the straw-filled mattress. It was old and so worn that there wasn't a lot of comfort to be had, but for now it would suffice.

He'd been hiding in the hunting cabin for nearly a week and was finally starting to relax. There had been no sign of anyone snooping around or coming to see who was in the place. Not that there was anyone else living in the area.

The cabin belonged to his father, and Jefferson had been there on many occasions as a boy. His father used it for his hunting trips and sometimes just to get away. Jefferson had never cared much for it. Hunting and fishing didn't interest him, and living without the amenities he was used to was unbearable. But he had had little choice in the matter. As an only son, he was expected to do whatever his father demanded.

The air was chilly despite it being the last Saturday in May. The mountains were always cooler, and mornings could be especially crisp. Jefferson checked the stove and found mostly dead ash and no warmth. He loaded up some kindling and a few larger pieces of wood and lit the fire. It crackled and popped as the kindling caught. After a few minutes, he could see that the rest of the wood was burning as well. It didn't take long for the tiny cabin to warm. He supposed he should be grateful his father had forced him to learn how to set a fire.

He got dressed, wondering how much longer he'd have to remain hidden. When the stage to Denver had stopped to change horses in Ft. Collins, he'd paid a man to take his place, knowing the driver would give little attention to the look of his passengers so long as the count was right.

Although only three years old, the military fort had been decommissioned the year before. Jefferson was more than a little familiar with the place. His father had conducted business with the army, and Jefferson had sometimes accompanied him when he did. On one trip there, some of the men had put together a hunting party, and Jefferson's father had gotten himself invited to accompany them. He'd fallen in love with the mountainous terrain southwest of the town and hired a man from Ft. Collins to build him the hunting cabin Jefferson now took refuge in.

After he'd left the stage, Jefferson had headed out on foot for a place not far from town where he knew he could discreetly buy a horse and tack. Then it was straight to the cabin. His father always kept the place stocked with supplies, so Jefferson knew he could live at the cabin for quite some time. No one from Cheyenne would ever think to look for him here, because no one there even knew the place existed. Jefferson figured after a few weeks, he could make his way down to Denver and then to wherever he desired to go.

So far everything had gone as he'd planned, and Jefferson couldn't help but be pleased with himself. When he'd first gone to Cheyenne the year before, he'd been enthralled with the wild and wicked ways of the town. He had heard that wealthy men were choosing Cheyenne as a new place to expand their fortunes, and Jefferson wanted to expand his fortune as well. Especially given his father's philosophy regarding each man making his own way in the world, even the sons of successful men.

On his twenty-fifth birthday, Jefferson's father had given him a hundred dollars and had the valet pack his bags. He could still hear his father's firm words over that last breakfast.

"I have the utmost confidence in your abilities, Jefferson. Return to me when you have a thousand dollars, and I will double it. Return when you have ten thousand, and I will give you tenfold. Prove to me you can double that, and I will turn over a portion of the family business to you."

The task was one that had both annoyed and challenged him. As an only son, Jefferson felt he was entitled to take on the family industrial interests anyway, but his father insisted he prove himself worthy. As if he hadn't always proven himself worthy by doing everything his father had demanded.

Standing at the stove, Jefferson held his hands out and rubbed them together for warmth. Surely in another week or two he could leave and head to Denver. Once there, he intended to see his parents and reveal the thousand dollars to his father in order to get it doubled. After that, he would head out and see what he might accomplish elsewhere. He was certain that with the money he could make a fresh start. Jefferson was also confident that he could, by some means, stretch that money into ten thousand dollars.

He smiled to himself. If not by a legal means, then he wasn't against another illegal one. His only regret, if it could be called that, was he'd been confident he could have talked

Melody Doyle into marriage . . . eventually. She was a beauty and wealthy to boot. Life with her could have had its benefits.

An image of Charles Decker came to mind. He had found Jefferson's embezzlement and, out of the goodness of his heart, hadn't brought in the marshal to arrest him. That had been his first mistake. The second had been in forgetting to demand the bank keys be returned before sending Jefferson on his way. Jefferson felt he'd had no choice but to take advantage of the situation. Decker was a fool, and fools always needed to be taught a lesson.

Saturday came all too soon. Melody had purchased a new plum-colored gown with a gored skirt and close-cut jacket. The black trim on the jacket's fitted sleeves and bodice was the only contrast to the dark red-purple hue of the dress. She had told Marybeth that she wanted to honor her father's wish that she not wear black while at the same time not shock the entire community. She didn't really care what the rest of Cheyenne thought, but it was difficult to dress for a ceremony when all Melody felt was sorrow.

As she stood waiting for the procession to commence, Melody couldn't help but remember gazing at her appearance in Marybeth's cheval mirror. The only thing that set her apart as a mourner rather than a well-dressed woman of means was the very small black hat she'd chosen to complement the gown. She'd been unable to find anything else that matched and knew Da would understand her choosing black. Now, all she could wish for was that the day would end, and this might all be behind her.

Charlie stood faithfully at her side. A well-brushed top hat adorned his head, and a double-breasted black coat covered his navy suit. Marybeth and Edward had come to support her, leaving Carrie at home with Granny Taylor. Jedediah, however, was there with more than fifty or sixty other railroad workers.

Finally, everyone was appropriately assembled. Her father had touched the lives of so many. The undertaker had told Melody that he'd had men stopping by all day on Friday to volunteer to carry her father's casket.

"It's like nothing I've ever seen before," he had shared with her.

Da was certainly well-known and valued. Even men who'd had run-ins with Da admired the man and had come to pay their respects. Da was a friend to all whose intentions were good and an encourager to those less trustworthy. Melody knew her father had changed the heart of many a man. He gave God the credit for it, of course, telling Melody that his role was just to help his fellow man see the truth of a matter.

She smiled at the thought, and Charlie squeezed her arm. "Pleasant memory?"

"Yes." She looked up at him. "I was just thinking of all the people who have come to Da's funeral. Some of them didn't start out as friends, and maybe still don't consider themselves as one to Da, but they respected him. Da would be pleased."

The undertaker climbed into the funeral carriage and had the driver start them down the road. Up and down Fifteenth Street, people who weren't a part of the procession stopped to pay their respects and wait for them to pass by. Men took off their hats and bowed their heads, while women hushed their children and bowed as well.

They walked all the way to the cemetery and gathered around the gravesite Da had chosen. The open land around them didn't have a single tree to break the landscape. Melody vowed then and there to plant a tree or two near Da's grave. Maybe she'd even arrange a bench beneath the trees so she could sit when she visited. Then another memory came to mind.

"*Don't ya be standin' at my grave all the time, weepin' and talkin' to me,*" Da had said one night a short time back. "*I won't be there, and I don't want ya to be there either. If ya have to be rememberin' me, go ride the train and enjoy the fine tracks me and the boys put down.*"

Again, she smiled. There'd be no trees or bench.

Once they were all assembled again and had Da's casket placed beside the open grave, Dr. Scott took his place and began to speak. "Dearly beloved, we have come here today to lay to rest our brother Clancy Michael Doyle. Most of you here called Clancy friend, and many of you worked alongside him for years. Others knew him from the help he offered his fellow man.

"Clancy was a man of God, but as he told me to remind everyone, that wasn't always so. He sowed his wild oats as a young man and nearly died in the process. He drank and cursed, lied and cheated, and fought anybody who was fool enough to cross him. But God had a plan for Clancy."

Melody had heard Da's story so many times she could recite it from memory. He'd gotten himself into a terrible fight and was stabbed several times. Half-dead, he knew his end was near, but help came in the form of an older church woman who had always been critical of him. Da said this woman despised him, or so he thought. Turned out she only despised his actions. She took him in and nursed him back to health, and every day she read the Bible aloud to him for hours and prayed over him.

Somewhere between the bandage changes, prayers, and readings, Da realized the life he was living was destined for a bad end. As the woman read from John one night, Da asked her if she thought the good Lord really wanted a worthless no-good named Clancy Doyle. The woman had closed the Bible and had the audacity to smile. Da said he'd never seen her smile before—not even on Christmas Day.

"That woman told Clancy that not only did the good Lord want him, He had a plan for Clancy to serve Him and help others to see the light. Clancy told her he'd never be a preacher. He knew God hadn't called him to speak from a pulpit each Sunday.

"She had laughed," Dr. Scott said, chuckling a little himself. "And she told him, 'Clancy Doyle, ya'll never be havin' it that easy. The good Lord is callin' ya to be servin' Him daily as ya go about yar life. There won't be any Sunday sermons from ya. No, sir. Ya'll be a livin' example of God, and when folks cross yar way, ya'll be feelin' God's presence and hearin' His words. The urge to share the good Lord and His Word won't let go of ya until ya give in and let God have His way.'" He smiled at the people gathered. "Sorry, my Irish brogue isn't as good as Clancy's, but I thought it important to try and tell it as he did."

Melody's eyes blurred with tears. Da had done his best to see to it that he lived his life in a way that would always turn people to Jesus. She wondered just how many lost souls had come to God because of Da's willingness to share the Bible. What a legacy. Oh, that she could be as much of a witness as he had been.

Dr. Scott told another story or two, then concluded with prayer. He encouraged the mourners to rejoice in the knowledge that Clancy was free of pain and no doubt was hearing the Lord tell him, "Well done, good and faithful servant."

Church friends and railroad workers alike came and told Melody how sorry they were to lose a man like her father. Most shared stories that she had never heard. Tales of how her father had helped someone down on their luck or shared a dollar to buy someone food or medicine. By the time the last man came forward, Melody was exhausted from standing and receiving each of them, but she knew Da would expect no less.

"Miss Melody, the boys and I took up a collection. It'll help see you through for a time and pay for the funeral."

"Oh, you shouldn't have. I . . . don't need . . . Da made arrangements . . . he, uh . . ." She looked to Charlie, uncertain what she should say or do.

Charlie smiled and took the pouch the man offered. "Thank you. This will be a blessing."

She said nothing but looked back at the man and nodded. "Thank you."

The man put his hat back on, and Melody could see his eyes were red around the rims. "I was one of them fellas your father helped. I made peace with God because of him. I'd probably be dead if not for Clancy Doyle."

Melody reached out to take hold of the man's hands. "Thank you for telling me that. It means the world to me to hear the things he did and see how he served God."

"He was a good man and friend. The world is a little worse off without Clancy Doyle."

Melody let him go and waited until he was well away from them before turning to Charlie. "I don't need their collection. They probably put in money they really needed for themselves and their families."

Charlie handed her the pouch. "They gave from their hearts knowing there wasn't any other way they could honor your father. You can't very well ruin the situation by throwing it back at them. Let them bless you."

She frowned and glanced at the men and women who were now walking back toward town. "But I don't need it. What should I do with it?"

"You could donate it to the church," Charlie said with a slight shrug. "The building fund could use it, and just imagine getting the church built all the sooner because of your father. Wouldn't he love that?"

Melody couldn't imagine a better plan. "Charlie, you're brilliant. It's absolutely perfect."

Marybeth had invited the church members to come back to the Vogels' house for lunch. The ladies of the church had cooked up a storm, and Edward, along with the help of some of the other men, had built temporary tables in the backyard to lay out the feast.

In the true fashion of those who knew what to expect, families furnished their own dishes, and some brought their chairs. They spread out around the yard and shared their stories and offered Melody their love. Never had she felt more cared for than that day.

Hours after everyone had eaten their fill, some of the men gathered near the back of the house with a variety of instruments and played a series of songs while the women worked to clean up the leftovers and other men helped Edward break down the tables.

When Charlie came to her, Melody didn't even question him as he took hold of her arm and led her to the front of the house. They climbed the steps and took a seat on the porch. It was the first time they'd been alone all day.

"They did all right by Clancy," Charlie said. "I hope folks love me even half as much when my time comes."

"I knew folks cared for Da, but I never knew just how much. People have told me stories all day long about things he did for them. I have no idea how he had the time or energy, not to mention the ability, to reach so many."

"God multiplied what was needed. Time. Strength. Whatever was necessary, God provided. Your father was just the willing vessel from which God could pour out those blessings."

"Sometimes all he did was listen to a man's sad story and pray with him. Just a little encouragement, Charlie. It changed everything. Just a few words or taking the time to pray for someone or with them."

"I guess a few words can be a lifeline to a soul who's drowning in a sea of troubles. Sometimes I don't think we realize that. We figure we must do something big, or it doesn't count. But sometimes it's the littlest thing that turns out to be big."

Melody knew he was right. How many times had it been true for her? Someone offered a word of kindness or just a hug. "Oh, Charlie, this was a perfect day despite losing Da. He was honored in the best of ways. I never thought I could come away from this day happy, but here I am content and filled with joy."

"Then let me add to that joy," Charlie said, slipping from the chair to one knee and taking hold of her hands. "I've fallen in love with you, Melody Doyle. I told your father that I was never one to believe in love at first sight. I thought a couple needed to have a foundation of friendship first. When I saw you, however, I knew there was something special about you. Something that I wanted to experience every day for the rest of my life.

"Your father told me he knew from the first moment I talked to him that I was the one—that I was his choice for you. I was humbled by that and scared too." He chuckled and took hold of her hand. "I wasn't sure that I was worthy of you, of your love, but your father was fully convinced, and that gave me courage to move forward."

Melody could see the love he held for her in his expression and the tone of his voice. She knew with this man she would always be cared for, always safe, and never forgotten.

"I love you with all of my heart. I don't know what the future will hold for us, but I know that if you're by my side, I can face anything. As I've prayed about asking you this question, God has continued to teach me what I need to know in order to be not only a better man but a better husband, and I want to be that for you and you alone. Will you marry me?"

She smiled and gave a nod. "I will. Through all of this you've been a dear friend to me. I told you about all of my other suitors and their shortcomings. I told you my fears and failings. I made accusations against you, and you bore them without fault and forgave me when God showed me how wrong I was. I cannot imagine my life without you. I love you, Charlie."

Charlie rose and pulled her to her feet. Wrapping his arm around her, he tilted her chin up. "I know this is bittersweet, but I also feel confident it is what your father would want."

Melody slipped her arms around him. "I know he'd be most pleased."

Charlie kissed her with great tenderness. Melody sighed and leaned against him as he pressed another kiss on her forehead. She could just see Da in heaven, elbowing the Lord and saying, *"That's me girl. That's me darlin' girl."*

21

Charlie paced nervously as he waited for the train to arrive on the evening of June 2. His father would soon be in Cheyenne, and who could say how things would go after that? Charlie was hopeful, however, that after the long train ride his father would be tired, and they could put off discussing the bank until tomorrow.

There was a part of Charlie that missed his parents' home in Chicago. Truthfully, the time he'd spent there had been good overall. His mother was a gentle soul, whose faith in God led her in all decisions and actions. When people in her circle of society needed advice, they always came to Abigail Decker, including Charlie. His father, on the other hand, although a man of faith, was far more severe and stern in his guidance. There was little in the way of sympathy or understanding for mistakes made, which was the reason for Charlie's anxiety now.

He heard the whistle before he saw the train. The evening skies were still light, and as the steam puffed heavenward from the locomotive, it formed little clouds against the purplish-blue heavens. For a moment, Charlie thought of a painting he'd once seen with a similar setting. Then the train whistle blasted again, and all pleasantries faded. He drew a deep breath and steadied himself as the train came to a stop.

Lord, I need strength to deal with this moment. Help me, please.

Charlie watched as the depot personnel went to work, and the porter stepped from the train, then turned around to assist others.

At nearly seventy years old, Bertram Decker cut a fine figure. He stepped onto the platform and secured his hat before looking around to find Charlie. His suit was impeccable despite having traveled for hours, and he looked as spry as a man half his age. When their gazes locked, Charlie called out, "Father!"

Charlie came forward and impulsively gave his father a hug. "It's so good to see you again. I wish the circumstances could be better." He bit his tongue. He hadn't meant to bring up the problem.

His father patted him on the back and pulled away. "I hadn't expected such enthusiasm." He surprised Charlie with a smile. A genuine smile. "But it's good to see you too, Charles. Your mother desperately wanted to join me, but I assured her this was to be a very quick trip."

There were few people arriving on the train this evening. Charlie retrieved his father's small trunk without much of a wait and then led the way to the hotel. He had reserved a room at the nicest hotel Cheyenne had to offer and hoped it would meet with his father's approval.

Father glanced up and down the street. "I wasn't sure what to expect. Jacob made it sound like Cheyenne was the very pit of hell itself."

"Up until a few weeks ago, it truly could be called that. So much has changed, almost overnight. The railroad moved west, and so did a great many of the troublesome characters. Of course, they're still close enough to Cheyenne that many come back on the weekends. But as the bulk of the gambling houses, brothels, and saloons move with them, that will stop, and there will be nothing Cheyenne has to offer that the new end-of-the-tracks town won't give them. By the way, how is Jacob feeling?"

"Much better, but I don't see him returning to Cheyenne. As I conveyed, he didn't find it much to his liking."

They secured Father's room at the hotel and deposited his things before Charlie suggested they go to dinner.

"I'm sure you didn't have anything decent to eat on the train."

"No, that's true enough."

"We have several decent restaurants here. Belham's is probably the best. I made a reservation for us. It's just a few blocks from here."

"Then lead the way."

Charlie did just that, pointing things out as they walked. "The town is growing quite rapidly. In fact, they call it the Magic City because it sprang into being like magic. Men who followed the tracks west said it was unlike any of the other towns along the way. We have a great many stores established, mercantiles, hardware, clothing, bakeries, and such. There are still more saloons than churches, but the latter are coming along nicely. The church I attend meets at the local school, but they plan to start building next year. Oh, and there are hospitals and doctor's offices—we now have nine doctors—and of course several banks, including ours." Again, Charlie wished he'd not mentioned anything to do with the dreaded subject. He hurried to continue.

"There is a fort nearby. Fort Russell. The soldiers are often in town for entertainment. Most stay on the west side, which is the seedier part of town. However, there are those who are of a better class."

They reached the restaurant and were immediately shown to a beautifully set table. Belham's had fine linens for the tablecloth and napkins and uniformed waiters to see to the customers' needs.

Charlie and his father took a seat and placed their orders for the steak dinner and coffee. The waiter had just left when Dr. Scott passed by the table. Charlie got to his feet and introduced his father to the man.

"Dr. Scott is a physician as well as the lay minister at our church. Dr. Scott, this is my father, Mr. Bertram Decker."

"Mr. Decker, I'm pleased to meet you. I'm a big fan of Charlie's. His Sunday school classes have been well received."

"Charles is a capable teacher, I'm sure," his father replied. "It's nice to meet you, Dr. Scott. How does a doctor of medicine end up taking the pulpit?"

"Need necessitates strange choices. We actually have another man who preaches from time to time too. It won't be long before there will be a need to replace me as well. I have no intention of filling the job indefinitely. Right now, however, it seems necessary, and I do enjoy it. Now, if you'll excuse me, I only stopped in to check on the owner." Dr. Scott turned to Charlie. "You might remember he had a stroke last week."

"I do. It was quite a surprise."

Dr. Scott nodded. "Since he and his wife live above the restaurant, it was easy enough to see to him on my way home."

"And is Mr. Belham doing better?" Charlie asked.

"He is. I'm happy to say the stroke was only a minor one, and I expect a full recovery."

"That is good news. We won't keep you, then. Have a good evening, Dr. Scott."

"And you and your father also," the man replied before heading out.

Charlie and his father reclaimed their seats as the waiter arrived with their soup and coffee. Charlie placed the napkin on his lap.

"I'll say grace, if you like." His father nodded.

Charlie offered a short prayer aloud, adding additional words in silence that God might allow his father to enjoy his trip to Cheyenne and understand Charlie's heart about teaching.

Father was already sampling the onion soup by the time Charlie picked up his spoon. He seemed pleased by the taste and gave a nod.

"Quite good. Better than I figured on getting."

"Belham's is the best. At least in my opinion. I don't eat out very often, but this is my first choice."

Father gave a quick glance around the large room. "As I mentioned, I wasn't at all sure what to expect. Jacob had given me insight into the town and the people, but he admitted the place was growing so rapidly that it would no doubt have changed a great deal by the time I arrived."

"They're pushing for this area to become a separate territory and, in time, a state. I believe given the railroad's actions in making Cheyenne their regional headquarters, there's a good chance Cheyenne will become the capital. After all, it is the main town for hundreds of miles around."

"It has been interesting to see the renewed push west after the war," Father declared. "As you know, it was your brother's idea to be a part of the westward expansion. Jacob believes there is a lot of money to be had, but I suppose he now realizes there's a lot to be lost as well. Why don't you tell me what happened? Start at the beginning."

Charlie had hoped to put off the discussion of the bank, but seeing his father was determined to know everything, he shrugged his shoulders.

"Well, you already know that Jacob left Jefferson Lane in charge of the bank when he returned to Chicago. When I arrived, I found Mr. Lane to be rather pretentious and self-serving. He clearly felt he should remain in charge and wasn't overly happy to see me. As I began to familiarize myself with the bank's records, I soon learned why. Jefferson had managed to embezzle nearly six hundred dollars. He took only a few dollars here and there, mostly from the wealthier depositors, knowing they would be less likely to worry over their totals being off by such small amounts. If anyone did question it, Jefferson must have either made it right and found another account to steal from or convinced the customer they were wrong."

"And this was going on from the time he was first employed?"

"As far as I can tell, yes. I confronted him about it, and he suggested Jacob had taken the money. I knew better and reminded Jefferson that Jacob had been gone for months and yet the embezzlement had continued. He had nothing to say. I fired him and told him I wouldn't press charges but expected him to return the money."

"You should have brought the officials into the matter immediately," his father said in a stern tone. "Criminals such as Mr. Lane have no conscience and will never endeavor to make such things right."

Charlie nodded and ate some of his soup. Finally, he put his spoon aside, sampled the coffee, and then continued. "My biggest mistake was in forgetting that Jefferson had keys to the bank. I just didn't think of it, and when he left in a huff, my mind was on other things."

He leaned back in his chair, shaking his head. "I am sorry, Father. I've never felt that I was called to be a banker, but this incident has made that even more clear to me. However, I want you to know that if Jefferson Lane and the money are not recovered, I will use some of my own inheritance to cover the loss. You aren't to blame for this tragedy."

His father finished his soup before speaking. "You have always been good about accepting responsibility for your mistakes, Charles. I have to say you do not disappoint regarding that matter. You never have."

He gave Charlie a look that could only be termed endearing. His reaction left Charlie momentarily speechless. He had expected his father to be quite disapproving and ready to point out all of Charlie's failings.

"You've also always been quite good at judging character. I'm impressed that you immediately sensed problems with Mr. Lane."

"His nature was off-putting, but I don't know that I would have thought him to be an embezzler had I not taken it upon myself to study the bank records. I thought that because the savings and loan was so new, reading back through the beginning transactions would help me to familiarize myself with the nature of the business done. I hadn't expected to find embezzlement."

"Nevertheless, you did a good job. The savings and loan here was always only an experiment in Jacob's interests with the West. I was never all that supportive, but the board felt it was worth checking into."

"I believe it is, if you are interested in my opinion," Charlie said. "Cheyenne is destined to grow, and here's why."

Just then, the waiter came to take away their soup. Without any delay, he returned with two large plates of food. He placed the dishes in front of the men and asked if they cared for anything else. Both men declined, and the waiter left.

Charlie picked up his knife and fork. The steak looked delicious, as did the potatoes and succotash. He decided to dig right in.

"You were going to share your opinion," his father said.

Pausing before cutting into the steak, Charlie nodded. "Just as I said. I believe the West is worth the interest. With the railroad connecting the eastern part of the nation with the western, people are going to be more inclined to settle the middle of the country. With the ending of the war, more and more people just long for peace of mind. Moving away from the battlefields and reminders of death and destruction has brought an influx of people that few could have expected.

"Added to this, they are now building a railroad line from Denver to Cheyenne, and as I understand it, we are soon to see ourselves a new territory of the United States. The growth will continue. There is no doubt. I see God's hand in it all."

"I could have figured on you to say something along those lines." His father smiled.

Charlie was again surprised by his father's actions. He'd never been one to smile so much in the past. At least not that Charlie remembered. Had something happened to mellow his father's more severe nature?

It was impossible not to say something. "You seem different, Father. Calmer. Less irritated. I have to say I fully expected your anger and frustration, yet here you are with a pleasant nature and smiles."

His father sobered. "I have been a bear to live with over the years. I've come to realize just how unpleasant I've been."

"And how did that happen?"

"Strangely enough by eavesdropping on one of your mother's teas. She had a small group of friends over one afternoon, and I had to interrupt them to retrieve something I'd left in the room where they were gathered. Your mother said something to me, and I reacted in my usual gruff manner. In my formal way, I acknowledged the women and made it clear I had no time for any of them. I don't even recall for certain what I said, but it wasn't charitable. As I left, I heard one of the women comment.

"She said to your mother, 'Abigail, I do not know how you live with such a disagreeable man. Have you ever known a moment's happiness?'"

Father shook his head. "That gave me pause. It was rather like a punch to the gut. Your mother replied by telling them that while my nature was more bitter than sweet, they needed to understand that I was a good man who had been wronged."

Charlie narrowed his eyes as he tried to understand. "Wronged? In what way?"

His father chuckled. Another inconsistency with his nature. "That was what I wondered. I had thought to just move on to my business, but I was frozen in place. Your sweet mother then explained to her friends that I had been forced into banking by my very strict father. She went on to share that I had wanted nothing to do with banking, but rather had wanted to farm."

"Farm? I never knew that about you, Father." Charlie

couldn't have been more surprised. The thought of his father out in the fields planting and harvesting was not a vision he'd ever considered.

"Few did, but your mother knew it and knew it well. She had walked the journey with me from the very moment when I decided that I had to do as my father bid me or suffer great consequences. She said that decision had robbed me of the joy and happiness life might have otherwise given."

Charlie had never heard his father ever once say that he didn't want to be a banker. All these years, Charlie had figured it was his father's passion. And in loving what he did, he had imposed it on his sons as well.

He looked up to meet his father's gaze, completely unsure what to say. Again, his father smiled. "You look completely baffled."

"I have to admit I am. I thought you enjoyed what you did. Banking had long been in the family, and I just presumed it was your choice. I thought when I found it tedious and boring that something was wrong with me. In fact, I fully planned to discuss my future with you while you were here. I wrote you a long letter, but then Jefferson stole the money, and Melody's father died."

"Melody?"

Charlie laughed. "That's an entirely different subject that we will definitely get to, but for now I have to say that after years of praying that you might understand my heart, I finally have hope that you do. You see, I want to be a teacher. I have been making plans to use my inheritance and build a small private school for boys. Around here there are so many children, and the public school has been overcrowded since its inception. I thought I could open my own school and teach maybe twenty or so to begin. I know it will never make me wealthy, but it is my passion and, I believe, my calling from God."

His father said nothing but cut into his steak.

Charlie couldn't bear the silence. "Did I offend you?"

Bertram Decker put his knife and fork down and met Charlie's concern with a clear expression of joy. "Quite the opposite, my boy. You've made me happier than I can say."

Charlie shook his head. "How?"

"You've finally taken a stand for yourself. For what's important to you. I've known for years that your heart wasn't in banking. Your brothers do seem to love it, and it makes me glad because I plan to soon be out of it altogether."

"You're resigning from the bank board?"

"Yes. Your mother and I discussed it, and it's time. After hearing her friends, I had a long talk with her. She was so supportive of my situation. Her words were nothing but kind and sympathetic. How deeply that woman loves me and for reasons beyond my understanding."

He picked up the knife and fork once more. "Let's eat, Charlie, and then we can discuss our plans."

Charlie's jaw dropped open. "You called me Charlie."

"That seems to be the name you prefer. I'd say it's about time I started listening to what pleases you rather than continue to impose my will upon you. Wouldn't you agree?"

Laughing, Charlie picked up his own silverware. "I do. It makes me happier than you could possibly know."

His father gave him a wink. "Oh, I think I understand pretty well."

Jefferson stepped outside into the sunshine. He walked to the small pen and lean-to where he'd put the horse. A nearby stream would supply the water, but Jefferson would have to carry full buckets to the trough in order to see the animal through the day. Thankfully there was also enough grain and hay left from their last trip that Jefferson wouldn't have to worry about feeding the animal for at least a week.

He had just come to the gate of the pen when he heard a noise off to his left. He glanced over, fearing perhaps a bear or other wild animal was upon him. The horse whinnied and took a little side step, furthering Jefferson's concern.

As the noise subsided, a different sound came from behind him.

"Jefferson Lane, hands up. You're under arrest by the authority of the Vigilante Committee of Cheyenne."

He slowly raised his hands as he considered making a break for it. If he could get beyond the cabin, there was a steep trail that led higher up into the mountain. He turned to find a man he didn't recognize coming forward with a rifle pointed at Jefferson's midsection.

"I've seen that look before. Don't even think of trying to run for it. You're surrounded. Come on out, boys!" the man called.

Men stepped out from the brush and trees. Jefferson could see they had fully encircled him. There wasn't any hope of escape.

"Roberts, go check the cabin and find that money. Davis, get the boy's coat and hat." Two men headed off to do the man's bidding.

"We're headed back to Cheyenne, Mr. Lane, where you'll stand trial for bank robbery."

22

"Let me grab my sunbonnet, and I'll help you with the laundry," Melody told Marybeth after they finished up the breakfast dishes.

Edward had gone to work before sunup, and now at nearly eight thirty in the morning, Melody felt she'd been lounging around all day. It wasn't Marybeth's normal routine to sleep so late either, but she said that Edward had encouraged her to go back to bed that morning since Carrie was still asleep, and she had complied.

Melody was glad for the extra rest. She'd been tired for so long. Da being sick had prevented her from sleeping deeply as she worried about his needs. These last few days since the funeral had been hard to face, but at least sleep had come.

Between sleeping and praying, there was always Charlie. His love and gentle encouragement had seen her through the worst of times. Marybeth and Edward's love had also helped. And that, along with Carrie's happy-go-lucky spirit and antics, was enough to chase away most of the sadness that surrounded Melody like a heavy blanket.

She had just started back from her upstairs bedroom when a loud knock sounded on the front door.

"I'll get it," she called out in case Marybeth was still in the house.

She opened the door and found Charlie standing there, handsome as ever, hat in hand. "Good morning, Charlie. I was just about to lend Marybeth a hand with the laundry."

"I want you to meet someone." Another man stepped up from the side. "This is my father, Mr. Bertram Decker."

"But you can call me Father, if you like," the man offered. "I hope that isn't out of line, but Charlie tells me the two of you would like to marry."

Melody smiled uncertainly. "Yes, we want very much to marry." She said nothing about calling him father. While she had never called Da *father*, it wasn't easy to think of this stranger as such.

"Won't you come in?" Melody said, stepping away. "As I said, I was just going to go help Marybeth with her laundry, but I can take a few minutes to visit with the two of you."

The men came inside, and Melody led them into the front room. "Have a seat, and I'll bring tea."

"Don't bother. We just had breakfast and drank an entire pot of coffee," Charlie said. "Sit with us for a moment."

She took a seat in Marybeth's rocking chair while Charlie and his father took the sofa.

"I've told my father all about Jefferson Lane and the robbery. The embezzlement too," Charlie explained. "I've also told him about us and my desire to own a school and teach."

She immediately feared the worst. Charlie had warned her about his father and his attitude toward having each of his sons follow him in banking.

"I can tell by the worried expression you wear," Charlie's

father interjected, "that you're concerned I would disapprove." He chuckled. "I must say that the old me very well would have."

Melody found his comment even more concerning. What did he mean by the "old me"? She shifted her weight and let the rocker move back and forth at a slow pace. It comforted her. She needed to let go of her growing fears that Charlie's father might start arguing for his side of the matter.

"You need not fear, my dear. I am a changed soul, as Charlie can confirm. Goodness, I wouldn't have even called him Charlie before my remaking. No, I assure you, God has taken hold of me, and I am a different man."

"It's true, Melody."

Charlie's smile caused her to immediately relax. Melody looked at the older man and could see the sincerity in his expression. "I don't know quite what to say."

"Don't worry about saying anything," Charlie began again. "Father and I talked long into the night. He is quite supportive of my plans. He even wants to help with the school."

"That's wonderful." Melody knew her tone was still guarded. She looked at Mr. Decker. "Charlie is quite good at teaching. I've heard nothing but enthusiasm for his Sunday school class endeavors. I would imagine running an entire school would suit him quite well."

Charlie's father nodded. "I believe Charlie would make an excellent teacher."

"Father has been so encouraging that he's offered to pay for the school to be built. I told him that I needed to discuss things with you first. And given all that you've been through this last week, I have no desire to burden you with it now."

"I don't think your dreams for the future are a burden, Charlie. You know I support them. I know that you've never enjoyed . . ." She fell silent. It wasn't right for her to comment on how Charlie felt about banking. That was entirely up to him.

"You know that my son has never enjoyed banking," Charlie's father said with a gentle smile. "Isn't that what you were about to say?"

Melody bit her lower lip and nodded. She felt terrible for having related such thoughts because now Charlie's father would know that he'd told her everything.

But instead of anger, Mr. Decker leaned forward. "Miss Doyle . . . may I call you Melody?"

"Please do." Melody continued to rock.

"Melody, I know that you must think me a terrible man."

"No!" she exclaimed, shaking her head. "I don't think that at all. I believe you to be firm, fixed in your thoughts. A man of opinion."

He chuckled. "Yes, to be certain, and those opinions were usually quite negative. But God has dealt with my bitter heart. As I told Charlie, much of my bitterness came from not seeking my own dream, but rather following the plan that my father put in place for me. I don't want to do that to Charlie any longer."

She glanced at her husband-to-be and found him smiling. She cocked her head to one side to silently ask the reason for his amusement.

He leaned forward and lowered his voice, as if trying to keep his father from hearing. "It's just so strange that he's calling me Charlie. He never would before. He said it wasn't fitting."

Mr. Decker leaned forward as well. "A lot has changed by the grace of God."

Melody felt the last of her tension ease. "God is good."

"To be sure, my dear." Mr. Decker eased back against the sofa. "Charlie has told me about your recent loss, and I am heartily sorry. He said that you were very close to your father."

"Yes." Melody folded her hands. "Da was a good man who always saw to our needs." She hesitated to say more lest she burst into tears. "I loved him very much. I still do."

Mr. Decker nodded. "It is never easy to lose anyone we care about, and even harder when it's someone who has touched your heart so deeply. I didn't have that kind of relationship with my earthly father. He was a man of rules and regulations who held no mercy for those who failed him." His joyful expression was replaced by a look of sorrow. "I am so sorry for having repeated his mistakes."

"Father, you were honoring Grandfather as you should. He was deserving of your respect."

"Yes, but I didn't have to become the very things I detested. Thank God you were strong enough to resist my bitter heart, Charlie."

Melody had never expected such confessions, and yet for a reason she couldn't explain, it comforted her. To see a man like Mr. Decker humble himself before her and his son was evidence of true contrition.

"You are forgiven, Father." Charlie squeezed his hand. "Now, let us speak of it no more. You have a new heart, and God will direct the days to come."

"I agree, son. Let us talk of your plans to marry this beautiful young lady."

"Melody and I haven't had much time to plan anything. I want to give her time to mourn. So many of our first experiences, even my asking her to marry me, have been mingled with sorrow. I want her to have all the time she needs."

Melody was again touched by Charlie's consideration of her feelings. However, she knew that her father had hoped to see her married right away. He hadn't wanted to leave her to manage alone and had said merely living with friends wasn't good enough to give him peace of mind in her remaining in Cheyenne. Not only that, but he had chosen Charlie for her.

"I'd like us to marry right away, Charlie. I don't want a big wedding. Something very small, with our friends. Maybe we could just get married on Sunday night after the church services. We wouldn't even need to announce it to anyone."

"But I've already heard about it," Marybeth said from the open doorway. She held Carrie in her arms, and the child was amazingly quiet. She looked at Melody. "When you didn't come out, I feared something was wrong."

"No, not at all. Charlie and his father stopped by to see me. Mr. Decker, this is my dear friend Marybeth Vogel and her daughter, Carrie."

Mr. Decker and Charlie were already on their feet. Charlie's father spoke in greeting. "It's very nice to make your acquaintance, Mrs. Vogel."

Melody didn't wait to continue. "Marybeth, I don't mind you knowing because you won't force me to have a big wedding with parties. You understand my feelings. You had a quiet ceremony yourself and have told me you didn't regret it at all."

"No." Marybeth shook her head. "I didn't. It was perfect for us."

Melody turned back to Charlie. "I've never worried about having a big wedding and fancy dress. The only thing that was ever important was the man I would wed. When Da suggested advertising for a husband and testing each applicant out, I wasn't certain it could work. But here we are, and I know you are the choice Da had for me. Let's marry Sunday, if Dr. Scott will do the deed." She looked at Charlie's father. "And maybe you would stand with me since my own father can't be here to be at my side?"

Bertram Decker gave her a solemn nod. "I would be proud to do so and even prouder to call you daughter."

The next day, Charlie was still struggling to get used to his father's change of heart as they sat at breakfast. Bertram Decker was a completely changed man. The father Charlie had known in the past would never have allowed for a quick wedding, much less been an enthusiastic participant. And all of this in light of the bank robbery made it all the more impressive.

"Your mother will be upset that she couldn't be here for the wedding," Father declared. "However, I know we could never get her here by Sunday."

"I wish she could be here. If you really think Mother is up to the trip here, I'll talk to Melody and see if we might wait a week."

His father's face lit up. "I know she could easily make the trip. She loves to travel, and I've denied her so many adventures. I could arrange for someone to travel with her so that she wouldn't have to worry about anything. My valet, Bixby, and her maid, Claudia, might do the job."

"Let me speak to Melody when we go to see the property later today. I'm sure she'll understand and want to wait. She would give anything if her mother and father could be with us. I know she won't refuse me mine."

"Wonderful. By the way, I think she'll love the property you have in mind. The house is quite grand."

"Grander than I had imagined." Charlie and his father had inspected it late the previous afternoon. The house was well built and quite nicely situated. "And the builder was happy to get right to work on the school."

"It was fortunate for you that he owned the lot next door. The contracts will be less complicated working with just one person rather than two."

"I agree, but what about the bank, Father?" Charlie had put off talking about the matter in light of his happy plans to marry Melody.

"I've given it much thought on the trip here as well as after going through everything with you. I believe the best thing is to dissolve the bank, especially since Jacob has no desire to return to Cheyenne. There aren't that many accounts left to worry about, and we can help the customers transfer to another bank."

"I'd like to think they'll find Jefferson soon. I don't see how he could have gotten that far."

His father gave a little shrug. "That is one of the differences with transportation being so readily available. People will have a much easier time getting away from bad situations."

"The men who went after him were the best of trackers and know a great deal about the area. At least, that's what Edward Vogel told me. He has worked with many of these men since last year. Edward's at work right now, perhaps we could go and ask him if there has been any word on the matter."

His father drank the last of his coffee and dabbed his lips with the napkin. "I think that's a good idea."

They walked the few blocks to the jail only to find a large gathering of horses and men outside. To Charlie's utter amazement, Jefferson Lane was at the very center of the gathering, positioned on the boardwalk between two rough-looking characters. Jefferson looked terrified and small compared to his companions.

"That's him," Charlie told his father. "That's Jefferson Lane."

"Why, he's just a child. What a sad beginning to a man's life."

They watched a moment from across the street, then made their way to join the noisy bunch at the jail. The men led Jefferson inside, and Charlie wasn't surprised to see Nathan Baker, owner and editor of the *Daily Leader*, race in behind them. He and Jefferson were the same age, or nearly so. Both came to Cheyenne from Denver. Yet they were as different as two men could be. Baker was married with a child. He was an upstanding citizen and popular with the townsfolk. Jefferson was now an enemy to all, especially those who had placed their trust in the Cheyenne Savings and Loan.

Charlie and his father pushed through the crowd and into the jail. He found Edward standing to one side while the marshal took charge of Jefferson.

They made their way to where Edward stood. The first thing on Charlie's mind was to find out if the money had been recovered.

"Glad you're here," Edward said. "We would have sent for you, and this saves us the trouble. They just brought him in."

"I figured as much since he was still outside the jail." Charlie glanced around. "Did they recover the money?"

Edward nodded. "They did. I don't know how much of it, but I'm sure the marshal will talk to you as soon as they get Jefferson locked up."

They didn't have to wait long. Marshal Sweeney approached them, ignoring Nathan Baker, who was already asking questions. Another man was at the marshal's side.

"Mr. Decker," Sweeney said, nodding to Charlie. "This is Johnny Barnes. He led the posse." The man was covered in dust and looked weary from his ride.

"Good to meet you." Charlie shook the man's hand. "Thank you for what you did." He turned to his side. "This is my father, Bertram Decker. He's the bank's owner."

Sweeney and Barnes gave a nod. Sweeney used his thumb to motion back over his shoulder. "The money's been recovered. All of it's there. Lane had an additional two hundred dollars and some change on his person, but the amount you told me about from the safe was all together in his suitcase. I'll send a couple of armed men with you if you want to take it back to the bank."

"That would be wonderful," Charlie's father answered.

"Where did they find him?" Charlie asked.

"We learned he'd gotten off the stage in Fort Collins," Barnes replied. "He paid a fella to pose as him and get back on the stage and continue to Denver. The fella took the money and then changed his mind. From that we learned Lane bought a horse and gear. We were able to track him from where he bought it and followed a trail up into the mountains. Apparently, his pa owned the cabin where we found him."

Charlie wasn't surprised that Jefferson had planned it all out. Lane didn't strike him as someone who would act willy-nilly.

"May I speak with him?" Charlie asked.

Sweeney shrugged. "Don't know why not. Ed, take Mr. Decker to Lane's cell."

Edward nodded. Charlie turned to his father. "I'll be right

back, I just want to . . . I don't know . . . say something to Jefferson. I hate how this all turned out."

"Go ahead. I'll be here."

Charlie followed Edward to the cells. Jefferson sat on a cot, staring at the wall. "Jefferson, I'm sorry things came to this," Charlie said, gazing through the bars of the jail cell.

Jefferson barely glanced up. He quickly went back to looking at the wall. "I don't want to sit here and listen to your lecture or have to endure your gloating over me."

"I didn't come for either of those reasons," Charlie replied. "I came to tell you that I was sorry things went the way they did and that I'd be praying for you."

"Don't bother. I don't believe in God."

"Well, I do, and since I'm the one doing the praying . . . I think that's enough for the time being."

Jefferson fixed him with a hard look. "I'm not sorry for what I did."

"Not even a little sorry?" Charlie asked in surprise. He couldn't imagine being in Jefferson's position without having a great deal of regret.

"I'm sorry I got caught," Jefferson replied. He got up and walked over to where Charlie stood. "You don't know anything about anything."

"I know that you're about to face a worse life than what you had. It seems like such a waste for someone like you. You're obviously capable, even smart in some ways."

"I'm very smart," Jefferson countered. "Smarter than most."

"I don't know that I would say that." Charlie could see his comment irritated Jefferson. "A smart man wouldn't have landed himself here in jail."

Jefferson's eyes narrowed. He seemed on the edge of

speaking, then returned to his place on the cot. "Like I said, you don't know anything."

"I suppose when it comes to throwing your life away, you're right. I don't know anything about it, nor do I want to." Charlie looked to Edward. "I guess I'm done here."

Two hours later, the money was back in the safe at the bank, as well as the keys. Charlie's father had agreed to an interview with Nathan Baker, while Charlie finally showed Melody the property he wanted to purchase for their future.

The builder worked upstairs while Charlie escorted Melody through the downstairs rooms. She was amazed at the size of the place.

"It's bigger than Marybeth's house, and I thought that was huge."

"You've been living in a tent for what, two or three years? Any other place would seem big," Charlie said, laughing. He showed her to the second of two parlors. "This could be a library or music room or whatever you want it to be."

"It's beautiful, Charlie. I can't imagine living here."

"But would you like to? I won't buy this house and the property next door if you don't like it."

"I like it very much. It would be a wonderful home."

She looked at him, and Charlie's heart skipped a beat. She was so beautiful, and he could easily lose himself in her blue-eyed gaze. Planning a future with her wasn't hard at all.

"There are four large bedrooms upstairs," Charlie said, moving her into the dining area. "The kitchen is just beyond this room."

"The dining room is quite big—and has its own fireplace," Melody said, looking around in awe. "I've never lived anywhere with this much room. Even the houses we lived in were much smaller."

"I figure we'll need the space. After all, I'm hoping for a large family," Charlie said, wondering how she'd react. They hadn't discussed having children, but he figured it was about time.

"Oh, I do too, Charlie," she said, giving his arm a squeeze. "I want an entire houseful. I was always so lonely as a child. There were always families around us with dozens of children, and I envied them so much." She met his gaze and smiled. "I'm so glad you want a large family."

"That brings me to another matter. I have a favor to ask you," he said, remembering what he and his father had discussed. "Would you mind if we married a week later than we discussed?"

She frowned. "Why?"

"I'd like my mother to be here. Father believes he can send for her and have her here by the end of next week, but not by this Sunday."

Melody's worried look faded as she reached up to touch his cheek. "Of course. How thoughtless of me. She must be here."

He pulled her into his arms. "I knew you'd feel that way, and I knew you'd love this house as much as I do. I'll get the details worked out, and we'll secure it and have the builder start on the school. I can't tell you how happy this makes me."

"It makes me happy too." She put her head against his chest and sighed. "I know Da would be happy as well. I can almost hear him saying, 'Good on ya, Charlie boy. Good on ya.'"

Charlie laughed and lifted her far enough to swing her in a circle. "I can hear him saying it too."

23

Melody found herself in tears at the strangest times. Mourning her father came in ways that she could never have anticipated or planned for. Sometimes just smelling the coffee brewing would set Melody awash in sadness. Da had loved his coffee. It was one of the first smells she could remember as a child. There was always a pot of coffee on the stove.

Once, when she was helping Marybeth clean house, a memory came to mind of her father and mother. Mother had just washed the floor of their little apartment, and Da had come in from a deluge of rain. He tracked mud into the house from one room to another until he came to where Mother was still mopping. He had looked at her and then the floor and the mess he'd made. Without a word, he slipped off his shoes, then took the mop from her hands and went to work, dancing a jig and cleaning at the same time. Melody had been very young, but she could still remember her mother's laughter. Why did they both have to be lost to her?

Through it all, Charlie was the epitome of understanding and concern. He would allow for her tears, offering comfort and love in return. He never grew impatient with her or chided her for her sadness, and it only served to endear him all the more to Melody.

Charlie's mother arrived on Friday the twelfth. Melody went with Charlie and Mr. Decker to welcome her and her servants to Cheyenne. Melody had feared the older woman wouldn't like her or would feel that she and Charlie had known each other far too short of time. However, Abigail Decker was a charming and loving woman.

"You are as pretty as a china doll," she told Melody. "But I have a feeling you're made of much sturdier material." She embraced Melody and whispered in her ear, "We shall be great friends, my dear." Melody immediately loved her.

They went for dinner at Belham's, and Melody listened to story after story about Charlie and their family. They had grown up with plenty and had never known want. But Melody felt she had been just as blessed. Da had always provided for them, and while they may not have lived in luxury, they did live in love. She related this when Charlie's mother asked to hear something of Melody's childhood.

"I was an only child," Melody said. "And my father's darling girl." She smiled at the memory of him calling her that. "Da loved railroad work and moving from place to place. He was a wanderer at heart and never seemed to settle down. My mother took it in stride. She loved Da more than life. I was always amazed at their love for each other. It devastated us to lose her. I was only ten, but I knew what they had was special and prayed I'd know that for myself one day."

"And do you think you have that with Charlie?" his mother asked.

Melody glanced over at Charlie and nodded. "I know I do. I sensed it in our first words. Charlie was the kind of friend I needed and wanted. I had other friends, but Charlie's friendship filled a void that I hadn't realized was present. I enjoyed talking to him about everything, and he was gracious about it all. Even when I told him about my experiences with other suitors."

Charlie's mother smiled. "That sounds like my Charlie."

"It wasn't easy to hear her speak of being with other suitors, let me tell you," Charlie interjected. "I was quite happy to hear of her misery on those outings." Charlie's parents laughed at this, and Melody couldn't help but smile.

They continued to eat and talk until finally it was time to leave, and Melody couldn't suppress a yawn. It had been good to be with Charlie's family, however. Her spirits were more uplifted in this small gathering than they had been since Da's death.

They walked Charlie's parents back to the hotel and bid them goodnight. Before they could part company, Abigail Decker spoke up.

"Melody, I wonder if we might spend some time together tomorrow. Just you and me. I know you probably have a lot to do to ready yourself for the wedding, but I would very much like to have some time alone with you. I also have a gift for you."

"You're very kind. I would be happy to see you tomorrow. Charlie, why don't you walk her over to Marybeth's around ten? Marybeth and Carrie will be gone with Edward doing the shopping and such. We can have the entire house to ourselves."

"That sounds wonderful," Mrs. Decker replied. "I promise I won't keep you but an hour or so."

The next morning at exactly ten, Mrs. Decker stood outside on the Vogels' porch. Charlie was at her side, carrying a large box.

"Good morning," Melody said in greeting. She eyed the box and then met Charlie's gaze. "Please come in." She showed them to the front room.

"Charlie, just leave the box on the sofa and go. You can come back for me in an hour."

He deposited the box and kissed his mother's cheek. "I'll see you soon." He then came to Melody and gave her a kiss on her head before heading for the front door.

Melody turned to Abigail Decker and motioned to the empty part of the sofa. "Please have a seat. I'm anxious to know you better."

"As am I to know you. I've long prayed for Charlie to find a wife." She took a seat and added, "And you seem a perfect fit for him and our family."

Melody pulled Marybeth's rocker closer and took a seat. "Why do you say that? You've only just met me."

"I can tell the sincerity of your heart. It's evident in your very nature. You are wholly unspoiled, and it no doubt drew Charlie's attention. He has long despised women who esteem themselves higher than others or demand to be the center of attention. Worse still were the ones who only showed interest in him because his family is wealthy and well-placed in society.

"You seem quite content to blend into a sea of people and draw no attention to yourself, and yet you are the very focus of their concern. I was touched at the number of people who stopped by the table to offer their condolences on your father's passing. It would seem you are both quite loved by this community."

"Da always had a way of making folks comfortable. He was a friend to all and never cared about social standing. Da left me quite an inheritance. He and his brothers had a business together in Ireland, and when Da knew he was dying, he sold his share back to his family. I'm not a pauper coming to Charlie for his money. I have no expectations of Charlie, in fact, except perhaps that he love the Lord."

"I know." She looked at Melody as if she had some special ability to see into her heart. "You are an exceptional young woman, and I believe you and Charlie will have a wonderful marriage." She lifted the box onto her lap. "I hope you don't mind, but when Charlie's father wired me that you were getting married, the first thing that popped into my head was about the wedding itself. Bertram mentioned that it would be a small affair, but I thought it important that you have a special gown for the ceremony. Have you already found one?"

"No, I don't have one. I figured to wear my Sunday clothes. It's not that I couldn't go to one of the shops and buy something. I just didn't feel like it, what with having lost Da. In fact, the last dress I bought was for his funeral."

Mrs. Decker nodded. "Well, I asked Bertram about your size. He said you were my size, and that made it rather simple. I do believe we are very nearly the same."

Melody had thought as much herself. The woman was quite petite and beautiful. Her face bore few wrinkles, and her salt-and-pepper hair seemed complementary rather than a reminder of age.

"Charlie is our last son to marry, and . . . well, I just wanted to do something special for you." She removed the box's lid and set it aside. Pushing back the tissue paper, she revealed a gown of embroidered white silk.

"I wanted you to have something lovely to start your new life. You've had your sorrows, and although you will continue to have moments of grief from time to time, I'm hopeful that marriage to my son will bless you with happier days."

Melody was touched by the gift, but more so by Mrs. Decker's words. "You speak as one who knows."

She nodded. "I do. I lost my father the year I turned twenty, and my mother died a year later. I miss them to this day. There are so many times I have wanted to speak to them, show them something, or just be in their presence. With the birth of each of my boys, I wanted more than anything to get my mother's advice . . . experience her approval and pride in her grandsons. With my father, I longed for his sage counsel."

Melody smiled. "My father was a wonderful counselor. I think I probably went to him at times when I should have gone to God. I have had moments of worry that God took him from me for that very reason."

"Never. That is not the nature of God. Yes, the Bible says He is a jealous God, but He is fully capable of winning our trust and affection without robbing us of the very loved ones He gave us."

A sense of relief washed over Melody. "It is reassuring to hear you say that. Da was just so very important to me, and without him, I feel a great emptiness. Sometimes the sadness just sweeps over me, and I realize once more that I'll never again have him here to talk to . . . to laugh with."

"And for a while, each reminder will be like the first moments after he left you."

"Yes!" Melody said, nodding. It helped so much that Charlie's mother understood.

"Over the years, that will ease, but it will never completely leave you. There will always be moments when he's the only one you long to speak to or share something with. And, my dear, that is quite all right. It neither offends God nor need separate you from Him."

"I'm so glad you came today. I was nervous as to what you might say. After all, we aren't well acquainted." Melody gave the older woman a smile. "But I feel as if we've known each other for a very long time. I feel you can see right into my heart."

"God has put us together for a very important purpose," Mrs. Decker replied. "I have long loved and cared for Charlie, and now I will turn that task over to you. However, just be aware that I will go on loving him, as well as you. Now, why don't you try on this dress, and we'll see if any alterations are needed."

Melody got to her feet. "I feel so very blessed. Here I lost my da, but now I'm gaining another set of parents. I'll once again have a mother and father who care about me. That's a completely unexpected gift, and I will cherish you both."

The next evening, following the church service in which Dr. Scott spoke of God's goodness and mercy, Melody joined Charlie at the front of the church. She had never felt more loved or beautiful. The gown given to her by Charlie's mother was perfect in every way. It was closely fitted in the front with a curved neckline that had been trimmed in delicately embroidered flowers. The sleeves were full to the elbow and then tight to the wrist. There was a full silk skirt with an overlay of lace, and tulle that gathered with a silk train to spill out behind Melody's tiny frame.

Marybeth had arranged her hair in a twist of curls and

topped it with the veil that Abigail Decker had included with the gown. The only thing missing had been the shoes, and Granny Taylor had managed to find a pair that were simple but perfect for the outfit.

Meanwhile, Charlie had dressed in a new three-piece suit. The dark gray color suited him and the occasion. Melody wondered if his mother had also brought it from Chicago.

Dr. Scott asked the congregation to stand as he offered prayers for the marriage. Melody was grateful that Charlie's father still held fast to her arm. The warmth of the room, despite the open windows, was causing her to feel a little uneasy. And the gravity of this lifelong decision was rather overwhelming. Even good things could be somewhat un-nerving.

Once the prayer was completed, the congregation took their seats and Dr. Scott continued. Charlie's father handed her over to his son and took his seat alongside his wife. Melody thought they were a lovely couple. Both had welcomed her into the family with such affection that she couldn't help loving them in return.

"Friends and family, we are gathered here today to join Charles Decker and Melody Doyle in holy matrimony," Dr. Scott began.

It seemed to only take a moment for them to pledge their lives to one another, and then Charlie was slipping a ring onto her finger.

She was surprised by the ring. They hadn't discussed it at all, and yet Charlie had produced the most beautiful piece, a gold band with a large diamond surrounded by smaller emeralds.

"With this ring, I thee wed," he said, and then leaned forward to whisper, "I thought the emeralds would remind you of Ireland and your father. I know he's smiling down on us today."

Tears pooled in her eyes. She felt her da's presence too. Whether it was just her desire to have him there or if he truly was looking down on them, she wasn't sure. Either way, she knew he would always be a part of their lives.

At the conclusion of the ceremony, Charlie offered her a chaste and gentle kiss before Dr. Scott turned them to face the congregation. "Let us pray.

"Father, we bring to You Charlie and Melody. They have married according to the laws of the land and the spirit of Your Word. May they be blessed and happy. May they serve You all the days of their lives and know Your peace upon their household. In Jesus's name, amen."

Melody and Charlie rode in a small horse-drawn carriage for the drive to their new house. The driver had said nothing to them as they took their seats. He saw them settled, then tipped his hat to them. Soon the horse was in motion to the cheers of the Methodist congregation.

Charlie put his arm around Melody, and she snuggled against him, feeling a great sense of satisfaction.

"I hope you like the surprise my father and mother arranged."

"Another surprise?" she asked, leaning away just a little to see his face. There was hardly enough light to make out anything but his outline. She lay back against him once more. "I think they've done more than enough."

"They have, but they're taking such joy in it that I could hardly say no. I wish you had heard my father as he helped me plan out the school."

"How wonderful that he wants to be a part of it."

"Wonderful and shocking all at the same time," Charlie replied. "I still can't get over the change in him. Only God could have done such a work."

The driver arrived at their house. Someone had gone ahead of them to light lamps. The soft glow emanating from the windows was most welcoming.

Charlie gallantly carried her from the carriage to the front door. With little trouble, he opened the door and carried her inside.

Melody gasped at the scene. The place had been completely changed since she'd seen it last. Someone had papered the entryway and completely furnished it with a receiving table and artwork on the walls.

"This is . . . Why, it's . . . stunning."

"You can thank Mother for it. She hired an army of people to decorate it in a fashionable way that she thought would suit our needs. She's made the local merchants quite happy with the inventory she demanded." He put Melody down and drew her into the front sitting room. "She somehow knew you liked shades of blue and did this room up accordingly. What do you think?"

Looking around the room at the lovely powder-blue upholstery on the sofa and chairs, as well as the darker blue patterned draperies and white sheers, Melody couldn't have been more pleased.

"I will be exploring this house for days—maybe weeks. It's beautiful."

"Not as beautiful as you are." He turned her to face him. "When I saw you in that dress, it took my breath away. In fact, every time I see you it's like seeing you for the first time."

She smiled up in adoration. "I still can't believe you're mine. What a precious gift from God."

"I was thinking much the same." He pulled her close and ran his hand gently down the side of her face. "I love you, and with all I have, I will endeavor to be a good husband to you and the best friend you could want."

"Oh, Charlie. You will always be my best friend and dearest love." She wrapped her arms around his neck, and Charlie tightened his hold on her for a long and very satisfying kiss.

Epilogue

NOVEMBER 1868

Mr. Decker, I need help with my arithmetic," a red-headed boy declared, coming to Charlie's desk.

Charlie was glad that Melody had already taken the rest of the class into the other room for lunch. "What seems to be the trouble, Isaac?" he asked the ten-year-old.

"Fractions," the boy answered. His expression was most serious. "They're perturbing me."

Charlie refrained from laughing. "Oh, I see. Well, I know that fractions often perturb people when they are first attempting to understand them."

"I just don't understand," the boy continued. "You want me to reduce them, but I can't figure out how. I have nine-thirds, and you said when the top number is bigger than the bottom it needs to be reduced, but I can't remember how to do it."

Charlie felt great affection for the boy. "Tell me, how do you feel about division?"

The boy's tense expression relaxed. "I like division. Makes sense to me."

"That's wonderful. I'm so glad you enjoy it." Charlie went to the blackboard. "Fractions are really nothing more than division problems."

The boy's look of stress was back. "How can that be a division problem, Mr. Decker?"

Charlie smiled. "Because nine over three is really just another way of saying nine divided by three. The bar is nothing more than a division bar."

The boy's eyes narrowed for a moment, then Charlie saw his eyes widen as understanding dawned. "A division bar?"

"Exactly. So when I ask you to reduce the fraction, what would the answer be?"

"Three," the boy said without hesitation. He looked up at Charlie for reassurance that he had answered correctly.

"There you are. That's right."

"Well, I'll be." The boy shook his head. "My ma is never gonna believe this."

"I think she'll be very pleased with you, Isaac. You're quite smart."

The boy stood a little taller. "Thank you for helping me, Mr. Decker."

"No problem. Fractions will get a little more complicated, but I know you're smart enough to handle it, and you can always come to me with your questions. Now you'd better go on and eat your lunch. Mrs. Decker will be waiting for you."

Isaac ran for the door and disappeared into the next room, while Charlie erased the problem he'd written on the board. He had a full school of twenty-two boys, all ranging in age from ten to sixteen. There was even a waiting list for people who wanted Charlie to take their boys on as well. It was quite a challenge to plan out lessons for each age group, but Melody had proven to be quite helpful. She seemed to enjoy working with various projects.

Charlie had no sooner reclaimed a seat at his desk than Melody appeared with his lunch in hand. He jumped back up as she placed the food on his desk. He took her in his arms, glanced around her at the open door, and then kissed her in a most loving fashion.

"Charlie Decker," she declared as he turned her loose. "That is not the way to conduct yourself in a schoolroom."

He laughed and sat back down. "I used to be jealous of boys who stole kisses from girls in school. I never had the chance to do that, and now I do."

"As the recipient of that kind of attention, I can tell you it was quite annoying. However, I don't mind your attention at all." She smiled and leaned back against the desk. "So what will you be teaching after lunch?"

"We're going to study how Wyoming became a territory and what the procedure is for statehood. After I talk about it, you can help us make a map. I think the boys will like getting an idea of where everything is situated. My father is arranging for a United States map that we can hang on the wall. It will be quite detailed and really give the boys a perspective on the country."

"That will be wonderful." Melody leaned over and kissed Charlie on the top of his head. "Oh, I'm wondering how you would feel about taking on another student."

"Now, Melody, you know we can't. There isn't room. Not only that, but we already have a waiting list."

"But this child won't start for a while. They'll probably need about five years before they'll be ready to sit in class."

Charlie was more than a little confused. "What are you talking about?"

Melody leaned over once again. Her eyes were wide. "I'm going to have a baby, Mr. Decker. That's what I'm talking about."

If she'd said the school was on fire, Charlie couldn't have been more shocked. "A baby?"

She nodded and straightened. "A baby. Our baby."

"When?"

"April, as best we can figure. I talked to Marybeth since she's also expecting around the same time. We calculated it and figured the babies will be born in April."

Charlie got to his feet and took hold of her shoulders. "I can hardly believe this. What a wonderful gift, and it's not even Christmas yet." He pulled her very gently into his arms. "Oh, how I love you."

"I love you too, Charlie." She wrapped her arms around him as best she could and sighed. "Maybe girls should advertise for husbands more often. I came out of the deal quite well."

Charlie chuckled. "Yes, but we had your father plotting and planning for you, and as you said, his discernment was a gift from the Lord."

Melody looked up. "Do you think if it's a boy we could name him after Da? Not Clancy, but his middle name, Michael."

"Michael Decker. Nothing would please me more," Charlie said, remembering the man he'd known for such a short time yet came to love.

A howling noise rose up from the direction of the lunchroom. Melody pulled away. "Time to go. Sounds like the boys have run out of food."

"I suggest we herd them outside for some fresh air. A little time in the cold and they'll be ready to come in and settle down to learning," Charlie suggested.

She nodded and left, calling out to the boys to clean up their messes and get their coats. Charlie leaned back in his seat, still in awe at the news Melody had just shared. He was going to be a father. The thought was terrifying and wonderful all at the same time. He glanced toward the ceiling.

"Thank you, Father. For the many blessings, but especially for Melody and the baby." He gazed out over the empty classroom and knew he'd never known more joy.

Melody awoke in the night. For a moment, she was back in time, listening for her father's moaning. She sat up on the edge of the bed, then remembered he was gone.

She slipped out of bed, careful not to wake Charlie, and went to the window. She looked heavenward, noting the vast, empty darkness. Snow clouds had moved in earlier in the evening and turned the pale blue skies a gunmetal gray. They figured to see snow by morning.

A smile touched her lips as her hands went to her abdomen. There was just the slightest rounding there. She'd been almost certain of her condition since September, but with Charlie so focused on getting the school started, she'd not wanted to say anything. With her expanding waistline, Melody had known she wouldn't be able to keep it quiet much longer.

It delighted her to know that she and Marybeth would have their babies around the same time. It would be good to have someone with Marybeth's parenting experience to help guide her. Of course, Granny Taylor would be there as well.

Oh, but how she wished Da could be with them. She missed him so much some days. Especially days like this when there was something special to share.

Lord, if possible, please let Da know how happy I am and that Charlie and I are going to have a baby. I know he'd be so delighted.

Warm arms encircled her. "Are you all right?" Charlie asked, pulling her back against him. "I woke up, and you weren't there."

"I'm fine. Something woke me, and I came to the window to see if it was snowing yet. Can't really see much of anything, but I don't think it's started."

Charlie nuzzled his face alongside her head. "Come back to bed. It's cold out here, and I always sleep better with you in my arms."

She turned and fixed her hands on either side of his cheeks. She couldn't see his face in the dark but knew he would be smiling at her. His blue eyes would have that wonderful twinkle to them. She stroked his chin with her thumb. He needed a shave. Not that it mattered. Charlie was perfect just the way he was. He was the perfect friend and the perfect husband.

And he belonged to her.

Read on
for a sneak peek at

Book three of
THE HEART OF CHEYENNE series.

AVAILABLE NOVEMBER 2024.

1

DECEMBER 1868
CHEYENNE, WYOMING TERRITORY

Laura Evans looked out the window at the snow-covered landscape as the train pulled into the Cheyenne station. After ten years living apart, she was about to be reunited with her father. At thoughts of Father, her fascination of the Western frontier faded, even as she surveyed the cowboy town that was to become her home.

Ten years.

Mama had died in November of 1858. Consumption, the doctor said. A debilitating depletion of her body for which he had no understanding. And just a week after they buried her, Father sent Laura to boarding school over fifty miles away. Where he got the money for such an endeavor was beyond Laura, but it had been her fate for the next decade.

In all those years, she'd only seen her father a handful of times. He had visited her at the boarding schools on several occasions and once during her college years. It had been six years since the latter visit. It came on the occasion of

Father settling her into the Tennessee women's college he'd chosen for her. Even with the war raging, he had figured her to be safe there. When that proved otherwise and the college closed, Father arranged for her to go abroad with a teacher to escape the ugliness of war. Now the world was set right again—or at least it was no longer pitting brother against brother in a war that Laura still found difficult to understand—and she would soon be with her beloved father once more.

Granite Evans was the light of her life. He was her hero. Despite having sent her away, Father had always meant the world to Laura. He was generous and kind, making sure she had everything she needed. His absence had been difficult, but Laura had reminded herself that Father hurt just as much, perhaps more, in losing Mama than she did. She respected that he had needed time alone to grieve and mourn. It hadn't been easy for her, but Laura had been determined to be strong. She owed him that much.

"Cheyenne!" the conductor announced as he moved through the car. "All out for Cheyenne!"

Laura stood, adjusted her cloak, then brushed down the skirt of her burgundy traveling suit with her gloved hand. She wanted to look her best when she met her father again. She hoped—prayed—that he would be proud of her.

With the help of the porter, Laura stepped from the train, her travel bag clutched tight, and her heavy wool cloak pulled close against her body. Father had told her that it would be cold in Cheyenne and to buy an appropriate wardrobe. She had taken the money he'd sent and did as instructed. As the December winds whipped at the hem of her cloak and skirt, Laura was glad she had listened.

She looked up and down the depot platform for some sign

of her father but found no one who resembled him. Six years was a long time, but she was certain he would look like he had when last he visited her.

Wouldn't he?

Making her way inside the depot, Laura shifted her bag from one gloved hand to the other. Quite a few people crowded into the building alongside her, and she allowed herself to be caught up in the flow of their movements. All the while she kept looking for the stocky, mustached man she knew would be there. And he was.

She spied him across the room, talking with a couple of other men. She called out to get her father's attention. "Father!"

He looked up and caught her gaze. He smiled and quickly dismissed the two younger men. Crossing the room to greet her, he held open his arms.

"Laura!"

She dropped her bag and rushed to him. A sigh escaped her as his arms closed tightly around her. It was here she felt the safest and most happy. She thought of how few times she had known his tender embrace over the years, but she refused to let such thoughts discourage her. The fact that they'd had so little time together only served to make this moment all the more precious.

"Father, I'm so happy to see you again." She breathed in deeply of his cologne and the unmistakable scent of cigars and coffee.

"I thought you'd never get here. Welcome home."

Home. The word touched a place deep in her heart. She hadn't had a home since Mama died. Oh, but Laura had longed for one. She had enjoyed very little consistency as a child attending boarding school. Year after year, her father moved her to a better, more stately and expensive school. As he was able to improve his own situation, he improved hers, never realizing that consistency would have been a bigger blessing than larger, more elegantly appointed rooms and educational halls.

Laura stepped back and studied her father from head to toe. He looked well and happy. "How wonderful it is to see you," she told him. "I worried that I might not recognize you, but then I chided myself for such doubt. Nothing about you could ever seem foreign or strange to me."

"And you." He shook his head. "I had no idea you'd grow into such a beauty. You always favored your mother, but the last time I saw you, there were still remnants of childhood in your face and figure. That, alas, is gone for good. You are no more a child."

"I was full grown last you saw me, or nearly so. Sixteen years old, in fact. Most of my fellow students were engaged to be married. I can't imagine there being any remnants of childhood remaining then."

"Well, there were. You were more gangly and awkward. Now you're full grown and a lovely young woman."

"Oh, Father, you do go on. Six years could not have made such a difference. You look the same as I remember you."

"I'm an old man, and change is slower."

She laughed. "You aren't that old. Not even yet fifty." She wrapped her arm around his. "I'm just so glad to see you again. I want to know all that has happened to you in the last six years."

He shook his head. "It's more important we plan a future than lose ourselves in the past. That was the reason for our separation in the first place. A separation that has been difficult but necessary."

She sobered. "And do you feel that time has healed your heart?"

"I will always have a place of emptiness where your mother once resided. She meant everything to me. You both did, but when she died, something in me died as well, and I knew I'd be no good to you. My poor, precious girl." He frowned, looking very close to tears.

Laura hadn't meant to make him so uncomfortable, and in a public place. What was she thinking?

"Forgive me. This is a talk better suited to a private parlor." She stepped back to where she'd dropped her bag and picked it up. Rejoining him, she gave her father a smile. "I have claim tickets for my trunks. Goodness, but I brought so much stuff. I got rid of as much as possible, but some keepsakes and pieces of memorabilia were impossible to part with."

"It's of no worry, as I told you in my letter. We are well-off now. I have a large home for you and staff to wait on your every need. I'll give these tickets to my driver, and he'll see to it that the trunks are delivered. For now, I'll take that bag you're carrying, and we'll be on our way."

She handed over her valise, then took hold of his arm. "I have dreamt of this day for so long."

He led her through the station and outside, where the wind again whipped at her cloak from every direction. Father approached an enclosed carriage as the driver jumped down from his seat in front.

"You have a landau." Laura observed as the driver opened the door. "What a treat. I came fully expecting buckboards or buggies at best."

Father assisted her into the carriage, and the scent of leather enveloped her.

Laura took a seat, and her father quickly joined her. He put her bag on the opposite seat and took up a blanket.

"I just had the landau delivered. It is a Christmas gift to us. As we rise to the top, it is only fitting that we travel in style."

"It's lovely." She ran her gloved hand along the leather upholstery. "I'm sure no one has a finer one."

"I have another smaller conveyance you can handle when you decide to move about town to see friends."

"You sound as though you are very rich, Father."

"I am. We are. It's for you that I've labored so long and hard. If we'd had proper money, your mother might not have died. Destitute patients get very little attention, in either the hospital or the church."

Laura hated to believe that her mother had died purely for lack of money, but Father had always insisted it was so.

"I've worked hard this last decade, bettering myself as I could. I invested heavily in the railroad, and it has done me well to be sure. There are, of course, other investments, and the ladies' store. I think you'll be impressed with what I've created there. I have items brought in from all over the world. Shipped right here to Cheyenne and made available to the women as if they lived in New York City or Paris."

Pride was evident in his voice. Laura smiled but refrained from telling him that luxury meant very little as far as she was concerned. Many of her friends at school also had money, but even those of lesser means had been far better off than Laura. They had family. Mothers and fathers who came and took them away for holidays and summers. Laura had been left to travel with old-maid teachers or matronly facilitators whose children were grown. More than once she'd remained with the head mistress at the school all summer doing little more than reading and taking long walks. She used to dream of her father showing up with a train ticket to take her away on some grand adventure. But he never came.

The carriage finally stopped, and the driver opened the door. Father was first to disembark, then he turned for Laura.

She gripped his hand and stepped from the landau to gaze up at a flat-faced white house. Snow lay all about the yard, where there wasn't a single tree or shrub.

The house wasn't anything elaborate on the outside. It was two-stories tall with a large square frame of white clapboard and multiple windows to break the lack of ornamentation. To one side there was a carriage house, but Laura couldn't see beyond that.

"This is only a temporary home," her father explained as they moved toward the front door. "I have property over on Ferguson and plan to build a us a mansion. You can see, however, the beautiful windows. Those cost a pretty penny."

"I know they must have, but they're lovely, Father. I'm sure you've made it a wonderful place."

"Well, it will be a home now for sure, what with having you here. There's so much I want you to know about me, Cheyenne, and this territory. I intend to do big things here, Laura. Big things."

She'd gathered from bits and pieces in his letters that her father had taken a strong interest in politics. He had left more than one hint at hoping to get involved rather than just be a sideline supporter.

"I've no doubt you will, Father. How could you not? You've done so well in just one decade. Imagine what you'll accomplish in another."

He fixed her with a proud look. "Exactly so. Now come. I'll show you the house and staff." He opened the door and ushered her inside out of the cold.

Laura was glad to find the house quite warm. She'd never much cared for cold weather. Mother often said the blood of Alabama women was much too thin for the colder climates. Laura didn't know if that was true or not, but she always suffered during her travels in Europe when they ventured where it was cold. She supposed she would just have to get used to it now.

"This is my housekeeper, Mrs. Duffy," Father said as three strangers entered the foyer. "She's agreed to act as your lady's maid until you can find someone else. She doesn't live with us as she has two teenage boys, but she comes every day from six in the morning to nine at night. Her days off vary."

Laura smiled at the dark haired woman. "I'm pleased to meet you, Mrs. Duffy."

"The pleasure is mine, Miss Evans." She had a small frame, but there was an edge in her voice that betrayed strength.

"This is our cook, Mrs. Murphy."

Mrs. Murphy was a stocky woman with a serious expression. Laura had often heard it said that she should never trust a skinny cook. There was no concern of that here.

Mrs. Murphy looked to be somewhere in her late fifties or early sixties. She gave Laura a nod, then looked her up and down as though trying to assess how much she would eat. The thought made Laura smile once again.

"I'm sure you are a blessing, Mrs. Murphy. Good food makes all the difference in a household." Laura saw her comment caused the older woman's expression to relax just a bit.

"And this young man is Curtis. Curtis does whatever needs to be done with the yard and stables. He often works with Mr. Grayson, my driver and stableman."

It was clear that Curtis was uncomfortable. He couldn't have been more than sixteen or seventeen. Laura took pity on him and offered him her best smile. "It's a pleasure to meet you, Curtis." The young man blushed and looked away after a brief glance.

Her father gave the trio a nod, and they all hurried away as quickly as they'd come. Laura untied her cloak since the warmth of the room proved more than enough. Father put aside his hat and gloves, then doffed his coat and hung it on a nearby coat-tree.

"Not a very elegant approach to outdoor garments," he said, reaching for Laura's cloak. "But as I said, next year I intend to begin building a new and luxurious place for us. We'll have a full staff to take care of everything."

Laura pulled the pin from her hat and set both aside on a nearby table. Last of all she drew off her gloves. "This looks like a lovely house, Father." She could see to his right that the pocket doors had been pushed back partway to reveal a large comfortable-looking room, complete with a hearth on the far wall. A fire blazed in welcome.

"It is sufficient for the time being, but I intend to better myself further. Many of us here feel the same. There are a great many quality families who have settled this growing community, and we intend to see that the elite make a clear and present mark on society."

Laura had never heard her father talk in this snobbish manner. She didn't feel it was proper to approach him on the matter her first day home and so gave a simple nod and followed him as he took her bag and led her upstairs.

"I'll show you to your room first. I hope you'll like it."

"I'm sure I will," Laura replied. "Everything seems perfect."

"I run a well-ordered house. Mrs. Duffy understands that and follows my instructions to the letter. I brook no nonsense, as I have a great many important people who come here from time to time."

She noted the highly polished oak banister and stairs. Mrs. Duffy apparently kept a very neat house. The upstairs hall was papered in a print of gold, beige, and green stripes, with prominent gold fleur-de-lis running down wide panels of powder-blue. It wasn't something Laura would have chosen, but it gave the hall a touch of elegance.

A beige hallway runner covered the oak floors nearly wall to wall. A few decorative tables were placed between the multiple closed doors.

"My room is to the right," Father announced pointing. "If you should need me for any reason in the middle of the night, do not hesitate to knock."

"Thank you, I will." Laura turned as he drew her to the left.

"The door to your right is a bedroom that has been appointed for sewing and storage. The next door is a bathing room. I had a copper tub brought in from Boston. It's situated beside a stove that can be used to heat the water and keep the room warm when in use. I find a hot bath to be one of those things I cannot live without."

"How very nice." Laura had wondered what kind of things would be available for their personal needs.

"And this door on the left is your room. It's actually two rooms. They seemed rather perfect to join together so I had a doorway created when I knew for sure you'd be coming home." He smiled. "One can be used as your sitting room and the other your bedroom."

He opened the door, and Laura stepped inside. The room had been furnished with a large wardrobe and desk of matching white oak. Dark rose-colored draperies were hanging at the windows, and a delicate print of pink roses on white paper trimmed the walls. It had been designed with a young woman in mind. On the wall to the right was a small but efficient fireplace trimmed in white tiles with the same rose pattern as the papered walls. A fire had been built up, and it, along with the lamps, gave the room a beautiful glow. A large chintz-covered chair waited in welcome.

"I shall be quite comfortable here." She turned to her father and kissed his cheek. "Thank you so much." She ran her hand along the back of the chair. "It's just perfect."

"Nothing is too good for you, my dear Laura." He patted her shoulder. "Now come see the bedroom."

Turning away from the fireplace, Laura found the bedroom door already open. Inside was a beautiful four poster bed and dressing table in the same white oak as the wardrobe and desk. The draperies and paper matched the sitting room.

"This is certainly everything a girl could want," she said, touched at all the details her father had put into the setting.

She went to the dressing table and found all sorts of bottles of perfume and lotions for her skin and a delicate silver hairbrush, comb, and mirror set. A large framed mirror was attached to the dressing table so that she could simply sit and survey her appearance at will.

"It's all so very nice, Father, thank you. I'm quite surprised by all of this. I read almost everything I could get my hands on about Cheyenne and Wyoming Territory, and I must admit, I wasn't hopeful of finding much, but I am pleased to be mistaken."

He chuckled. "We have worked hard to improve the situation in our little town. Mark my words, Cheyenne will one day be as fine a city as any other. Important people are making their mark here, and incredible things will be accomplished. You are to be a part of all of that, my dear."

She could see the excitement in his eyes. This was significant to him, and she intended to join in as much as she could. If only to please him.

* * * *

Granite Evans settled into the leather chair behind his desk and considered the young woman upstairs. His daughter. His only child. He'd hardly seen her in the last ten years, and now she would be his constant companion. Could he still manage to accomplish all that he had planned with her under his roof?

All of Cheyenne's society would adore her. The men would line up to court her. He could probably arrange a lucrative betrothal. It was something he hadn't given much thought to, but now that she was here, he could see she was a valuable prize. There weren't that many women in Cheyenne, and certainly none as beautiful as Laura. She favored her mother more than he liked to admit.

When he'd first seen her in the depot, she had startled him. For just a moment, he thought Meredith had returned in all her youth and beauty. Cinnamon red hair framing a lovely oval face. Dark brown eyes and full lips. Laura was the spitting image of her deceased mother.

Then again, Laura had always reminded him of her mother. It was the reason he had sent her away. He couldn't bear the constant reminder of what he had lost. Meredith had been his entire world. He had been nothing of value prior to meeting her. She had transformed him with her love, and her death had forever changed him. Even now, remembering her and what she had gone through stirred undiluted anger, as though he'd lost her only yesterday.

Granite would never forget the attitude of the doctors and

hospital staff when he'd sought help for Meredith. With no money to pay up front for the needed treatment, they had been given nothing more than the smallest bit of attention and then sent on their way. Knowing his wife's faith, he had gone to the church, as well, but found them equally callous.

With nothing left to do, he had contacted her well-to-do parents in Birmingham. Meredith had defied them and run away to marry Granite. They denounced her as their child and refused to even listen when Granite begged for help. They told him she'd be better off dead than married to a low-life gambler. Rejections from the doctors, church, and family had left Granite hard and angry, and when his beloved wife died, he vowed to make a success of himself in such a way that he could get back at those who had denied her help.

Her parents had died before he could do anything to them, and their wealth had passed on to a distant cousin. But then the war had come, and opportunities arose on every side. Granite had never been afraid to step over the line where laws were concerned. As the South's needs grew, he found ways to accommodate, using the persona of an Irishman named Marcus O'Brien, while Granite Evans kept his hands and name clean. Eventually, Granite had a team of men working for him. They smuggled goods, robbed warehouses and shipments of supplies, and did whatever it took to put money in their pockets.

Granite didn't care about the outcome of the war. He wasn't a patriot in any sense of the word. Let there be slaves or none. Let the states be in control or not. The only things he cared about were himself, Laura, and getting back at the people who had failed him.

Already he'd had some of his revenge on the hospital back in Alabama. After the war, he had pledged to give them an endowment and help rebuild and expand their facilities. There had been a front-page photograph showing Granite with the smug-faced hospital board members to announce his decision. He felt a great sense of satisfaction in knowing they were confident of good things to come. But that satisfaction could not equal the feeling of accomplishment that came when he denied them the gift based on trumped-up charges. His accomplices had been able to create quite an ordeal for the board with declarations of moral lacking and scandals too great to mention in mixed company.

It had satisfied Granite's sense of revenge—to a point. They had no idea of the real crime he held against them. But he had no intention of reminding anyone of where he'd come from. Instead, Granite let them think what they would and suffer his decision as the reputation of their hospital was lessened in the public eye.

A dull thump sounded from upstairs, catching Granite's attention and reminding him that he was no longer alone. Having Laura here would create complications. Hopefully she'd be cooperative and easy to manage.

He poured himself a drink, then went to the window. Winter wasn't his favorite time of year. The weather was unpredictable—even deadly. Sandwiched between vast prairies and the Rocky Mountains, Cheyenne was at the mercy of a variety of elements. The wind in particular could be most annoying. Throughout the year, winds often caused a great deal of misery, but when combined with snow, the town could find itself seeking shelter for days.

For tonight, though, the winds were calm, and the weather at peace. Granite walked to the fireplace and finished his drink. He would meet with some of the business leaders tomorrow and put forth his proposals for town improvements to benefit as many as possible. He knew if he could convince the others that his concepts were beneficial not only to him but also to them, they would go along with his ideas and remember Evans when it came time to vote in future elections. His popularity would also be sure to reach the ear of the president, who was charged with choosing a governor for the new Wyoming Territory. Thankfully, President Johnson had never gotten the job done, and the November election had given the office to Ulysses S. Grant. Grant was a man who was indebted to Granite. They'd met on many occasions during the war when Granite had shared information with Grant and produced supplies for the North. Of course, he'd provided them for the South as well, but Grant didn't know that.

With the money he made through underhanded means, Granite had been able to create a credible way of making money. Investing in the railroads had been a sure thing, especially after the war. The country was desperate for ways to unite it once again. And of course, there was his idea for a large emporium. It was the perfect solution for moving products purchased both legally and otherwise. He'd started small at first, then increased in size—always selling at a large profit when he sold and moved to another location. Lady Luck was clearly his companion, and when he reached Cheyenne, the stage was set for the Cheyenne Ladies' Department Store. A grand and glorious emporium with multiple departments, focusing on all that any woman could ever desire in fashion, home management, and entertaining. He'd even put in a seasonal department just for Christmas decorations and gifts. That had proven quite popular.

Granite deposited his glass on the table, then headed to bed. He was quite satisfied with how he'd overcome the obstacles in his life, but now a new element had entered in.

Laura had come back into his daily life. At first he'd been rather alarmed when she'd written to say she'd completed her studies. But the more he thought of her being in Cheyenne, the more benefits he could envision. Tomorrow, he'd start to figure out what role Laura would play in his schemes.

Tracie Peterson is the award-winning author of over one hundred novels, both historical and contemporary. She has won the ACFW Lifetime Achievement Award and the Romantic Times Career Achievement Award. She is often referred to as the "Queen of Historical Christian Fiction," and her avid research resonates in her stories, as seen in her bestselling Heirs of Montana and Alaskan Quest series. Tracie considers her writing a ministry for God to share the Gospel and biblical application. She and her family make their home in Montana. Visit her website at TraciePeterson.com or on Facebook at Facebook.com/AuthorTraciePeterson.

Sign Up for
Tracie's Newsletter

Keep up to date with Tracie's latest news
on book releases and events by signing up
for her email list at the link below.

TraciePeterson.com

FOLLOW TRACIE ON SOCIAL MEDIA

Tracie Peterson   @AuthorTraciePeterson

More from Tracie Peterson

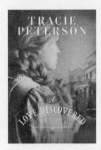

Marybeth and Edward are compelled by their circumstances to marry as they trek west to the newly formed railroad town of Cheyenne. But life in Cheyenne is fraught with danger, and they find that they need each other more than ever. Despite the trials they face, will happiness await them in this arrangement of convenience?

A Love Discovered
THE HEART OF CHEYENNE #1

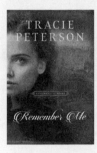

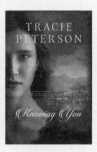

Bestselling author Tracie Peterson transports readers to early 1900s Seattle where three Brownie Camera Girls must face their pasts in order to embrace their lives, their futures, and their hope in God in her new series PICTURES OF THE HEART. Rich in history and faith, fans of Francine Rivers and Janette Oke will feel uplifted and inspired by these seamlessly woven novels.

PICTURES OF THE HEART: *Remember Me, Finding Us, Knowing You*

BETHANYHOUSE

 Bethany House Fiction

 @BethanyHouseFiction

 @Bethany_House

 @BethanyHouseFiction

 Free exclusive resources for your book group at BethanyHouseOpenBook.com

Sign up for our fiction newsletter today at BethanyHouse.com